After graduating from the University of Oxford, Catherine Bruton began her career as an English teacher and later went on to write feature articles for *The Times* and other publications. She started writing *We Can Be Heroes* in 2009, inspired by her research for an article about children whose parents died on 9/11, and by the manga fans in her Year 9 class. *We Can Be Heroes* is her first novel for Egmont. Catherine lives near Bath with her husband and two small children.

CATHERINE BRUTON

WE CAN BE HEROES

EGMONT

EGMONT

We bring stories to life

We Can Be Heroes
First published in Great Britain 2011
by Egmont UK Limited
239 Kensington High Street
London W8 6SA

Text copyright © 2011 Catherine Bruton
Inside illustrations copyright © 2011 David Shephard

The moral rights of the author and illustrator have been asserted

ISBN 978 1 4052 5652 0

1 3 5 7 9 10 8 6 4 2

www.egmont.co.uk

A CIP catalogue record for this title is available from the
British Library

Typeset by Avon DataSet Ltd, Bidford on Avon, Warwickshire
Printed and bound in Great Britain by the CPI Group

For Jonny, Joe-Joe and Elsie Maudie,
and all our lovely grandparents,
with love xx

A FEW THINGS YOU SHOULD KNOW

My dad was killed in the 9/11 attacks in New York. I was only two at the time so I don't really remember him much, although when people ask, I say I do. People ask about my dad a lot. I usually respond with a shrug or by looking at my shoes. But no one seems to mind: it's OK if I'm rude or even a bit weird at times, because I'm the boy whose dad died on 9/11.

But the stuff in this book is not about that. It's about the summer my mum went away; the summer that me and Jed and Priti tried to catch a suicide bomber and prevent an honour killing; the summer that Stevie Sanders disappeared and we caused a race riot. It's about how we built a tree house and joined the bomb squad; how I found my dad and Jed lost his; and how we both lost our mums then found them again.

So it's not really about 9/11, but then again none of those things would have happened if it hadn't been for that day. So I guess it's all back to front. Sort of . . .

JULY 13TH

THINGS I'D LIKE TO KNOW ABOUT MY DAD

1. Who was his favourite *Star Wars* character? Was he a fan of the Dark Side? Darth Vader or Maul? Young Obi Wan or old?

2. If he could choose for England to win the World Cup or for Aston Villa to win the treble, which would he go for?

3. Who did he think was the greatest ever Sports Personality of the Year?

4. Could he light a fire by rubbing sticks together?

5. What was his record for keepy-uppies?

6. Was he a morning person or an evening person?

7. Would he have been good cop or bad cop? (Mum says she gets tired of trying to be both.)

8. What did he smell like and what did it feel like to hug him?

9. What did he think about me?

10. I can't think of another one, which is pretty rubbish. You'd think I'd have loads and loads of questions

about my dad since I hardly remember him at all and he died in such tragic circumstances, but I can't even think of ten. What does that say about me exactly?

*　　　*　　　*

This used to be my dad's room. When he was a kid, he shared it with his brother, Ian. They stuck the glow-in-the-dark stars on the ceiling, and the Smurf stickers all over the window frame. On the shelf are some trophies my dad won – chess champion, Under 12 Most Improved Player, that sort of thing. And on the wall is a second place pennant he once won in a rowing regatta, covering up a doodle on the wallpaper. So maybe he liked drawing, like me.

I'm going to be sleeping here, just like last time. And, just like last time, I don't know how long I'll be staying, and it's not worth asking Granny and Grandad because they don't know either.

So I'm sitting on the windowsill, drawing cartoons. That's what I do when stuff like this happens: I draw things. Doodles, mainly, and cartoons, whatever comes into my head. I don't know why, but it sort of helps. First I doodle the birds on the telephone wires. I draw them with mobile phones held up to their beaks, then I draw phone numbers circling their heads, spinning round them till they go goggle-eyed. Then I start to draw a girl with the phone, but she ends up looking like my mum so I stop because I don't want to think about my mum.

I put down my pencil, run my finger over my dad's faded Smurf stickers and stare out of the window.

Downstairs I can hear my grandparents talking.

'How was she?' That's my granny.

'The same as last time,' Grandad replies.

Which doesn't tell me anything I don't already know.

I pick up my pencil and look out of the window again for something else to draw.

The cul-de-sac is empty except for the little chav kid (that's what my grandad calls her, but I think her real name is Stevie) riding a pink bicycle with tassels on the handlebars round and round her driveway. She's been there for ages, all on her own. I draw a

5

picture of her – a cartoon girl with big Bambi eyes and a tiny body in outsized shoes. I make it look like she's riding her bike through a twister in the sky – just like the witch in *The Wizard of Oz* – then I draw things whirling and twirling around her: a washing machine, a pair of wellies, *click-clackety* knitting needles, a hula-hooping cow, a fish bowl on a piano.

I glance over at the house opposite. My grandad says an Asian family have moved in. Most of the neighbours on the cul-de-sac are as old as my grandparents, except the Sanders (Stevie's family) next door and now the Asian kids in the house opposite.

I'm just wondering whether any of the kids are my sort of age when the door of the Asian House (Grandad again) opens and out comes the oddest-looking girl I've ever seen.

She's about ten, I reckon, maybe eleven. Skin the colour of toffee, massive bunches attached to the sides of her head with frilly pink things that make her look like a poodle. She's wearing her school uniform so I guess her school hasn't broken up yet either. I suppose I should be pleased that I'm missing the last week of term, but I'm not – not really. On top of her school uniform, the bunchy girl is wearing this red tutu thing, and on her feet she has trainers that, from the way she's zooming around, I guess must have wheels in them. They're bright pink and look very new.

She looks up, sees me in the window and ignores me. Then she wheelies up and down her drive, twirling in neat circles before coming to a stop in front of her doorway with a little flourish – like she's an Olympic gymnast or a figure skater or something. Stevie stops to watch her, but the bunchy girl just ignores her too and keeps on wheelie-ing.

I draw a cartoon of a wheelie-wearing superheroine – giant bunches flying, the wheels in her heels going at the speed of light, whizzing past Stevie on her flying bike and the hula-hooping cow and the upside-down fish-bowl piano.

And then, suddenly, the wheelie girl stops, tips back on her heels, hands on hips, and stares up at the window where I'm sitting. Stares right at me. And waves.

* * *

7

Five minutes later, the wheelie girl is standing on my grandparents' doorstep, resting back on her wheelie heels in a way that makes her whole body tilt slightly backwards. She's checking me out.

'I'm Priti,' she says, looking at my granny and deliberately ignoring me. 'Although my big sister says I'm not. Pretty that is. She reckons we should swap names, but she's dead vain and totally into herself, so she would say that, wouldn't she? Anyway, my mum says I should ask your boy if he wants to hang out.'

I don't say anything.

Granny smiles. 'Well, I think you are *very* pretty,' she says. 'And very kind to ask Ben to play. What do you think, Ben?'

I should say that I'm tired (because wheelie girl is obviously way younger than me – and a girl) but I don't. Instead, I go really red and suddenly can't say anything at all.

'Can't he talk?' Priti asks, giving me a funny look. She clearly thinks I'm some sort of weirdo.

'He's just had a difficult day,' says Granny gently.

8

'What do you say, Ben? Do you want to "hang out" with Priti?'

I shrug my shoulders. (I can feel my face turning the colour of a pickled beetroot now.)

'Well, that looks like a yes to me, Priti,' says Granny brightly.

My heart sinks. I know she's trying to help, but this was not the answer I wanted.

Priti grins from ear to ear.

I imagine doodling a Cheshire cat with a face like Priti and giant bunches for ears. Wearing pink wheelie shoes.

Priti whizzes off down Granny's path, leaving me to follow behind.

'So what do you want to do then?' she says, when I finally catch up with her.

I shrug.

We both look around the cul-de-sac. Little Stevie's fallen off her pink bike and is crying. I wonder if we ought to go over and help her, but her mum leans out of the window and screams at her to shut up and get inside right now. Stevie gets up and hobbles back in, leaving the pink bike abandoned on the pavement. She has blood coming out of her knee and her face is streaked with tears. Once she's gone, there's not much else to see.

Priti turns and looks at me with her nose screwed up and says, 'You *can* talk, can't you?'

'Yeah!' I say, my face getting hot again. 'I'm not stupid.'

'Good, I was beginning to worry. You talk funny though. Where you from anyway?'

'Somerset,' I say.

'Never heard of it. That's the country, right?'

I nod.

'That explains why you talk funny.'

'Except I don't,' I say.

'Yes you do. You say "oi" instead of I.'

'I do not!'

'You just did. You sound like a farmer.'

I want to tell her that she speaks through her nose only she doesn't give me the chance.

'Why you here then?'

'I'm staying with my grandparents.'

'Yeah, I got that. But why?'

'Does there have to be a reason?'

'No, but there is, isn't there? I can tell.'

I just shrug because I don't want to talk about it, but Priti isn't taking the hint. 'What is it? Did your mum and dad get divorced? Or is it swine flu? Or foot and mouth or whatever it is you have in the country?'

'No, it's nothing like that.'

'So there is something!' she says. 'I knew it. You can always tell.'

'How's that exactly?' I say.

I imagine doodling a giant cartoon piano descending from the sky and landing on her head.

Crash! Tinkle! Tinkle!

'You've got the look of one of those dog-is-for-life-not-just-for-Christmas mutts,' she says.

'At least I don't have hair like a poodle,' I mutter. She ignores me.

'You've got OK clothes,' she says, then adds, 'although they don't really suit you.'

'Thanks a lot,' I say, trying to sound sarcastic, but not really succeeding.

She's probably right though. Most of my clothes are hand-me-downs from my too-cool-for-school cousin Jed. His mum always passes things on to my mum. Or at least she used to, until last year. And Jed mostly wears labels and I'm not exactly a label person. Which Priti can obviously tell.

'Does your mum buy stuff for you?' she asks.

'No!' I say quickly.

'Mine tries to, but I don't let her,' she says. 'She's an academic so she's got no sense of style. Obviously.'

'What's an academic?' I say, glancing at what Priti is wearing.

'A professor thingy. She works at the university and thinks fashion is a feminist issue.'

'Right,' I say, even though I've got no idea what she's talking about.

'So this is about your mum then,' she says.

'What is?'

'The "Ben's had a difficult day" bit. The reason you're here. I'm right, aren't I?'

'My mum's sick, OK? She had to go to hospital. Happy now?'

'Happy would be weird,' says Priti solemnly. Then she grins. 'But it's always nice to be right!' She tips back on her wheelie shoes. 'We could take turns on my skateboard if you like?'

As Priti prepares for launch, I fish my notebook out of my pocket and doodle a superheroine with bunches somersaulting through the air on giant wheelie shoes surrounded by a swirl of exclamation marks and asterisks.

Then Priti takes off and suddenly she's in the air for real. Then she lands bum down on the tarmac.

For a moment, I think she's going to cry, but instead she starts laughing. 'Too many wheels,' she says, kicking off her shoes and going at it again with just her socks on. This time she clears the ramp and lands easily.

'I'm eleven and a quarter,' she says as she lands. 'How old are you?'

'Twelve,' I say, 'and eight months.'

'You're pretty short for your age,' she says, standing in front of me in her white socks on the hot, dirty

13

tarmac. 'Bet I'm nearly as tall as you.'

'Only cos you're standing on your tiptoes.'

She glances down at her feet – she doesn't seem that bothered about the state of her socks – and shrugs.

'What're you drawing?' she asks, staring down at my notepad.

'You,' I say.

'Oh.' She twists herself to take a look. 'Cool! I look like a midget Lara Croft.'

'With a tutu and bunches,' I say.

'You're well good.'

'Thanks.'

'My mum would say that drawing cartoons offers you an escape from your troubled existence.'

'I don't have a troubled existence.'

'If you say so.' She shrugs again. 'Your turn,' she says, handing me the skateboard. 'You can do it, can't you?'

'Course I can,' I say, taking the board from her. She raises one eyebrow (which I know from trying it is harder than it looks) and folds her arms. I can tell she's waiting for me to mess up.

Luckily, I actually can skateboard, though not as

well as Priti. I clear the ramp and land a little awkwardly on the other side.

'Not bad,' she says as I hand back the skateboard. 'And I've just figured out why you're here.'

'I told you why.'

'Yeah, but then I thought, if his mum's so ill, why isn't he with his dad? And I figured that your dad could be an international spy or an Arctic explorer or a contestant on a reality TV programme, or maybe just divorced or in a coma or something boring like that. But then I remembered.'

I look down, knowing what's coming.

'I remembered that my brother said that he heard my mum say to my dad that the pink bike kid's mum said to her that your gran's boy was killed on September 11th,' she says, without taking a breath. 'And that must be your dad, right?'

I nod.

She pauses for the briefest of seconds. 'So what does that mean anyway?'

I look up. 'Have you never heard of September 11th?' I ask.

'Nope!' She shakes her head and her bunches flap around like giant dog's ears.

'But everyone's heard of September 11th!' I say, trying to work out if she's lying. 'Don't they do it in your school?'

'Is it a "racially sensitive" topic?' asks Priti, picking sticky tarmac off the bottom of her sock.

'I guess,' I say.

'Cos our teachers generally steer clear of those.'

'Why?'

'High ratio of Asian pupils of immigrant backgrounds to white teachers of newly qualified teacher status,' she says quickly, sounding like she's quoting something she read in a newspaper. 'My mum reckons all our teachers are "white and green" – that means newly qualified, not really green, like aliens. That would be cool too, but you probably couldn't mess them around so much. Anyway, Mum reckons they're all frightened of saying something racially offensive. That's why they keep things pretty much uncontroversial. Personally, I think it's a shame because informed discussion is a valuable educational tool, but what can you do?'

'I see,' I say.

'So are you going to tell me what's so special about this September 11th thing or not?' says Priti, still picking at her socks.

Actually, I'd rather not, but I take a deep breath and do anyway. 'These men flew their aeroplanes into some tower blocks in America and knocked them over. Loads of people were killed.' Then I add, 'Including my dad.'

I imagine drawing cartoon aeroplanes flying into cartoon tower blocks. Cartoon flames and speech bubbles filled with *AAAAAAAAAAH*s.

'Oh, you mean 9/11,' she says, looking up. 'You should have said.'

I stare at her. 'Um, I did.'

'Yeah, well, everyone's heard of 9/11,' she says. Like I was the one who'd said I didn't know.

'I told you they had,' I say.

'And you reckon your dad was one of the ones that died?'

In my head I'm drawing cartoon flames coming

from the tower blocks. Stick men jumping through the air, falling.

'I don't *reckon*,' I say. 'He was.'

I grab the skateboard and take off in the direction of the ramp. This time I don't quite make it and my ankle twists painfully as I hit the tarmac. I want to cry out, but I don't.

'You are so making this up,' I hear Priti saying.

'You were the one who said your brother heard it from your mum or whoever,' I say, getting up and trying not to show how much my ankle hurts.

'Yeah, well, your granny must have made it up in that case.'

'Why would she do that?' I shove the board in her direction.

'I dunno. To get free meals-on-wheels? To have something to talk about with her pals at bingo? To get herself through to the next round on *The X Factor*? How should I know?'

'Well, she didn't,' I say.

'I mean, you don't exactly look like someone whose dad got killed by terrorists, do you?'

'What am I supposed to look like then?'

'I dunno – just different.'

I glance down at my shoes. Imagine doodling sad faces on the toe of each one.

'Would it be better if I had a leg missing or a big sign on my head saying *9/11 Boy* or something?' I say.

'All right. No need to get upset just cos I don't believe you! Which I don't by the way.'

'I'm not getting upset,' I say. 'It's not my fault that you're too young to remember it.'

'I so am not!' says Priti. One of her bunches has come loose and is hanging much lower than the other so it makes her look lopsided. 'My dad says I've got a memory like an elephant, and that's pretty big.'

Even though I'm fairly sure that elephants have small memories, I don't argue with her; I just say, 'I'm going in.'

Most people, when they find out about my dad, are super nice to me in a way that's really creepy. Even my friends go all weird on me every September, like I've got a contagious disease or something. But no one has ever accused me of making it up before. And it's really annoying.

Priti jumps to her feet. 'Don't go,' she says. 'If you go in my mum'll make me do my homework. She's dead hot on that sort of thing.'

Part of me wants to go back inside just to get her in trouble. But then I glance back at my grandparents' house and I can see my grandad sitting in his favourite armchair watching daytime TV and eating ginger biscuits. My granny's probably in the kitchen, fixing tea and worrying. And I realise I don't want to go back inside, not just yet.

'If you stay, I won't ask you any more about what happened with your mum, or about your dad . . . or your Twin Towers fantasy,' Priti says in this super-nice voice.

I look at her. She looks at me.

'AND I'll tell you a secret! A BIG one!'

I glance back at the house again. I don't want her to think I'm a pushover.

'OK,' I say with a shrug.

So she does.

'My brothers are going to kill my sister,' Priti

whispers, squatting down dead close to me, like she's my girlfriend or something.

I give her a look. 'That's the secret?'

'Yup,' she says. 'Good, innit?'

I stare at her again. 'Yeah, right!' I say.

'They are!' she says. 'It's going to be an honour killing.'

'What's that anyway?'

'It's when they kill her because she's got a boyfriend.'

'My mum's got a boyfriend,' I say. 'He's called Gary.' An image of my mum laughing with Gary flashes through my mind. I push it to one side. 'So are they going to kill her too?'

'Don't be stupid. My sister is, like, sixteen. And anyway, it's a Muslim thing.'

'Are you a Muslim then?'

In my head I draw Priti in one of those giant burkhas, her wheelie shoes peeping out of the bottom.

'Yep,' she says, tugging at her bunches until one ends up slightly higher than the other. 'I know it's a bit confusing because I've got a Hindu name – apparently there was a big row about it at the time, but my mum loved it and her great-great-grandma was half Hindu or something. And it's not like we're dead religious anyway, so I don't know what the big problem was – except Priti is a hard name to live up to, you know!'

She looks at me like I'm expected to say something here, but I don't. She tuts loudly.

I look over at Stevie's house. She's waving to us from her bedroom window. She's wearing her pyjamas and holding a princess doll. I wave back. Priti doesn't.

'So what makes you think they're going to kill your sister?' I ask. 'Did they tell you?'

'No, but she's got this totally unsuitable boyfriend called Tyreese. Now *there's* a stupid name! Anyway, I'm the only one who knows about him and I have to keep it a secret or she'll be dead!' Priti tries to sound really serious, but she can't stop grinning. 'Zara let me have some of her lipstick and a packet of cigarettes if I promised not to tell because it's a matter of life and death.'

'Why doesn't she just break up with him if it's so dangerous?' I say.

'She reckons she's in love with him.'

'Is she?'

'No way! She's too in love with herself.'

'So has she got some kind of death wish then?'

'Nah, she just reckons she's being cool and rebellious. Combination of having an overachieving mother and watching too much *Hollyoaks*.'

'And they'll definitely really kill her if they find out?' I say, still unconvinced.

'They might just send her to Pakistan and force her to marry some old bloke. Or they might kill her. Depends, I s'pose.'

'On what?'

'Dunno.' Priti shrugs. 'Want some bubblegum?'

She passes me a bit of gum, pink like her shoes. We sit and chew for a bit and she picks more bits of tarmac off her socks. 'Won't your mum mind?' I ask, pointing to her socks.

'She's going to be well mad. My dad says the sooner they can pack me off to Pakistan and get *me* married to some poor fool the better. He reckons he's joking, but I know better. Dads!' she says.

And the way she says it reminds me of the way my

grandad said 'Asians!' earlier and that makes me smile
– because it's hard to imagine anyone who is *less* like
my grandad than Priti.

At bedtime, I ask Granny how long I'll be staying, but
she doesn't really give me an answer. I know it's going
to be a while because, if it was only for a day or so, I'd
have been sent to Grandma's (Mum's mum, who lives
near to us, but she's got arthritis and has to have help
with cooking and washing and stuff) or to stay with a
friend. My mum doesn't like troubling Rita and Barry
(that's Granny and Grandad) unless she has to. She
says it's because of the distance, but I know that's not
the real reason.

'Let's not worry about how long you'll be staying
for the moment,' Granny says. 'Let's just concentrate
on having a nice time while we've got you.'

'Can I call Mum later?' I ask. I know what the
answer will be.

'Maybe tomorrow,' she says.

'Right.'

After she's gone, I draw a cartoon of Priti on her

skateboard, being chased by two balaclava-wearing assassins, also on skateboards, waving giant swords. Then I draw me, dressed as a commando, taking out the assassins with a flying karate kick.

Kerpow!

THINGS PEOPLE WANT TO KNOW ABOUT MY DAD DYING IN 9/11

1. What was he doing in New York that meant he happened to be there on that day? (He was at a meeting in the World Trade Center.)

2. Did he make any phone calls before he died? What did he say and did we keep any messages he left? (No. Nothing. No.)

3. Have I been to Ground Zero (the place where the Twin Towers used to be) to see where it happened? (No.)

4. Which tower was he in and what floor and did anyone on that floor escape? (Tower One. 102nd floor. No.)

5. Why haven't I seen any TV footage of what

happened? (I have actually. My mum just tells people I haven't because she always turns off the TV when it comes on, but I've seen clips and it wasn't so bad watching as I thought it would be.)

6. Did they ever find any bits of him and what did we do with them? (No, so nothing – obviously.)

7. What do I think about the people who did it? (I'm not sure – which I don't think is the right answer.)

8. What would I do if I ever met the people who did it? (Which is a silly question because they're dead anyway.)

9. Do I miss having a dad? (I always say yes, but I don't remember having one, so I don't really.)

10. What do me and my mum do on September 11th each year? (I get the day off school, and we pretend to do nothing much and just have a 'normal' day, which actually means doing stuff like blackberry picking and building papier-mâché volcanoes – things we never normally do. Then Mum tries to talk about it, gets upset, I change the subject, we do normal stuff some more. That's about it.)

JULY 14TH

Old people fall asleep in the afternoon. This is something I've discovered living at Granny and Grandad's. After lunch today, I do the washing-up so they can put their feet up, then I sit and draw cartoons: Granny flying an old-fashioned aeroplane, wearing a cap and goggles, her scarf flapping in the breeze; Grandad in a cape with a jet pack on his back, shouting, 'To infinity and beyond!'; then my mum lying on a bed with thorns growing up all around it.

The doorbell rings and I quickly scribble over the picture of my mum before going to answer it. Because you can't wake old people suddenly, can you? They might have a heart attack or something and I can't afford to lose any more family members.

So I open the door and there's Priti, standing on the doorstep next to an older girl who's wearing cropped jeans and a white T-shirt with little black ballet pumps on her slim brown feet. She's maybe fifteen or sixteen, and she's dressed so differently from Priti that you have to look closely to see they actually look alike.

This must be the sister who's going to be honour-killed.

'Zara says she'll take us to the park if you want to come,' says Priti, who is wearing a pink velour tracksuit top and what looks like her school uniform skirt rolled up short and worn over a pair of patterned leggings. She has her wheelie shoes on again, this time with orange and pink fluorescent laces.

'I'll have to ask my grandad,' I say.

'Well, get a move on then!' says Zara, who is chewing gum and doesn't even bother to look at me.

So I leave them waiting on the doorstep and poke my head into the lounge. Both grandparents are still fast asleep and they look like big wrinkly babies.

'Grandad,' I whisper, shaking him gently on the shoulder. Grandad lets out a little snort and then stares at me, confused.

'Priti's sister says she'll take us to the park. Can I go?'

I expect him to say, 'How old is she?' or, 'When will you be back?' or one of those things my mum usually asks, but instead he says, 'You sure you want to get pally with that lot?'

Granny stirs in her sleep and mutters something. Grandad glances at her.

'They're nice,' I say.

'*Hmmph!*' says Grandad. 'Those are the sort that killed your dad!'

'Barry!' says Granny, awake suddenly.

'I'm just saying,' says Grandad.

'Well, it's not helpful,' says Granny. 'Don't listen to him, Ben.'

I stare from one grandparent to the other, wondering whether they mind being stuck with me all summer. Not that they'd say if they did.

'Can I go then?' I ask.

'Of course,' says Granny.

I glance at my grandad. 'Yes, yes. Get along with you.'

'Thanks,' I say. 'I'll see you later.'

My grandad mutters something about closing the door, so I do. I get the feeling they're going to keep on talking about me after I've gone.

'Right, come on then. I'm late,' says Zara and she's already heading off down the drive before I've even had time to put my shoes on. Priti follows her, so I'm left, half running, half hopping at the rear, as the two sisters cross the road and make their way down the alleyway that runs alongside Priti's house and leads to the park behind.

As I catch up with them, Priti whispers loudly, 'Zara's meeting her boyfriend. We're her cover.'

Zara glances back at us and glares.

'What do you mean?'

'Zara tells Mum she's taking me to the park to get me out from under her feet, then she texts Tyreese and he meets her there. We have to be the lookouts.'

Zara turns around and looks at me. 'Is that OK with you?' she asks sarcastically.

I look at her and feel myself going red as I nod.

Priti giggles. Zara tuts and turns away.

When we get to the park, Priti tells me we have to sit on top of the climbing frame or the slide, but the best view is from the climbing frame and you can fit two of us up there – then if we see anyone coming, we have to run and tell Zara.

'Do you just have to sit here?' I ask.

'Yeah. It's dead boring. That's why I thought I'd ask you to come.'

'Right,' I say.

I get out my notepad while she dangles upside down.

'By the way,' she says, defying gravity. 'My dad says it's right what you said about your dad and the whole 9/11 thing.'

'I wasn't the one who said it wasn't,' I reply.

'Yeah, well, I was well impressed. Just like a movie. Do you reckon that's where the blokes who did it got the idea?'

'No,' I say. I start to doodle a little paper aeroplane.

'My dad got really mad when I said it was a cool way to die,' says Priti, her long bunches almost touching the tarmac. 'He said the people who did it are a disgrace to Muslims like us.'

I don't say anything, but Priti doesn't seem to notice. 'Mik – he's my brother, the cool one; he's really called Mikaeel, but everyone calls him Mik –

anyway, he said the terrorists certainly got the world to sit up and listen and my dad went mad at him. He said, "If I ever hear any son or daughter of mine talk that way in this house, I will disown them!" It was well cool!' She swings herself upright suddenly, and her face is bright red with all the blood that's gone to it, and she's grinning.

'What did Mik say then?' I ask, drawing another aeroplane, a Boeing 767 this time. Little windows with faces at each one.

'He said there were plenty of other Muslims who thought the same as he did and my dad said, "Shame on them and shame on you if you take notice of people who talk that way!"'

'What happened then?'

'I thought it was all going to kick off, but then Shakeel, he's my eldest brother, he started talking about boring wedding arrangements – he's getting married soon – so it never did get into a big punch-up.'

Priti leans back so that she's horizontal and lifts up her legs, twirling her feet around so she can admire her shoes from all angles. I scribble over my aeroplane pictures.

'My grandad said your people killed my dad,' I say after a minute.

'Why did he say that?'

'Dunno. That's just what he said.'

'Well, they didn't,' she says, sitting upright now. 'None of my family live in America anyway.'

'Well, my dad didn't live there either,' I say. 'He just had a meeting in New York that day.'

'And none of my family can fly a plane!' she retorts.

'If you say so.' I look down at my shoes – tattered old Converse, all faded, nothing like Priti's garish footwear at all.

'So do you reckon the people who did it are dead?' she asks, swinging upright suddenly.

'Obviously!' I say.

'Unless they parachuted out of the aeroplanes just before they crashed. Or had those ejector seat things that sent them flying out of the cockpit,' she says. 'Hey! If they escaped, they might be on the run somewhere. Wouldn't it be dead cool if we could catch them and turn them in to the police?'

Once I drew one of those thumb-flick cartoons of planes flying into the Twin Towers. The ones where there's a little picture on the corner of each page and you flick through them with your thumb so they look like they're moving. Only I drew mine backwards – manga style – so you saw the toppling towers gradually rebuild themselves, saw the planes fly back off into the distance until they were just a speck on the horizon. I wish it was as easy as that: turn the book back to front and erase history, rebuild the towers, end the war.

Bring my dad back.

Priti keeps talking and I'm thinking about all this stuff, so neither of us is watching the path and then suddenly Priti says, 'Oh, no! It's Shakeel!' She heaves herself up quickly before jumping in one swift movement from the top of the climbing frame down on to the spongy green tarmac below. She lands on her wheels and narrowly avoids going head over heels by grabbing on to the fireman's pole to steady herself.

'Go!' she shouts up to me. 'You go tell Zara. I'll keep him chatting.'

'Why me?'

'Because he doesn't know you and you can hardly string two words together. How are you going to keep a conversation going?'

I have no answer to this, so I jump down and leg it in the direction of the woods where Zara and Tyreese are doing whatever they're doing.

Behind me I hear Priti counting in a loud voice. 'One . . . two . . . three . . . four . . .', pretending we're playing hide-and-seek, I suppose.

I stop running when I reach the edge of the wooded area. The earth between the trees is dusty and bare save for a few discarded cigarette cartons and empty beer cans.

I stop running because I can see Tyreese leaning back against a tree with Zara pressed up against him. In one hand he's holding a can of cider while the other hand is resting on Zara's bum. From where I'm standing it looks as if she's kissing him rather than the other way round.

I expect them to stop when they hear me approach, but they don't. Behind me I can hear Priti saying,

35

'sixteen . . . seventeen . . . Hi, Shakeel . . . we're playing hide-and-seek . . . eighteen . . . nineteen . . . Want to join in?'

I try to say something, but no words come out.

'Mum wants you and Zara to come and do your study,' I can hear Shakeel saying. 'Where is Zara anyway? I thought she was supposed to be watching out for you.'

'She's hiding. Twenty . . . twenty-one . . . twenty-two . . .'

I open my mouth and stammer something, but the snoggers don't hear.

'In my day we stopped at twenty,' Shakeel says.

'Maybe that's why you got so old so quickly!' Priti retorts. 'Twenty-three . . . twenty-four . . .'

Still Tyreese and Zara don't turn round.

'Come on, Priti. I don't have time for this. Mum wants you in now and I have my own studies to complete. '

I cough as loud as I can.

They stop snogging and turn to stare at me. Zara's mouth is wiped bare of lipstick.

'Whazzup, kid?' says Tyreese, who is tall and lanky,

his head shaven to a stubble and his jeans hanging off his bum so I can see most of his pants.

'Just looking, were you?' Zara asks, pushing a strand of hair off her face.

'Blood go rushing to your head, lil' bro?' Tyreese laughs. 'Or maybe it go somewhere else?' He grins and takes a swig of his cider. I go even redder.

Just then Shakeel shouts, 'Come *on*, Priti! I haven't got time for this!'

Zara leaps up at the sound of his voice. 'Oh, shit. What's *he* doing here?'

'Twenty-seven . . . twenty-eight,' I can hear Priti saying.

'Get the hell out of here,' Zara hisses at Tyreese.

'Ain't in no rush,' he says with the same slow, lazy grin he aimed at me.

'Twenty-nine.'

'Hide-and-seek,' I say.

'You what?' They both look at me like I'm an idiot.

'We're supposed to be playing hide-and-seek,' I say with an effort. 'Priti is looking for us.'

'Thirty. Coming, ready or not!'

'Shit! Quick!' Zara grabs me and pulls me into a bush to her left. Jammed up close to her, I don't know where to look or what to do with my hands.

We can hear Priti talking to herself as she pretends to look round the park for us.

Tyreese doesn't move. He grins and takes another swig of cider. Zara is breathing quickly next to me. 'Will you just go, Tyreese,' she hisses. Her blouse is still unbuttoned and I catch a flash of white bra against brown skin.

Tyreese takes another gulp before discarding his can. Then he starts to move off. 'So long, gorgeous!' he drawls.

Then he turns back and says, 'And keep your hands to yourself, kid!'

I feel my cheeks go redder than even I thought was possible.

'Text me,' Zara whispers.

But Tyreese doesn't reply, just blows her a kiss without even turning round.

Then it's just me and Zara. I turn my face away as she buttons up her blouse.

'Thanks,' she says.

In my head I doodle the words *No problem* and *My pleasure* over and over again in different fonts, but nothing comes out of my mouth.

Priti is coming now, making a big song and dance about not being able to find us. She stomps around the thicket, looking behind every bush but ours, exclaiming out loud about the empty bottles being a hazard to young kids. I concentrate on doodling words in my head to avoid looking at Zara.

Then, finally, Priti discovers our hiding place and it's all over.

Shakeel is the elder of Priti's two brothers. I think she said he's about twenty-three, but he seems older because his hair is thinning and he wears glasses. He doesn't look like a potential sister-killer to me.

I expect him to be mad when we get back to the swings, but he just shakes his head and laughs at Priti. 'She's going to Bollywood, this one!' he says.

'About bloody time too!' shouts Zara, standing up and dusting herself down. 'You know how long

39

I've been babysitting these two?'

Priti mutters something under her breath about Bollywood divas which makes Zara glare at her. I rise slowly to my feet, still unable to look at Zara.

'I seem to remember having to babysit *you* not so long ago, little sister,' says Shakeel with the same smile he gave to Priti. He actually seems nice.

'Well, unlike you, big bro, I got better things to do with my time than hang out with babies!' And, with that, Zara marches off towards the house. I watch her go – she looks flushed and her shirt is a bit lopsided. I want to write a caption for her, but I can't think of one.

'You saved her skin then, I reckon,' says Priti when Shakeel's far enough ahead not to hear us. 'She owes you a life debt now.'

'They wouldn't really kill her, would they, your brothers?' I ask.

'You obviously don't know anything about honour killings!' says Priti. 'They're going on all over the place. I mean, I don't *actually* know anyone it's happened to, but everyone knows it does, don't they? Shakeel

40

might seem all nicey-nicey Mr Big Brother, but he's well into all the tradition and that. If my sister brings shame on the family then . . .' She draws a hand across her throat in a slitting motion and chokes. Then she says cheerily, 'Gotta go do my homework. You up for hanging out tomorrow?'

I shrug my shoulders and say, 'Sure, why not.'

'Cool,' she says. 'I'll text you.'

'I don't have a mobile.'

Priti stares at me in astonishment. 'No way!'

'My mum reckons they're really bad for you,' I say.

Priti shakes her head. 'I figured something must be seriously wrong with your mum,' she says. 'Now I know I'm right!'

My mum has never let me have a mobile phone. She reckons the radio waves will fry my brain or something. I'm not allowed an iPod or a games console either. And I must be the only kid in the whole of Year 8 who doesn't have a computer at home. We've got a TV, but we only really watch *Coronation Street* and reruns of *Friends* and old cartoons on DVD. And we have a landline telephone, but my mum never makes calls and always gets me to answer it when it rings.

My mum hates all that stuff. She says she doesn't like being bombarded with unsolicited sounds and words and images. She reckons it saps us of our creativity and does God-knows-what to our brain cells.

But I don't think that's the only reason. I reckon it's to do with 9/11 too – like the time she turned on the radio in the car and they were playing answerphone messages that the victims had left for their families. She never put the radio on again after that.

When other kids at school ask, I just say it's because she's a painter. Because artists are supposed to be a bit wacky, aren't they? Which also explains why my mum forgets things, like parents' evenings and permission slips. And also why she's so thin.

My friend Lukas offered to give me his old mobile phone. He reckons he knows a way to top them up without paying. I nearly said yes, but I knew it would upset my mum, so I didn't. Only now I wish I had. Because maybe if I had a phone, he'd have texted to see why I haven't been in school, and when I'm coming back. And if Mum had one too, I could have texted her. But she doesn't, and I know she won't call, so I have no idea how she is.

Which feels rubbish.

JULY 15TH

When the doorbell rings, I know it's Priti because I've already worked out that no one else ever calls at the house. Sure enough, when Granny opens the door, Priti is standing there, only this time she's got the Honour Killer in tow. He's wearing a long white dress thing over his trousers and a little hat on his head.

'Good morning, Mrs Evans,' he says. 'I'm Shakeel Muhammed. I am the eldest son of your neighbours.'

'Hello, Shakeel. It's nice to meet you,' says Granny.

'And also you,' says Shakeel.

'Hello, Mrs Evans!' says Priti with an expression on her face that I bet she only puts on for adults.

'Hello, Priti,' says Granny. 'And I must say you *are* looking very pretty again today.'

Priti grins at me. She has a new hairstyle – a single ponytail high on her head, fixed with floaty pink things that make her look like she might take off at any minute.

'Mrs Evans, I am taking Priti to the newsagent to

spend her pocket money,' says Shakeel. 'She wondered if Ben would like to come with us.'

Priti grins at Granny.

'That's very kind,' says Granny, smiling back.

So Granny gives me a pound for tidying my room – although I haven't exactly had time to get it untidy – and the three of us head off down to the parade.

The Peacock Parade – which is the name Granny gives to the little row of shops nearby because they are on Peacock Street – is a five-minute walk away, where the last of the quiet cul-de-sacs meets the busy main road. Behind the parade are the rows of terraced houses (full of Asians, according to Grandad) and then beyond that, the city starts with its tower blocks and shopping centres and busy roads. My grandparents don't often go into the city centre these days.

'Too fast,' says Granny.

'In every sense of the word,' says Grandad.

As soon as we get out of the cul-de-sac, Priti tugs me ahead and whispers, 'I've got to run on ahead and warn Zara. Can you fall down and hurt your knee or something? Give me a bit of time?'

But it's not really a question – or even a request – because before I can answer, she's shot off down the road, veering dangerously close to the edge of the pavement.

'Slow down, missy!' shouts Shakeel. Then, turning to me, 'Why is she in such a hurry?'

'I think she saw someone she knew,' I reply, bending down and pretending to tie my lace. I can feel myself going red. I'm not a very good liar.

'Girls, eh!' Shakeel laughs. 'She's a bit crazy that sister of mine. No man will want a crazy-head like that! It's a good job she has brains otherwise we'd have to pay someone to take her off our hands.'

I'm not sure if he's joking, so I don't laugh.

Down at the parade a group of teenage boys with shaved heads are sitting on motorbikes, laughing and revving their engines. Among them is Zara's boyfriend, Tyreese. Zara is sitting on a bench only a few metres away, flicking through a copy of *Heat* magazine and pretending to ignore them. Priti is perched next to her, swinging her legs and checking the bikers out.

As Shakeel and I walk past the bikers, I can feel them staring at us, but none of them says anything.

Zara looks up and stares accusingly in our direction. I feel myself starting to blush.

'I thought you were supposed to be looking out for Ugli here?' she says to Shakeel, completely ignoring me. 'She's cramping my style with this Asian Jordan look she's got going on today.'

Priti pulls a face at Zara.

'And she's not supposed to run off and cross the road without me,' says Shakeel, looking at Priti, who gives him what I think is supposed to be a kooky grin, but which just makes her face look a bit lopsided. 'What are you doing here anyway?' he asks Zara, glancing at the bikers who are laughing raucously.

'Buying tampons, if you must know,' says Zara.

Shakeel goes red and looks uncomfortable and I can feel myself doing the same.

Then one of the lads on the bikes calls out to Shakeel, 'Nice dress, mate!'

They all start laughing and Tyreese revs his engine. Zara colours, but doesn't look at him.

Shakeel doesn't respond or even turn in their direction. 'Just ignore them,' he says.

'Hey, loser! Watcha doing hanging out with a load of Pakis?' Tyreese shouts.

I feel hot and uncomfortable because I know he's talking to me and because my mum always tells me that's a word you should never use, but I don't say anything.

'Hey, you little runt!' says Tyreese when I don't answer. 'I'm talking to you. Dontcha know it's disrespectful not to answer you' elders?'

Still I don't say anything. I imagine a caption over my head, reading, *What ya gonna do now?*

'What you doin' hanging out with Mussies anyway?' Tyreese goes on. 'Dontcha know they all terrorists?'

I imagine my face morphing into a giant cartoon tomato.

'Oi, leave off him,' says Priti.

I see Zara kick her.

'Got yourself a mouthy little Paki bit of stuff there, have you, kid?' Tyreese says.

The other bikers laugh and one of them shouts, 'Don't fancy yours much, kid, but I'd give her sister a go!'

Zara turns to stare furiously at Tyreese, but he just laughs.

Then I hear a voice from behind me say, 'You want your skull caved in, just keep talking to my sisters like that.'

I turn round to see a teenage boy who looks like a tall, spikey-haired version of Priti. He's wearing jeans that hang almost as low as Tyreese's and he steps towards the bikers as he speaks to show he means business.

'Leave it, Mik,' Shakeel says. 'We don't want any trouble.'

'You might not, big bro. Me, I'm gagging for it!'

'You want a beating, Paki boy?' says Tyreese.

'You got nothing I want, white trash!' says the boy called Mik, who I figure must be Priti's other brother.

I glance at Priti. She doesn't look the least bit scared.

'Come on, Mik, we are going,' Shakeel says, putting an arm round his brother.

'You trying to shame me, bro?' Mik pushes him away.

'You bring shame on yourself by fighting in the street,' says Shakeel.

'So you'll let them insult your sisters, your family, your people. That's supposed to be honourable, is it?'

'There are better ways of keeping our honour than this!' says Shakeel. As he says it, he touches his brother on the arm again and the two of them stare at each other for a moment.

Next to Shakeel, Mik looks really young and really angry. He shakes Shakeel's hand away.

'Not worth getting my hands dirty for anyway!' he says, furious, turning away.

'You can leave your sister here for us if you want,' says Tyreese. 'I wouldn't mind a bit of that myself.' He laughs.

Mik swings round and is about to go for him, but Shakeel pulls him back, more forcefully this time. 'Let them keep,' he says, speaking right into Mik's face now. 'There are better ways to deal with this kind of scum than with your fists.'

But there's a look on Mik's face as his brother

drags him away – his clenched jaw, furrowed brow, the cartoon daggers flying out of his eyes – that makes me think this is not over for him. Not by a long way.

Somehow Priti manages to persuade Shakeel to let us get our sweets, despite the fact that a race riot is about to kick off at the parade, but he makes us go straight home after. Zara's mad at him, but Mik is even madder. As I watch him marching on ahead with Zara, I get the feeling Mik doesn't like having to do what his older brother tells him.

Priti and I hang at the back, munching on our sweets.

'That was well cool back there, wasn't it?' she says, sucking a fizzy pink strawberry lace through her teeth.

'Nothing like that happens where I come from,' I say.

'No?' She turns and looks at me curiously. 'Aren't there any Muslims where you live?'

'What's that got to do with it?' I say.

'Not sure,' she says, slurping in the last of her lace. 'Aren't there?'

I think for a moment. 'Not sure.'

'People don't like Muslims much,' she says, trying to lick a stray bit of pink sugar from her nose with the tip of her tongue. 'I don't think your 9/11 thing helped our image, to be honest.'

'It's not my 9/11 thing,' I say.

'You know what I mean. And they don't like the headscarves either.' She stretches up her tongue again, tantalisingly close to the sugar grains this time.

'Why don't you wear one?' I ask.

'Cos I'd look minging,' she says, scrunching her nose to try and shift the pink sugar closer to her mouth. 'Zara reckons she's "emancipated", but that basically means she thinks she's too cool for one.'

Priti stretches out her tongue one last time, without success. 'Bum!' she says, wiping the sugar away with her sleeve. 'I'm sure my tongue has shrunk!'

'Why did Tyreese have a go at her?' I ask after a moment. This has been bothering me. If he's supposed to be her boyfriend, why did he let his mates talk about her like that?

'It's like foreplay, I reckon,' says Priti. 'Gets them both hot and steamy!'

'Foreplay?'

Priti looks at me like I'm some kind of idiot. 'You really don't know much, do you?' She shakes her head. 'Zara's into the whole forbidden love thing. She reads too many of those soppy vampire romance novels, I reckon, so now she figures Tyreese is like one of those repressed bloodsuckers who gets off on seeing girls in danger. Which is a load of misogynist nonsense if you ask me, but you know what teenage girls are like.'

I imagine doodling fangs and a hooded cape on to Tyreese, drops of blood dripping inkily down his chin. I don't bother asking her what misogynist means.

We're nearly back at the close now and Priti is opening a packet of pink space dust. 'Anyway, my dad says we're going to Pakistan for a holiday next year,' she says. 'And you know what that means, don't you?'

I shake my head.

'He's going to get Zara into a forced marriage. And maybe me too. Go on, ask me what a forced marriage is. I know you want to!' She pours space dust on her tongue and keeps it out, watching the bright pink grains exploding.

'What's a forced marriage?' I say, pulling a face.

'He's gonna find some old, ugly bloke and make us marry him. Want some?' she says, offering me the space dust.

'Are you sure?' I say. 'Both of you?'

'Not to the same bloke obviously.'

'Obviously,' I reply.

'That's why Zara's into the Tyreese thing. It's her last chance to mess up her own love life.'

'So why doesn't she get to choose who she marries?'

'Cos that's how it works, duh. Your dad chooses for you.'

'Why not your mum?'

'Patriarchal oppression!' Priti says solemnly, emptying more space dust into her mouth then giggling as it explodes.

'Do you even know what that means?' I ask.

Priti licks her lips before saying, 'I so do! It means the men get to decide everything and women are like glorified slaves. Not that it's like that in our house. My parents have a marriage of equals – only my dad still blatantly reckons he gets to choose the husbands. Which is probably good because my mum'd be rubbish at choosing anyway. Psychiatrists are the *worst* judges of character.'

I'm about to ask why, but Priti doesn't give me a chance.

'*And* my mum went to university,' she says. 'Which no one is ever allowed to mention because my dad didn't. She wants me and Zara to be educated and have careers before we get married, so she's the one making us memorise the dictionary and learn speeches from the classics while my dad is off doing the whole matchmaker thing – although I bet she ends up getting the last word in that too, like she does about everything else. If you ask me, there's a lot of gender role reversal going on in our house!' Priti finishes, looking really pleased with herself, then runs her finger round the inside of the space-dust sachet to pick up any stray grains.

'Does your mum really make you memorise the

dictionary?' I ask, imagining Priti with her head in a giant book, long words circling about and heaped up in piles all around her.

'Yup. I have to learn ten new words a week. Then every Friday we have a spelling bee, with definitions and everything. And it can be any of the words I've learned over the last six months. Zara really hates it. She says it would be way cooler to fail all her GCSEs than know how to spell "phosphorescence", but I reckon it just drives her nuts that I'm so much cleverer than her.' Priti swallows quickly and says, 'It's not all bad though. My mum has some cool books that I get to read when she's not looking.'

'What sort of books?' I ask.

'About how all kids want to do it with their dad, and how all girls wish they had willies – which I totally don't agree with because willies are the most pointless, ugly little things. And I bet even *you* don't want to do it with your dad.'

'Course not!' I say.

'No, I reckon that'd probably be too weird even for my mum's books – maybe not though,' she says, looking thoughtful. 'Do you want to do it with your mum?' she asks, looking at me curiously.

'No!' I say, angry at her for reminding me of my mum who I've been trying not to think about.

We're back at Priti's house now and she clambers up on the front wall and starts walking along it, arms akimbo, like she's on a tightrope. To change the subject, I say, 'Can't your mum stop your dad from forcing Zara to get married then?'

'Not if she finds out about Zara and Tyreese!' Priti replies, wobbling on her wheelies. 'She'd rather see us not graduate than get knocked up by some random trash boy before we've finished school.' The way she says this reminds me of my grandad again. 'Anyway, it's tradition. Your dad's supposed to decide who you go out with.'

'Well, my mum's got a boyfriend and I know for a fact her dad didn't pick him out,' I say.

An image flashes up from the other morning: Gary helping my mum into the car on the day she left. She was wearing a fur coat, even though it was the middle of summer, and she was carrying a suitcase. That was when I noticed that more of her beautiful hair had fallen out.

'It's a Muslim thing,' says Priti, who is raising one leg then the other in the air as she walks. 'I guess your mum didn't have to check with anyone before she started carrying on with this Gary bloke then?'

'She asked me if I was OK with it.'

Another image: of my mum's face the morning she left. Red eyes, lipstick as dark as blackberries. Her lips mouthing the words, 'Miss you, darling,' although no sound came out.

'Really?' Priti looks surprised and abandons her performance for a moment. 'What did you say?'

'I said it was fine with me.'

'And is it?'

'I suppose so.'

'That's cool!' Priti says. 'You get to choose who your mum goes out with. I reckon I'd choose a wicked husband for my mum. One who dresses up as Elvis and knows how to make candyfloss and sticks his used bubblegum under the bed till it goes hard, and lets us have chips every day and go to sleep whenever we want and wear wheelies to school and never do any homework!'

'I didn't exactly get to choose,' I say, imagining a Willy Wonka Elvis with a quiff and a giant stick of candyfloss walking down the aisle with my mum.

'No, but you still get to say if you don't like him, don't you?'

I'm not really sure that I do, but I don't bother trying to explain.

'I guess my dad would have to die before I get a candyfloss Elvis,' Priti says thoughtfully.

'Yeah, there is that.'

'That'd be a bummer. Still, it'd be pretty cool to have a dad who could blow bigger bubbles than you. So how did your mum meet him then, this Gary?'

'They met at the village fete committee,' I say.

'That is so country!' says Priti. 'Still, I suppose you don't have speed dating and Internet matchmakers in the sticks. Boy, am I glad I don't live in the country!'

'My mum's on loads of committees,' I say defensively. 'She's a pillar of the community.'

Actually, she's a serial committee member who

59

spends all her free time setting up trestle tables, decorating church halls, bulk-buying burgers and getting people to volunteer for things. Which is all great – I mean, I'm dead proud of her – but I don't get to see much of her. Well, I do, but only while we're both helping out with things. I've lost count of the number of times I've fallen asleep in the corner at a committee meeting or sat late in the headmistress's office because mum was running late from organising something or other.

'She sounds pretty needy, if you ask me,' says Priti, tipped back on her wheelies now, but still balancing on the wall in a way that seems to defy gravity.

'What's that supposed to mean?' I ask. I can feel my bag of sweets getting hot and sticky in my pocket and my face doing the same.

'Anyone who volunteers that much clearly has a desperate need to be needed,' she says, authoritatively, like it's something she's read in another of her mum's books.

'You've never even met her,' I say crossly, digging my hands deeper into my pockets.

'OK, keep your hair on. I was only saying.' She's still tipped back at a precarious-looking forty-five degree angle, her arms folded across her chest.

'Well, don't!'

I stare down at my feet and wonder if she's right. Before dad died, my mum was always 'a willing volunteer', but not like she is now. Now her friends are always telling her she does too much, but she just laughs and says, 'I know, but someone's got to do it.'

I wonder how all the committees are doing now she's in hospital. The parent-teacher association and the village fete committee and the gardeners' club and the Save the Post Office committee and all the rest? Will they fall apart without her? I wonder if she knows that I need her too.

'OK, so why don't you tell me what she's really like then?' says Priti, tilting back and forth on her wheelies on the narrow strip of wall, staring down at her feet as she does so to make sure she doesn't fall off.

I hesitate. What else is there to say about my mum? 'Um, she's called Hannah. She's thirty-nine years old,' I say, wrapping my fingers round the hot bag of sweets in my pocket, feeling their shapes sticky against the paper. 'She's pretty short and she has long hair down to her waist.' Little girl hair she calls it. It makes her look younger from the back than from the front. But I don't say that.

'Yeah, but I mean, what's she *like*?' Priti glances up from her balancing act and nearly topples backwards, righting herself just in time. 'Like, what does she do – when she's not picking up men at village fete committees, that is?'

I stare at my feet some more. I want to tell her that my mum can do anything – she can make a light sabre from a toilet roll or save a nest of baby birds that have been abandoned by their mother. But I don't. I say, 'She's an artist.'

'What sort of artist?'

'She makes pictures of the countryside where we live to sell to tourists.' Then quickly, before Priti can interrupt again, I add, 'But she has loads of other jobs too: she cooks these nut-free-gluten-free-meat-free-soya-free meals for a little girl down the road who's ill; she does some landscape gardening; she works as a PA for a charity fundraiser and runs play-scheme projects for the council. And loads of other stuff too.'

'Wow!' says Priti, tilting herself forwards on her toes one last time before launching herself off the wall and landing next to me with a clatter. 'Maybe my mum's books are right,' she says with a triumphant grin.

'What about?'

Priti scrunches up her nose and parks her bum on to the wall next to mine. I notice that her tongue is bright pink from the strawberry lace. 'Not about the whole "all boys are in love with their mums" stuff – that's just obvious,' she says. 'More the one she's reading at the moment. About how women who care too much screw their kids up.'

I want to think of something clever to say in response to this, but I can't.

'So are you going to share those sweets before they melt and make it look like you've wet yourself or what?'

When we get back from the parade, there's a new arrival.

'You look just like your dad did at your age,' says

my uncle Ian who's sitting in Grandad's chair. 'He was skinny and scrappy like you. Used to do whatever I said, but I still beat him up pretty regularly!'

Uncle Ian laughs. Grandad laughs. Granny tells him to watch what he's saying. And I remember why I don't like Uncle Ian.

He and my cousin Jed turned up while I was out with Priti and Co. 'A surprise visit,' says Uncle Ian.

'Cos we didn't have anything better to do,' says Jed.

Jed is only a year older than me, but it always seems like more. He's bigger than me and cooler and better at pretty much everything. I haven't seen him for ages and he seems to have grown about half a metre since last time and his hair is all long and scraggly.

Jed's OK (so long as you always agree with him) but I've always been a bit scared of Uncle Ian. He has this habit of knowing exactly what to say to make me feel really small and stupid. I've seen him do it to Granny too, and to Jed – it's just what he does. He used to be in the army and, even though he isn't any more, he's still got what Jed calls his 'Corporal Bollocking voice'.

'Why don't you boys go and play in the garden?' suggests Granny after about five minutes. Jed is climbing all over the sofa like a great big gangly toddler, his feet in dirty trainers, looking as if they're about to smash into her favourite glass cabinet.

He pulls a face and says, 'Play?'

'Oh, you know, hang out,' says Granny. 'Or whatever you young people do.'

Jed glances at me like he'd prefer not to and says, 'Do we have to?'

'Do as your gran tells you,' says Uncle Ian.

So the two of us head out into the back garden and I'm surprised to find myself wishing that Priti was here too.

'My dad says your mum is turning into a nutcase just like mine,' says Jed in a big loud voice as he bounds out through the patio doors, leaping so high he nearly takes his head off.

'No, she's not!' I say, wishing I'd grown a bit more. And wishing my hair wasn't so short.

'That's what my dad says. He reckons your dad and him were both stupid enough to fall for women who are soft in the head.'

'My mum's not soft in the head – she's ill,' I say.

'Yeah, that's what they would tell you, isn't it?'

Jed's brought a ball with him and he starts doing headers and keepy-uppies. He's wearing a puffa jacket several sizes too big for him and it hangs off his shoulders. All his clothes hang off him, and not just because he's wiry – although he is – more like he's too cool for clothes. When I wear his hand-me-downs they don't look the same on me at all, although my mum says this is because I actually bother to do up all the buttons.

I sit down on the patio and picture a cartoon Jed, swamped in a giant puffa so large it drags along the floor while he does keepy-uppies. 'What's wrong with your mum then?' I ask.

'She's a bitch,' says Jed and, as he says this, he lets the ball fall from the air, catching it in his hands and looking straight at me. It's like he's daring me to challenge him for swearing.

'Why? What did she do?' I sort of know already because my mum told me, but I ask anyway.

'She tried to take me away from my dad.'

'How?'

'She took him to court, but he showed them she had a screw loose, which she does.' Jed kicks the ball hard against the fence. 'I don't want to see her anyway,' he says.

'Why not?'

'I don't want her turning me soft in the head. It's bad enough I've got her genes, I reckon, without her hanging around messing with my mind!' He tosses the ball at me so quickly that I don't see it coming and I miss it. 'I bet you miss *your* mum, don't you?' he says.

'No,' I say quickly, picking up the ball, my face reddening.

'I bet you do. I bet you cry for her at night, don't you?' He shrugs. 'Don't worry about it. I used to as well, but now I've got tough. Come on, let's do penalties.'

So we play for penalties for a bit. I'm in goal and

I'm not very good, but I soon realise it's better if I don't actually stop the goals anyway cos when I do, Jed gets really pissed off.

'My dad says your dad was the falling man,' Jed says after he's shot three goals in a row.

'What?' I'm standing between the plant pots that Jed has set up as a makeshift goal and suddenly I see a picture of a stick man slowly falling in loop-the-loop motions, like a leaf from a tree.

'The falling man,' Jed repeats. 'You must have seen him on the telly. He's the guy who was the first one to jump out of the Twin Towers.' He stares at me as if I'm an idiot. 'You know, in 9/11?'

'Yeah, I know,' I say.

He pauses, stares at me, then starts grinning. 'You haven't seen it, have you?'

I can feel myself going red again. I'm not supposed to have seen any of the 9/11 footage – my mum doesn't want me to – but I have anyway. My friend Lukas showed me the falling man on his laptop. We watched it over and over again. It was after that I made the thumb-flick cartoon.

'God, mums are so lame!' says Jed. 'Wrapping you up in cotton wool – pulling the wool over your eyes more like. OK, so it's like this,' he continues. 'After the planes crash into the buildings, they're like a towering inferno. You must have seen pictures at least?'

'Of course I have,' I say quickly.

'Right, well there's this one guy who decides he'd rather jump out and die than get burned alive. So you see him jump out. Just this little man falling through the sky.'

I see it again, the little stick man, curling through the air.

'Then some others do it too, but that first one, he's the coolest, I reckon, and that's your dad.'

I feel more blood rushing to my cheeks so I stare really hard at the ball that Jed's about to kick.

'I reckon I'd do the same,' Jed goes on. 'I'd rather die jumping out of a building than get burned to death. At least it'd be a laugh on the way down. And it'd be pretty cool to be the first one to jump. What do you reckon?' He looks at me.

'I don't know,' I say. In my head, a giant boxing glove pings out on a spring and catches him square on the jaw.

'Well, my dad's watched that falling man over and over and he says it's definitely Uncle Andrew. I think so too.'

'Does he look like my dad then?' I ask, glancing up quickly.

'Yeah!' says Jed.

I pause and then say, 'So do you, like, remember him? What he looked like and all that?'

'Yeah. Don't you?'

Now I see a midget with a giant hammer clubbing him over the head.

'Course I do,' I say. But I've taken my eye off the ball and Jed kicks it hard so it goes straight past me into the flower bed behind.

'Goal!' cheers Jed.

A giant anvil falls out of the sky and flattens him to the ground.

THINGS I'VE ALWAYS WANTED TO KNOW ABOUT THE MEN WHO FLEW THEIR PLANES INTO THE TWIN TOWERS AND KILLED MY DAD

1. What did they look like?

2. Did they actually come up with the idea themselves or did someone else think of it and they just agreed to do it?

3. Did they have brothers and sisters and families and kids and homes and stuff? And did they tell those people what they were going to do?

4. Were they scared of dying? Or was it that they didn't like being alive and had rubbish lives so didn't mind dying?

5. And if not, how did they end up being the ones picked to do it?

6. What did they do in the day before it happened?

7. Did they ever have second thoughts?

8. Did they hate my dad and all the people in the Twin Towers when they did it?

9. Did they hate the kids like me who had dads and mums in the towers too?

10. Did they make it to heaven or wherever they

thought they'd get to? And, if not, did they ever regret what they did?

❖   ❖   ❖

Jed is going to stay all summer. Uncle Ian has to work and Jed can't go to his mum for the holidays ('for obvious reasons,' says Jed, rolling his eyes) so I suppose Granny and Grandad have no choice but to say yes. Granny says it will be like having her two boys back again. Grandad says it will be 'bloody noisy!' and I think I agree with him.

Jed and I are sharing a room, and within five minutes, Jed's stuff is everywhere and he's climbing all over the furniture. I can tell he isn't impressed about having to stay. 'I don't see why I had to come here anyway. I could have looked after myself,' he says. 'I do it every day after school – sometimes Dad's not back till well late.'

'It'll be fun,' says Granny brightly.

'I doubt it,' says Jed, glaring out from under his hair. Then he says, 'I'll stay for a bit, but if it gets boring, I'm off. I've got my own key you know.'

It turns out that Jed gets bored *really* quickly and isn't into Granny's idea of fun. Or mine. I suggest things to do, but he says they're for little kids. Granny suggests things, but he says they're for wrinklies. Grandad says it's going to be a long summer.

While Grandad is in the garden, Granny goes to make a phone call. When she comes back, she's smiling. 'I've made an appointment for you tomorrow, Jed,' she says cheerfully. Jed looks up from our game of snakes and ladders. (Jed cheated – I'm pretty sure he knows I noticed too – but neither of us said anything.) 'Perhaps we can do something nice on the way back,' Granny suggests.

'Whatever!' says Jed.

Then the doorbell rings and there is Priti wearing a bubblegum-pink ra-ra skirt and a T-shirt which says *My imaginary friend did it*.

'You coming to play, Ben?' she says.

'I can't. My cousin's here.'

'Who's the kid?' asks Jed, coming up behind me.

'This is Priti,' I say. 'She lives across the road.'

Jed takes one look at her and says, 'So you're the Asian invasion?'

'Well spotted,' says Priti. 'You must be the hand-me-down cousin?'

They stare at each other for a moment.

Priti seems less impressed by Jed than I expected. 'You can come too, I suppose,' she says.

'Why would I want to hang out with a pair of kids?' says Jed.

'Don't then,' says Priti. 'You coming, Ben?'

I look from one to the other.

'I dunno,' I say. 'Jed's just arrived.'

'Suit yourself,' she says. 'But Shakeel's gonna help us build a tree house in the garden.'

I glance at Jed. 'She's OK,' I say. 'Even if she is a girl.'

'Thanks a lot!' says Priti.

Jed tosses his hair back off his face and checks Priti out again, then shrugs his shoulders and says, 'There's nothing better to do here, I suppose.'

I breathe a sigh of relief and off we go.

* * *

Granny insists on walking over with us to Priti's house to make sure we're not imposing. It's Shakeel who opens the door.

'Hello, Mrs Evans,' he says. Then he glances at Priti. 'I do hope my sister has not been causing you any trouble?'

Priti grins at him and sticks out her tongue. He grins back.

'No, no, quite the opposite,' says Granny. 'She's been very kind to Ben, and to my other grandson, Jed.' She puts a hand on Jed's arm, but he shrugs it away. I see Shakeel take in the gesture. 'Priti has very kindly invited them both over to play,' Granny goes on, 'but I just wanted to check with your parents that it wasn't an imposition.'

'I'm afraid my mother and father are both out at present,' says Shakeel.

'Oh, I see,' says Granny. She seems uncertain suddenly.

'But I know my parents will consider it no imposition whatsoever to have your grandsons here,' Shakeel goes on. 'And neither do I.'

'That's very kind of you, Shakeel.' Granny smiles.

'It will be our pleasure to have them.'

Granny hesitates, glancing back to our house.

'Perhaps your husband is not comfortable with this arrangement?' asks Shakeel.

'Oh, no, no,' says Granny hurriedly, bright spots of colour appearing in her cheeks. 'I was just concerned. Will there be someone around to look after them?'

'I don't need looking after,' says Jed crossly.

Shakeel smiles. 'Be assured. My brother, sister or I will be here to supervise at all times.'

'Well then, I'm sure the boys would love to come in and play, Shakeel,' says Granny, smiling brightly. 'Please just send them back if they are any trouble at all.'

'I don't need anyone to look after me!' Jed repeats.

'Then it is agreed,' says Shakeel with a smile. 'Thank you, Mrs Evans. I know Priti is delighted to have the boys as playmates.'

Jed is scowling at Shakeel, but Granny seems satisfied.

'Just remember your pleases and thank yous,' she

76

says to us, before she heads back across the road.

'Don't worry. We'll look after them!' says Priti with the biggest grin I've ever seen. Ever. Jed looks furious.

Priti's house is laid out just like my grandparents', but it doesn't feel the same at all. I know that an old couple called the Moons used to live here, so the carpets and wallpaper are the sort old people choose, but the curtains and pictures and stuff have obviously been chosen by Priti's mum and they are totally different – lots of bright colours, all shiny and silky.

And there's loads and loads of stuff *everywhere*. My granny likes it all neat with just one or two ornaments and some pictures in silver frames, but this house has tons of knick-knacks and more books than I've ever seen in my life, with weird titles like *The Crescent and the Couch: Counselling the Modern Muslim* and *Listen to the Heron's Voice: Gender, Feminism and Islam* – even *The Sheikh's New Clothes: Psychoanalysis of the Suicide Bomber*.

There are photos of Priti and her brothers and sister over every available surface and pinned up on all the walls. Massive pictures, some of them in big gold frames. There's even an oil painting of them all which must have been done when Priti was a baby. Jed laughs at it and even I can see that the artist wasn't very good because it doesn't really look that much like any of them. Priti just gives me a look like everything Jed does is my fault because I brought him along.

'Where are your mum and dad anyway?' asks Jed.

'At work,' says Priti.

'So your brothers and sister have to look after you? That's pretty lame.'

'No lamer than your grandparents looking after you,' says Priti, raising an eyebrow.

'My dad's job is pretty dangerous. There could be people after him – or me – so it's not safe for me to be home alone.'

'Yeah?' says Priti, who doesn't look like she believes him for a minute. 'What does he do then?'

'Can't tell you,' says Jed. 'Don't want to compromise his security.'

'If you say so,' says Priti, rolling her eyes. 'Anyway, I basically get to do what I want. My siblings are *not* happy about the babysitting so they're pretty hands-off. Zara's the worst, she's well mad about it, so she basically ignores me all day, but it's Shakeel's turn today and he's cool. Well, he's not – he's a total geek, worse than you, Ben – but he lets me do cool stuff.'

'What like?' says Jed. 'I thought you said we were building a tree house or something.'

'We've got to wait till Shakeel's finished tinkering around with his radios, or whatever he's doing,' says Priti.

'How long will that be?' says Jed, picking up a china dolphin and throwing it from hand to hand.

'Impatient, isn't he, your cousin?' says Priti, looking at me.

'Why don't we hang out in the garden while we wait for him?' I say, watching Jed pick up a crystal mermaid that looks as if it might be worth a lot of money.

So we go outside and Jed starts kicking the grass and making loads of bits of mud fly up in the air and Priti starts making little holes by digging her wheelies into the turf, like it's a competition as to who can make the biggest mess of the lawn (my grandad would HATE this!) and I just stand there feeling awkward. In the end, to break the silence, I say to Priti, 'Tell Jed about the honour killing.'

As soon as it comes out of my mouth, I regret it. Priti glares at me.

'What honour killing?' says Jed, kicking a lump of turf up into the air. I can tell he's trying hard not to look like he's interested.

'Do you really want to know?' Priti asks. She looks at him with a hint of challenge in her voice and he looks right back. He's all dressed in khaki and military fatigues and she's in pink, but they both look pretty fierce.

'I don't know,' he says. 'Do I?'

'Go on. Tell him,' I say, although I don't really know why I'm pushing it.

So Priti tells Jed all about forced marriages and Zara's boyfriend and the honour killing and, by the end, I can tell Jed is into it even though he pretends he's heard it all before.

'That's why we need the tree house,' says Priti,

getting excited now and jumping from foot to foot in a little dance as she talks. 'It's going to be a lookout. From up here you can see the park and the house and who's coming down the alleyway. We'll have a secret signal or something.'

Jed is already scaling the tree trunk to the makeshift platform that's been erected there. 'We can be lookouts,' he says.

'Yeah, that's the idea.'

'Does that mean we get to see your sister, like, making out?' he asks, grinning.

'I hope not,' says Priti.

'Is she fit?' he says, looking at me.

I don't answer.

'No,' says Priti putting her fingers in her mouth and pretending to vomit.

'Shame,' says Jed, who is now standing on the platform. 'Hey, look at me!'

He raises his arms in the air. 'It's too hot in here!' he shrieks in an American accent. 'I'm gonna die! I can't stand it any more! I've gotta jump!' Then he flings himself headlong off the platform, arms outstretched, wailing as he falls, 'I'm the falling man!' He lands with a thud on the floor and bursts out laughing.

Priti glances at me, but I don't say anything.

Then Shakeel comes out so we start making the tree house. But afterwards, I can't get the image out of my head – of my dad crying out like a baby and falling through the sky – just like Jed did.

Shakeel does most of the work on the tree house. Me and Priti and Jed spend the time messing about, climbing up and down the trunk and getting in his way. When he gets fed up with hammering planks and answering questions (about tree houses – me; forced marriages – Jed; and when it's going to be finished – Priti) Shakeel asks if we want to look at the radio he's building.

Priti groans and says it's boring, but we haven't got any better ideas so we all follow him inside. Up in his ultra neat-and-tidy bedroom, Shakeel has all this equipment – circuit boards and wires, cylinders, headphones, knobs, screws and even a soldering iron. He tries to explain to us how it works, but Priti isn't listening – she's probably heard it all before – and Jed just fiddles with everything. But I like listening to Shakeel talk. I don't really understand it all, but it's kind of cool hearing about radio waves and frequencies and all that.

'Your dad used to build radios, didn't he?' Jed says, interrupting Shakeel and putting down a fragile-looking bit of equipment with a thud. I realise he's talking to me.

'Did he?' Shakeel also turns to me. He looks really interested.

I'd never heard this before, so I just say, 'Yes.'

'My dad says Uncle Andrew was always tinkering around with stuff like that,' says Jed. 'Bit sad, if you ask me. So what are you, like, building exactly?' he asks Shakeel, picking up a circuit board and staring at it, even though Shakeel has spent the last ten minutes telling us exactly that.

Shakeel explains it all over again. 'This is a simple FM receiver, but I'd like to try my hand at a transmitter.'

'What and then do like a pirate radio station or something?' asks Jed.

'That's not really my style,' says Shakeel, laughing. 'I just like the challenge.'

Jed nods. 'You're just not really cool enough, are you?'

Priti starts to look offended, but doesn't say anything. She probably realises there's no point.

'Guilty as charged!' laughs Shakeel.

When we get home, Gary has sent me a letter. Well, it's really only a postcard with a picture of a pig wearing sunglasses on it. On the back, in Gary's writing, it says, *Missing you more than flying pigs, kid!* Then there are three kisses. It doesn't really make any sense, but it's nice of him to send it anyway and I like the idea that it might have been posted in the box at the end of our road (Gary lives round the corner from us). Jed wants to look at it, but I don't let him. I tuck it into the notepad where I make all my lists, but I can't help feeling sad that even Gary has bothered to write me a card when my mum still hasn't been in touch at all.

There was this one time when I was sitting in the

corner of the village hall, drawing cartoons while
Mum was at one of her committee meetings, taking
minutes and stuff, and this little kid came up and
stared over my shoulder, checking out what I was
drawing.

'Draw one of me!' she said. So I drew a cartoon of
her as a princess, then as a fairy, then a mermaid and a
cheerleader. I asked her what she was doing there and
she pointed at a skinny, bald bloke in a leather jacket
and said, 'That's my dad. He's called Gary.' I hadn't
seen him at any of the meetings before and she said
that's because he'd just moved to the village. After the
meeting, he and my mum talked for ages and my mum
laughed a lot. The little girl – whose name is Blythe
– made me show him the pictures of her and he said,
'These are really good!'

A few meetings later, my mum and Gary were an
item and I knew the names and costumes of every
Disney princess. And I had a new four-year-old best
friend.

So that's how my mum met Gary.

THINGS ABOUT MY MUM I SHOULD HAVE PAID MORE ATTENTION TO

1. She was getting all weird about cutlery again. She told me once – ages ago – that I mustn't let her do this. It's my job to lay the table and she said I should just lay whatever cutlery came to hand. But I could tell she was getting funny about it again. That she was finding it hard to eat if she didn't have the knife with the ivory handle and the fork with the initials on the end. So I started laying those ones out for her every time and pretending it just came out like that. She didn't say anything and neither did I. And she seemed to find it easier to eat that way, so I thought it would be OK.

2. She started running. She's not supposed to really, but she said it made her feel so great. So in control. And she always came back on such a high. But then she started running more and more, and she stopped looking like she was enjoying it. More like she was doing it to punish herself. I should have known that was a sign too.

3. She was always wearing bright red lipstick.

Sometimes even dark purples or raspberry reds with a dab of blusher on each cheek that made her look like she was hot and flustered. And too much mascara.

4. She began forgetting things: my school trip letter, putting out the dustbins, wearing a coat. So I started doing a few things to make it easier for her, like the bins and making sure there was milk in, and doing my own letters for school. But when she realised, she got upset and said I shouldn't have to be doing all those things and that she'd let me down.

5. She took up smoking. She didn't think I knew because she always did it outside or when I wasn't around, and when I asked her, she denied it. But I knew she was. Because of the smell mostly. And because she's done this before. She's done it all before. But it's never been quite as bad as this time.

       ❖   ❖   ❖

'I don't see why we have to go every time I come and stay.'

Jed is arguing with Granny in the bathroom. I go upstairs to get my notebook and I can hear them, speaking in low voices behind the closed door. Grandad is downstairs, watching kids' TV.

'If you don't want to go then I can ring up and cancel,' I hear Granny saying.

I imagine her standing next to the crocheted toilet-roll holder, looking nervous like she always does around Jed.

'Whatever,' says Jed. 'It's not like I'm bothered. Might as well get it over with.'

I really want to stay and listen, but I figure I'm not meant to be hearing this.

I'm turning to go when Granny's voice rises slightly. 'You know you can't tell your father, or even your grandad,' she says. 'You know that, don't you, Jed?'

'My dad's gonna be well mad if he finds out,' I hear Jed say. I imagine him climbing over the bathtub and the toilet, leaving muddy footprints over Granny's spotless enamel.

'We don't want to cause an upset,' Granny goes on.

'If he found out, I'd tell him I never really wanted to go,' Jed says, louder now. I imagine him standing on top of the toilet, towering over Granny. 'That you made me.'

There's a pause. I'm halfway down the stairs now but I stop because I don't want them to hear me and think I was listening. And because part of me still sort of wants to know what's going on.

'Of course,' says Granny. There's a pause before she says, 'And if you don't want to go . . .'

'Whatever,' says Jed.

Five minutes later, Jed comes downstairs. He flops down on the sofa and pretends to be engrossed in some babies' TV programme about a family of pigs that Blythe likes, only he doesn't look like he's really watching.

I draw a picture of Jed and Granny, both wearing pig disguises, tiptoeing along like undercover spies. Jed's pig looks really angry, but Granny's one ends up just looking old and sad.

* * *

'You know it's not for making radios, all that,' Jed says when we're both in bed. He still seems to be in a bad mood from before.

'What?'

'All that stuff Shakeel has. It's not for radios.'

'How do you know?' I say. I'm busy doodling cartoons of him and Priti dressed as Princess Leia and Han Solo and duelling with light sabres.

'I just do.'

'What is it then?' I ask.

'It's for making bombs,' he says.

'Don't be stupid,' I say, looking up from my sketch pad and glancing across to the other bed where he's playing with his games console.

'He's a Muslim, yeah? That's what they do. My dad told me.'

'That's stupid. Why would he want to build a bomb?'

'To blow up loads of British people.'

'And how's he going to do that then?'

'He'll strap it all on to himself, then put on a big coat so no one can see and then he'll go somewhere really busy, press the button and – *boom*!'

'He'll get killed himself then,' I say.

'Duh! That's the point!' says Jed. 'Haven't you ever heard of suicide bombers?'

'Of course I have,' I say.

'My dad's always going on about them. He reckons there are loads of them out there, plotting stuff even worse than what happened to your dad. He reckons we need to hunt them all down and string 'em up.' Jed sniffs and stares up at the ceiling then says, 'I reckon he might be in some counterterrorism intelligence unit actually. Undercover.'

'Really?' I say. I'm sort of used to him making stuff up; he's been doing it ever since I've known him. When we were little, before his mum and dad split up, we used to see him loads and my mum told me not to believe everything he told me. (That was after the time he said he could hold his breath under water for ten minutes and dared me to try it too.)

Jed just shrugs. 'Maybe. Cos there's no way the army sacked him, so I reckon he's undercover.'

I don't say anything.

'I don't really get it myself.'

'What?'

'Terrorists. Like, why don't they just plant the bomb somewhere then press the button when they're safely away? Or maybe they're too stupid and haven't thought of that.'

'Shakeel seems really clever,' I say.

'Or maybe the sniffer dogs can't find bombs if they're on people, only if they're in shopping bags or suitcases or whatever.'

'Maybe.' I do some more drawing. Of Shakeel as Yoda, then as Darth Maul with zigzags on his face.

'Oh, man!' says Jed, tossing aside his controller as his games console plays the music for 'Game Over'. He flops over on to his back and stares at me crossly. 'What's that all about anyway?' he asks, waving in the direction of my notepad.

'What?' I say.

'The drawing stuff.'

'I just like doing cartoons,' I say.

'Show us then,' says Jed.

He reaches out a hand across the gap between the two beds. I hesitate before passing him my sketchbook.

He flicks through it with a bored look on his face. 'These are all right.'

'Thanks,' I say. 'You're meant to read it backwards.'

'Why?'

'It's manga. You know, Japanese comic strips.'

'I know what manga is.'

'Well, you read them backwards, don't you?'

'I don't do reading either way,' says Jed, staring up at the ceiling again.

'My English teacher says it's not real reading,' I say. 'Because there aren't enough full sentences.'

But Jed isn't listening. He's come across the pictures of him and Priti in *Star Wars* outfits. 'Cool!' he says. 'Reckon I'd be a better Anakin though. Can you draw me as him?'

'I can try.'

Jed tosses the book back at me. 'Glad to find there's something you're good at. I was beginning to think you were a total no-hoper. When did you start this mango thing anyway?'

'Manga,' I say. 'I dunno.'

I could have told him that when I started getting

pocket money, I bought *The Beano* (which Mum said was my dad's favourite when he was a boy) and that's when I started drawing my own stuff. Just doodles at first, then my friend Lukas got me into manga and I started doing little comic strips, mainly about me and Lukas as superhero kids, defeating loads of baddies. I could have told Jed that it was about the same time my mum met Gary and then got into doing her stuff again that I started thinking in comic strips. But I don't bother explaining any of that because I don't think he's listening anyway.

'So you just, like, make it up?' he asks.

'I suppose so,' I shrug.

I don't tell him about the doodling in my head either: how, when I'm watching stuff going on – everyday things – I find myself adding captions or doodles; how I imagine drawing pencil moustaches and specs on teachers' faces and see things people say in speech bubbles above their heads. Because if he did listen, I know he'd only laugh.

'So do you reckon Shakeel is a terrorist or what?' says Jed, losing interest in my notepad.

I shrug again.

'If someone held a gun to your head and said they were going to shoot you unless you decided, what would you say?'

'That's stupid,' I reply.

'Yeah, but what would you say?'

'I'd say: if Shakeel is building a bomb, why would he show it to us?'

'He reckons we're just kids and we won't realise what he's up to,' says Jed.

We both lie in bed and I stare at my dad's star-sticker constellations on the ceiling. I can make out Orion, the Bear and the Seven Sisters. I don't know any of the others, but I decide to ask Granny tomorrow if she has a book I can look them up in.

I glance over at Jed. He's holding a tatty bit of old baby blanket close to his face and is still for the first time all day. He looks different somehow.

'I don't think Shakeel is a suicide bomber,' I say. 'He's nice.'

'Yeah, well, I bet that's what people said about the men who killed your dad,' says Jed.

JULY 16TH

This morning, Granny's taking Jed to his appointment. She doesn't say what it's for and Jed avoids talking to me over breakfast, so I guess he doesn't want me to ask.

Granny makes Jed put a belt on before they go, so his trousers don't hang down and show his pants. She even makes him do his coat up, which I know he hates.

She seems a bit nervous about going: she gets in a muddle about the bus times and numbers when she talks to Grandad. (He doesn't offer to drive – he says that being summoned to pick me up at five in the morning was enough driving to last him all year.) Jed looks a bit weird too. He rolls his eyes at me as they leave and when Granny tries to put a hand on his arm, he shrugs it off impatiently.

Later on, Priti comes over and we hang out in my bedroom.

'He thinks he's it, doesn't he? Your cousin,' says Priti, checking out some of Jed's things, which are scattered all over the place. In fact, apart from the extra bed and a stack of manga comics, it hardly looks as if I sleep here at all.

'No, he doesn't,' I say. For some reason, I don't want Priti saying bad stuff about him.

'Don't pretend you don't agree.'

'I don't.'

'Yeah, right. Anyway, Zara doesn't reckon he's cool. She reckons she saw him out the window yesterday, doing keepy-uppies on your driveway like he thought he was some kind of Premiership footballer. She says he looks like a tramp. And I agree with her.' Priti is wearing a red and white cheerleader's outfit with a huge picture of some teen movie star emblazoned on her bum and red and white pompom bobbles holding up her pigtails.

'She says you can tell he doesn't have a mum,' she goes on.

'How do you know?' I ask.

'I'm right, aren't I!' She grins. 'You can always tell.'

'Anyway, he does have a mum,' I say. 'He just doesn't see her.'

'Same difference.'

Priti flicks through one of Jed's football magazines. I pick up my notepad, but I can't think what to draw.

'So can you tell I don't have a dad?' I ask.

'That's not the same,' says Priti, without looking up from the magazine.

'Why?'

'It just isn't,' she says.

'So you can't tell then?'

'Yeah, you can. But it's not the same. He talks funny too, your cousin.'

'He talks the same as you.'

'He so does not. He sounds like a total chav,' she says.

'You both talk through your noses,' I say. 'My mum says that people in the city do that because of the pollution.'

'Yeah, well, at least *I* can talk about my mum without looking like I'm going to have a heart attack.' She flicks the pages of the magazine, her red and white bobbles bouncing up and down with each turn.

I imagine the bobbles morphing into giant red and white basketballs, crashing down around her head.

'How can you tell then?' I ask after a moment.

'What?'

'That I don't have a dad.'

She stops flicking and looks thoughtful. 'Well, you're crap at climbing trees and you're way more polite than most boys I know. Oh, and you're always drawing those pictures.'

'Is that it?'

'And you walk differently.'

'I do not.'

'Not like a girl. But not all swaggering and sticking out your crotch like most boys do. I guess they must get that off their dads.'

'That's pants,' I say.

'Don't blame me if you've got unresolved issues about this! Hey!' she says, suddenly leaping to her feet, looking very excited. 'Do your grands have a computer in the house?'

'Yes. Why?' I still have a picture in my head of myself swaggering like a cowboy with chaps on.

'We should do some research.'

'What are we researching?' I ask.

'You,' she says. 'The whole 9/11 kid thing. You never talk about it. So I reckon we should find out more about it. Then I can help you.'

'I don't want to be helped.'

'Try telling that to my mum.'

Priti makes out that her mum is this terrifying professor type, but I met her yesterday after Shakeel finished showing us all the radio stuff, and she's actually a tiny little woman with a soft voice and long hair down to her waist, like my mum. She wears hippy tie-dye stuff and dangly earrings, and she seems all right to me. Priti says that I'm not the one who has to carry around 'the weight of maternal expectations', so what do I know.

If Granny had been here, she'd have made a fuss about supervising Internet access, but Grandad is too busy reading an article about benefit fraudsters to care about cyber-stalkers. He just says, 'Don't blow up the computer!' and lets us get on with it.

So Priti makes herself comfortable in the big swivel chair in Grandad's office (really the spare room) while I get to perch on a kitchen stool, which is dead uncomfortable and too high.

'Right, what shall we type in?' She doesn't even pause for my answer before saying, '9/11.Then what?'

I shrug. Staring at the screen, thinking of paper aeroplanes and cartoon towers.

'Bereaved children,' she says.

'Bereaved?'

'That's what my mum called you. "He's bereaved," she said. She reckons that's why you don't talk much. B-E-R-E-A-V-E-D. Bereaved,' she says, with a slight American accent as she types in the word.

Priti turns to me and grins as she jabs at the enter button and almost immediately a whole scroll of links comes up.

'Bingo!' she says. I imagine a fruit machine coming up with three little aeroplanes. *Ching! Ching! Ching!* 'Right, let's just click on the first one.'

I don't look at the screen. I look down at my hands, but Priti opens the link and reads out the contents in a loud voice, so I don't get much choice but to listen.

'*Nearly 3,000 children under the age of 18 lost a parent during the terrorist attacks of September*

11 2001,' she reads. 'Wow! So there are loads of you out there.'

'Most of them are in America,' I say.

'Still, there must be some over here. I bet you didn't know there were so many of you.'

'I hadn't thought about it,' I say, which is almost true. I've never considered how *many* other kids there are like me out there, although I've sometimes wondered what I'd do if I ever bumped into one.

'*The average age of the "9/11 kids" when the Twin Towers fell was 9*,' Priti reads. '*But some were mere babes in arms (or in their mothers' wombs) when they lost a parent that day.*' She turns to look at me and says, 'So if some of them were born after it happened, they must never have met their dads at all.'

'I guess so,' I say. At least they've got a decent excuse for why *they* can't remember their dads.

'That must be weird,' says Priti. 'I wonder if they met them on the way down.'

'What?'

'The babies on their way down to earth and the

dads on their way up to heaven. Maybe they crossed on the way.'

'I don't think it works like that,' I say.

'How do you know?'

'I don't – obviously!'

'Well, there you are then.'

I don't bother to argue as Priti carries on reading from the screen. I've got to admit – but not to her of course – I'm impressed at what she can read for a kid her age. '*A recent study showed the rate of psychi–*' she hesitates – '*psychi-atric disorders is more than double the norm among children who lost loved ones in the 2001 terrorist attacks,*' she goes on. 'Psychic-hat-trick means mental cases. Nutjobs. The sort of people my mum deals with. Right?' she says, glancing at me like she's looking for signs I'm going mental.

There must be a better word for it, but I can't think of one, so I just nod.

'Wow, you're screwed then.'

'What else does it say?' I ask, ignoring the loony tunes face she's pulling at me.

'*Researchers found that more than 50 per cent were*

displaying signs of an anxiety disorder, while a third had symptoms of post-trau–' She pauses and, for a moment, I think she may finally have come across a word she can't read, but then she continues, '*Post trau-mat-ic stress disorder.*'

'I don't even know what that means,' I say.

'Nor do I,' says Priti. 'D'you reckon you've got it?'

'How should I know?'

'Well, if you've got it without realising it, it can't be that bad, can it?'

'I suppose not,' I say.

Priti turns back to the screen. '*More than 27 per cent of the bereaved children showed symptoms of separation anxiety, while 14 per cent had a major de-press-ive disorder,*' she reads, spelling out the longer words carefully. '*The rate of simple pho-bia in bereaved children was also double that of non-bereaved children.*'

'Well, there you are then,' says Priti. 'That explains why you look so miserable a lot of the time.'

'I do not!'

'And you get well scared about stuff.'

'That's not true!'

'When Tyreese and his gang were yelling, you were bricking it.'

'So would any normal person!' I say. 'Just because you get a weird kick out of that kind of thing doesn't mean I have an anxiety disorder or whatever they called it.'

Priti sighs. 'Have you got any phobias then?' she asks in a sort of I'm-trying-to-be-patient voice, which makes me want to lamp her one.

'I don't like spiders much,' I say.

'Nor do I,' says Priti, shivering. 'So I suppose that doesn't count. What about "separation anxiety" or whatever it is? Do you miss your mum?'

'Course I do.'

'Jed doesn't.'

'That's different.'

'You're right. He's weird,' says Priti. 'So where does this leave us with you?'

'None of that stuff applies to me because I don't remember my dad,' I say, not looking at her as I say it. 'Which means I can't be "bereaved" or whatever your mum called it.'

I sometimes wonder if I should be feeling all those things the other bereaved kids are feeling. Should I be terrified of snakes or heights or shaking like a bag of nerves or being carted off to the loony bin? And if I'm not, what does that say about me?

'My mum reckons you're never too young to feel the pain of loss.'

'I might be bereaved, but I'm not bonkers,' I say.

'You're obviously getting upset,' says Priti. 'Perhaps we should leave it for now.'

'I am not getting upset!' I say, annoyed at her for acting like she knows it all, when she doesn't.

'Whatever you say,' she replies, sounding just like my mum.

In my head, I draw her being attacked by a giant, hairy, goggly-eyed black spider, which sucks all her blood. And a speech bubble saying, '*Yum! Yum!*'

My school once suggested to my mum that I see a counsellor. The pastoral head rang her up one day when I was in Year 7 and said perhaps I'd like to talk to someone about 9/11. They didn't tell me they were going to call her. And if they had, I'd have asked them not to because I knew it would only upset her, and she'd been so happy since she started seeing Gary.

So the first I knew about it was when I came home to find Mum crying in the kitchen. 'Why didn't you tell me you were finding things hard?' she said.

'I'm not,' I replied.

'You could have talked to me.'

'But I'm OK, Mum.'

'You know I'm always here if you need to talk, don't you?'

'Course I do,' I said.

She sighed and looked like she was going to cry again. 'I've let you down.'

'You haven't, Mum.'

She started crying properly then. I put down my schoolbag and went to sit next to her.

'I've tried to give you a normal life,' she said.

'You've been brilliant. The best mum in the world.'

'I didn't think you wanted to go raking over the past.'

'I don't, honest.'

'Because if you want to see this counsellor then of course you can.'

'I don't, Mum. I don't even know why the school said that.'

'Maybe you said something to one of the teachers? Or maybe this is to do with Gary?' she asks. 'Because I'd understand if you were finding it hard.'

'I'm really not. I like Gary,' I said. 'Everything's OK, honestly.'

'I thought we were doing so well. I just don't know if I can –' and then she started to cry again.

And she just went on crying like that for what seemed like hours. I kept trying to tell her nothing was wrong, but she just cried and cried until I thought she'd never stop.

I wanted to call Gary, but she wouldn't let me. 'I don't want him seeing me like this,' she said.

'But he'd want to help.'

'No, this is just us,' she said. 'You and me. We can deal with it, can't we?'

'Course, Mum,' I said.

But she didn't stop crying. Then, or for about a

week afterwards. And pretty soon after that, she started doing her stuff again. The stuff which meant she wasn't OK. And I wasn't sure we could cope with it on our own. Not really.

I finally persuade Priti to take a break from the 9/11 research and she persuades me that Granny won't mind us raiding the biscuit barrel. So we sit eating biscuits in the kitchen.

'Jed reckons Shakeel's going to blow loads of white people up,' I say.

'What?' Priti looks up from licking the sticky middle bit out of her custard cream.

'He reckons Shakeel is making a bomb not a radio and that he's actually a suicide bomber.'

'Why would he want to do something stupid like that?'

'He reckons all Muslims see Britain and America as the enemies of Islam,' I say, repeating something he'd said last night.

'Yeah, I get all that stuff about Holy War. But why would *Shakeel* want to do it?'

'You said he was religious,' I suggest.

'Yeah, he's well into the mosque and that. But he wouldn't kill anyone. He's too much of a wimp.'

'He's got all that electrical equipment up there. I suppose it could be for building a bomb.'

'No, Shakeel is way too boring to be a terrorist.' She goes back to licking her biscuit, lapping up the cream filling like a cat.

'Jed says it's the quiet ones you have to watch,' I say. 'His dad knows all about it apparently.'

'Oh, yeah? How?'

I hesitate. 'I suppose because he used to be in the army.'

'Yeah, and what does he do now?'

'He's a mechanic.'

Priti laughs. 'I knew he was blagging.'

'Yeah, but Jed reckons that's just a cover and he's really still working for army intelligence.'

'Undercover?'

'I guess so.'

Priti looks vaguely impressed.

'Jed says the army only pretended to sack him so

no one would know he had gone underground.' Then I add, 'But you know what Jed's like. He might just be making it up.'

Priti ignores the last bit. 'So he's, like, bomb squad or something?' she says, perking up suddenly.

'Maybe. But only if you believe Jed.'

'And he's on to Shakeel?'

'Jed didn't say that exactly.'

'Cos if the bomb squad is on to him, he must be up to something.' She wriggles excitedly on her chair.

'I don't think Jed said the bomb squad exactly.'

But Priti is clearly no longer listening. 'I reckon it'd be pretty cool if Shakeel was building a bomb!' she says with a big grin on her face.

'It was just something Jed said.'

'I wonder if he'd let us help,' she says excitedly. 'It'd be so cool!'

'Yeah, right,' I say.

'Of course, we can't let him actually blow himself up. I'm not having him do a Twin Towers on me,' she adds, glancing at me. 'I mean, he's the only half decent sibling I've got. We have to keep an eye on him.'

'How are we meant to do that exactly?'

'We'll go undercover too: spy on him, find out what he's up to.'

I have an image of us both in trench coats peering through giant magnifying glasses.

'We can pass on all the information to Jed's dad in the bomb squad, then when they catch him, we'll get medals,' says Priti happily. 'We can be heroes!'

'We're not even sure Uncle Ian is in the bomb squad. He could be doing something else.'

'Like what?'

'I dunno.' I shrug. 'Mending cars, like he says he is?'

'Whatever,' says Priti who has now licked off all the cream filling and is eating the rest of her biscuit in little tiny bites all round the edge. 'We can be the moles – and turn Shakeel in before he does anything stupid.'

'And what happens if the bomb squad or the police or whoever actually catch him? He'll be in massive trouble.'

'If he hasn't actually blown anything up, they can't be that mad at him, can they?'

'My mum says it's the thought that counts.' An image of my mum pops into my brain and I can't make it go away.

'Thinking about bombs isn't going to do anyone any harm, is it?' says Priti. 'It's only if you actually press the button that things go *boom*, innit?' I've noticed that when Priti gets excited, she sometimes starts speaking like a gangsta rapper.

'I don't think that's how it works. We could get him in loads of trouble,' I say. 'And us too!'

'Then we'll get him a fake passport and he can escape somewhere far away. We'll still get medals because of all the people we'll save, and Shakeel will be sunning it on a beach with loads of ladyboys.'

I want to ask her what ladyboys are, but I know if I do, we'll never finish the conversation.

'Wouldn't it be easier to just ask him if he's building a bomb?' I say.

'He'll just go underground if we blow his cover,' says Priti, like she does this sort of thing all the time. 'Besides, it'll be no fun! And I've always wanted to be a spy!'

And I know it's probably a load of rubbish, but when Priti gets excited about something, it's hard not to get carried along too. And I have this picture in my head of Shakeel dressed in white robes, riding a paper aeroplane with a bomb strapped to his torso. And laughing.

So I go along with it. Because it's only a game, so what harm can it do?

When Jed comes back, he's wearing a new Liverpool football top and is in a weird mood.

'Nice top,' I say. 'Did Granny get it for you?'

'Of course, dumbo! Who else would it be?' he replies quickly.

I ask him if his appointment was OK and he tells me to mind my own business. Then he flops on to the sofa and pretends to be watching the TV, but I can tell he isn't really.

When Granny comes in a minute or two later, Grandad asks her, 'Good?'

'Oh, yes, very,' she replies in an ultra-cheerful voice.

'The usual NHS fob-off then!' says Grandad.

'No, no,' says Granny. 'He was very good. Very helpful. We have another appointment to see him up at the hospital again, don't we, Jed?'

Jed just grunts.

'In about six months' time, I'll bet,' says Grandad.

'Next week,' says Granny, blushing slightly as she says it.

'Fine,' says Grandad. He seems almost disappointed at not having something to moan about. After that, he gets back on with watching his daytime quiz show.

As I help Granny with her coat and bag, I ask if she has any binoculars. She looks a bit flustered, like she hasn't heard me at first, so I say it again.

'Sorry, dear,' she says. 'I was miles away. I think I've got a pair that used to belong to your dad.'

'Oh,' I say. Then, 'That'd be good.'

So she goes off and gets them. It's a nice pair, in a leather case with my dad's name written inside the flap. I try to imagine him using them, but no image comes into my head.

'He used to take them to the cricket,' she says. 'He'd be happy for you to have them.'

She gives a sad smile and I don't really know what to say, so I just take them and say, 'Thanks, Granny.'

Then I go up to my room – or Jed's room with a spare bed for me, which is what it feels like these days – and sit on the windowsill to try them out. I twiddle with the focus a bit until I can see clearly then look out at the cul-de-sac. It's a bit weird holding them, knowing the last person to use them was my dad. Weird, but sort of nice.

Little Stevie from next door is out on her bike again, going round and round in circles. She always seems to be out playing on her own, while her mum sits and smokes in front of the TV by the window. Like my grandad, except for the smoking bit.

Stevie reminds me a bit of Blythe, who is a bit crazy and silly and is always hugging me and being annoying, but I kind of miss her. I wonder if I should do her one of the cartoons she likes and send it to her, but then I remember that she's away with her mum all summer, so she probably wouldn't get it anyway.

'What you looking at?' Jed is right behind me when he says this. I must have been deep into my daydream because you can usually hear him coming five minutes before he arrives.

'Nothing,' I say.

'Give me a go,' he says, grabbing the binoculars. He's up beside me now on the windowsill. He always moves so quickly that, when I was little, I used to think he had superpowers. I imagine him now with a cape and a superhero suit, whizzing through the clouds, one hand punching the air.

'You been keeping an eye on the Unabomber?' He jerks his thumb at the Muhammed house across the road.

'You can't see his room from here.'

'Shame,' says Jed. 'Reckon we need to get inside. Snoop around a bit. I bet he's got stuff up there. Information about his terror cell and that. Bet you don't even know what a terror cell is, do you?'

'Course I do,' I say.

'What is it then?'

'Like a club for terrorists,' I reply, repeating a phrase Priti used earlier.

'Exactly. He won't be operating on his own, will

117

he? There'll be loads of them in on it. You said they were going to Pakistan, didn't you? They've probably got links to a terror network over there. What we need to do is infiltrate their cell then bring it down.'

'And how exactly do we find out who's in the cell?' I say.

'We'll have to hack into his computer and bug his phone and go through all his things looking for clues. Should be cool!'

He's obviously not going to give up the binoculars, so I slide off the windowsill on to the bed.

'Jed,' I say after a moment. 'Are you sick?'

He pulls a stupid face. 'Do I look sick to you?'

'No,' I say. Because he doesn't. Not really.

'Why you asking a stupid question like that then?'

'I just wondered, that's all.'

'Well, quit wondering. Are you any good at computer hacking?'

'No,' I say.

'Bugging devices?'

'Can't we just ask your dad?'

Jed hesitates before saying, 'What?'

'You said he was into all that stuff. Counterterrorism and that?'

Jed hesitates. 'Yeah, he is.'

'So he'd have all that surveillance equipment, wouldn't he?'

Jed pauses again. 'We can't bother him until we've got some concrete intel on the suspect.'

'Right.'

'In the mean time, we'll have to do this the old-fashioned way. Should be great!'

'Great,' I say.

THINGS I'D LIKE TO KNOW ABOUT JED

1. Why is he called Jed when his real name is Geoffrey (spelt with a 'g')?
2. Why does he talk so loud?
3. Why will he only eat white bread and nothing that's green or orange?
4. Why doesn't he get a haircut?
5. Why does he think his dad's so great?
6. Why does he think his mum's so awful?

7. Why doesn't he ever see his mum?

8. What are the appointments about and why can't he tell his dad or Grandad about them?

9. Is he ill and, if so, why doesn't he look ill?

10. What is he dreaming about when he cries in his sleep?

JULY 17TH

'We need to sneak into Shakeel's room and look for incriminating evidence,' Priti says.

'Yeah, that's what I said!' Jed agrees.

We're all sitting in the tree house, keeping lookout for Zara and taking turns with the binoculars to spy on Shakeel.

'You really think he's a suicide bomber?' I say.

'You can just bet that if he is then the day he decides to do his bombing Mum will say he has to look after me and then it'll be yours truly being blown to smithereens.' Priti does a funny little bounce and pulls a face which I think is supposed to be her being blown up.

Jed laughs, but I don't.

'I wonder if Ameenah knows about it,' Priti goes on.

'Who's Ameenah?' asks Jed. It's meant to be my turn to use the binoculars, but he shows no sign of handing them over. He's been staring for ages at the copse where Zara and Tyreese are hanging out.

'Shakeel's fiancée. They're getting married in a few weeks.'

'She's probably part of the cell then,' says Jed without taking his eyes off the copse.

'But if he's getting married in a few weeks, why would he blow himself up?' I ask. 'My mum says her wedding day was the happiest day of her life.'

'My dad says it was the worst mistake of his!' says Jed.

'I reckon it's an excuse to get out of all the wedding stuff,' says Priti. 'We go well overboard on weddings. Loads of parties that go on all week – it's dead boring.'

'What about the wedding night?' says Jed. 'He won't want to miss that!'

'*Eugh!*' says Priti. 'You are sick. That's my brother you're talking about.'

'So you reckon he's done it with this Ameenah already then?' says Jed.

'I don't want to think about it,' says Priti, pulling a face. 'But, knowing Shakeel, probably not.'

'Why? Is she a moose?' asks Jed.

'She's all right. Dresses a bit boring, but she's not a real minger.'

'So he'll wanna wait till after his big night before he blows himself up then?' says Jed. 'When's the wedding?'

'Beginning of August,' says Priti.

'That's only a couple of weeks away,' I say.

'So we'd better keep an eye on him then,' says Jed.

When we go back over to Granny's for lunch, I find another card from Gary. This one has a picture of a potato decorated to look like Darth Vader and on the back it says, *The force connects all living things – even me and you. Feel the force, Ben!* It sounds like the sort of thing my mum would say which makes me feel really sad. And it's also a bit like Gary's pretending to be my dad (cos everyone knows Darth Vader is actually Luke's father) which is a bit weird too. Jed asks me to show it to him, but Granny says I don't have to talk about it if I don't want to. So I don't.

After lunch, Jed and Grandad clear off pretty

quickly, so it's just me and Granny left to clear up as usual.

'Granny,' I say as she leans over me to pick up the salt and pepper pots. 'Have you heard from my mum?'

She stops what she's doing, so she's standing there, holding the two little ceramic pots shaped like chickens, and it's like she hasn't heard me because she doesn't answer for ages. I'm about to ask her again when she says simply, 'No, not yet, dear.' And then it's as if she suddenly remembers what she was doing and busies herself again tidying away.

'It's worse than before, isn't it?' I ask.

'A bit.' Granny turns to the cupboards and stops again, like she can't remember which one the salt and pepper go in.

'Is she going to die?' I ask, keeping my voice very quiet. I'm staring at the painted feathers on the chickens, tracing the patterns of colour with my eyes.

'No, dear.' She turns round quickly to face me. 'No, of course not. They won't let her.' She looks really upset.

'Sorry, Granny,' I say.

'*You've* nothing to be sorry for,' she says. Then she sits down next to me again and puts her hand on mine. 'Now go ahead, ask me whatever you like,' she says, trying to look cheery again.

But I just say, 'No, it's OK, thank you.' And then, 'I know she'll be better soon anyway, so I'm not worried about her.' And I smile and look at the chicken pots and try to imagine them as real chickens, only I can't.

And Granny just smiles and pats my hand. And that's the end of the conversation.

It's Zara's turn to keep an eye on Priti this afternoon, but she tries to palm it off on Shakeel.

'Give me a break, Shakeel! I'm supposed to be meeting some friends.'

'I have things to do too, little sister.'

'Like what?'

'Making an improvised explosive!' Jed whispers in my ear.

'All you do is study and sit and fiddle with your radios. It's no skin off your nose to keep an eye on the rug rats.'

'I have people to meet,' he replies.

'What people?'

'That's no concern of yours.'

Jed mutters the words 'terror cell'.

'Come on, Shakeel, do me a favour,' says Zara, who is wearing a dress and smells of perfume.

'I'm sorry, Zara. I have to go to the library. I'll try and get back early so you can see your friends.' He turns to us and says, 'Try and entertain yourselves and don't get under Zara's feet – OK?'

But Zara is still angry with him and slams the door behind him as he leaves. 'Don't think I'm looking after your kids when you start sprogging with Professor Ameenah!' she shouts after him.

As soon as Shakeel is safely out of earshot, Jed says, 'Why don't you let me look after these kids while you go and shag your boyfriend?'

Zara turns round quickly and glares at him.

'Who told you I had a boyfriend, shrimp?' The 'shrimp' doesn't quite work because, without her heels on, Jed is nearly as tall as she is.

'I have my sources!' says Jed with a swagger. 'My

sources also tell me you could do a lot better. Have you ever considered going for a younger man?'

Zara makes a funny gesture with her head and laughs. 'Oh, I didn't realise you meant you. The word "man" must have confused me. I don't go for boys. Sorry!' She laughs again.

'You will be,' says Jed, sounding a bit like his dad. 'What do you see in that loser anyway?'

'Um, let me see!' she puts a finger to her lips. 'He's fit. He's funny . . . His balls have actually dropped.'

'I think you'll find everything in order in that department!' says Jed. 'But if you'd like to check . . .' He reaches for the belt of his jeans.

'Like I wanna go grubbing around in your skiddy little pants!' she says. 'How old are you anyway, kid?'

'Fourteen,' Jed lies.

'That figures.' She laughs. 'Now out of my way, kiddo!'

Jed steps to one side with a little bow and Zara looks like she's going to walk on past him, but then she comes right close to his face and says, 'And if you tell anyone I've got a boyfriend . . .'

'You'll what?' says Jed.

Zara pulls herself up straight, sticks her boobs out and I can see her looking at him, wondering what to say next. 'Are you trying to blackmail me, kid?'

Jed shrugs.

'Oh, what the hell, if it'll shut you up!' Then she grabs his head, presses her mouth to his and moves her lips around for about half a minute.

Priti lets out a giggle. I just stare.

When Zara finally pulls away, Jed's face is doing a good impression of my beetroot red, and for the first time since I've known him, he's lost for words.

Zara quickly rubs her sleeve over her lips and says, 'Right, well, if you ever want that to happen again, you keep quiet, you hear?'

Jed just nods and she turns away.

Priti bursts out laughing. 'Like that's gonna keep him quiet.'

But Jed doesn't say anything and neither do I.

After Zara has disappeared into the bedroom she shares with Priti, we sneak upstairs to check out

Shakeel's room for hidden explosives or detonator devices. It feels like we're playing bomb squad, but Jed says it's not a game because Shakeel is a potential terror suspect so this is totally for real. And I don't bother to argue because he and Priti actually seem to agree on something for once.

The door to Zara and Priti's room is ajar and we can hear Zara on the phone to Tyreese as we crawl past, commando style. (Why don't soldiers use their knees to crawl on? Is it because they've been shot off – as Jed says – or in case they get a bullet in the bum – Priti's suggestion?)

Glancing in as I crawl by, I can see that the girls' room is a tip. The beds are unmade, the curtains are still shut giving the room a purple glow and there are clothes strewn everywhere. They've got loads of posters on the wall: goth bands and film stars who look like vampires (Zara's, I guess), girl bands and pretty-boy popstars (must be Priti's) and there's make-up and underwear scattered all over the floor.

Zara is on her bed, lying back on some pink furry cushions. Above her hangs a pink and black gauzy thing like a mosquito net. She looks like some sort of gothic princess as she whispers into her mobile. I imagine evil-looking black fairies fluttering in the air around her.

'Will you two stop ogling my sister so we can get on with spying on my brother!' whispers Priti impatiently.

Jed and I both snap to attention.

Shakeel's room is at the end of the corridor and the door is closed but not locked. I imagine a skull and crossbones sign and the caption, *Beware all who enter here!*

'Mum won't let us have locks on our bedrooms,' Priti whispers. 'Says she'd rather see the nonsense we get up to.'

Jed and I stand guard while Priti opens the door. Jed is holding two fingers up to his chest, like a pretend revolver. Priti gently eases down the door handle and we all pile into Shakeel's bedroom.

The room is really neat, not like his sisters' at all. There's not much space to move though because a large double bed touches the wall on both sides and there are bookshelves built up all round it which make me wonder how it feels to sleep there. I imagine an avalanche of books burying Shakeel alive while he sleeps.

'After they get married, Ameenah's gonna come and live with us. Just till they get a place of their own,' Priti whispers. 'That's why he gets to have a double bed!'

'*If* he gets married,' whispers Jed, staring at the desk with all Shakeel's law college books on it, then over at the bench beneath the window where all the radio equipment is laid out.

'What are we looking for?' I ask.

Priti shrugs so we both look at Jed.

'Anything suspicious,' he says. 'I've brought my phone so we can take pictures and pass them on to my dad.'

'So, Jed, what *does* your dad do exactly?' asks Priti, looking straight at him.

'He's a mechanic,' says Jed, opening Shakeel's underwear drawer and lifting out a pair of boxer shorts. 'Reckon we should check for skid marks?'

'So is he in the bomb squad or what?' asks Priti as

Jed waves Shakeel's pants in front of my face.

Jed shrugs.

'I thought you said he was in the bomb squad.'

'No, I didn't.' Jed drops the pants back into the drawer and continues rifling through it. Shakeel's stuff is all very tidy and I can't help thinking that he's going to notice someone's been in here messing it up.

'Then how does he know about terrorists and bombs and stuff?'

'Even if I knew, I probably couldn't tell you. All that sort of stuff is classified, innit?' He looks right at her. Priti narrows her eyes and stares back. 'So stop asking stupid questions and get on with it before we get caught.'

'We've got to put everything back exactly where it was,' I say.

They both turn to look at me, like I'm some kind of freak.

'You said if he knows we're on to him, he'll go underground,' I say.

'That's true,' agrees Jed. 'Make a mental note of where things are before you pick them up.'

So that's what we do and it's quite good fun. I try to measure the exact position of everything on the desk and replace things really carefully. Jed isn't so careful and keeps forgetting and Priti doesn't actually do that much searching. She sits on the bed and quizzes Jed. 'Ben said your dad's bomb squad – or whatever it's called – had identified Shakeel as a suspect,' she says.

'No, I didn't,' I say.

'But if he's not even in the bomb squad then this is a waste of time.'

'Everyone knows that a Muslim tinkering about in his bedroom with home-made electronics is dodgy,' says Jed.

'So what exactly is your dad gonna do when you tell him anyway?' asks Priti.

'Hey, look at this!' I've opened this folder and inside is a list – all typed out neatly in columns. Names, addresses, phone numbers and emails accompanied by little ticks and crosses in columns.

'What do your reckon it is?' I ask, handing it to Jed.

'This must be a list of all the people in his terror cell!' says Jed, forgetting to whisper.

'*Shh!*' says Priti, looking at the list of names. 'That's creepy Uncle Aatif,' she says. 'I can totally believe he's a terrorist.'

'Exactly,' says Jed, folding up the list and putting it in his pocket. 'Keep it in the family. Like the Mafia.'

'Hey, you can't just take it,' says Priti.

'Yes, I can. I'm gonna give this to my dad and he can check these people out.'

'Won't Shakeel notice it's gone?' I say.

'He's got it on computer. He can just print off another copy.' Jed glances at Shakeel's laptop. 'Next time we should bring a memory stick – download stuff off his hard drive. Now come on, keep searching!'

Me and Jed keep up our search and Priti stares out of the window, humming.

'Wow!' exclaims Jed suddenly. He pulls something out of the bottom of a drawer from under a pile of neatly stacked pyjamas and holds it up. It looks like a belt of some sort – one of those wide belt things that bullfighters wear – only this one is black and rubbery and lined with compartments: five or six of them, spaced out along its length.

'Woah!' says Priti. 'What is that?'

'I think it's pretty obvious what this is,' says Jed.

'What?' I ask.

'It's a strap-on bomb!' says Jed. 'I've seen them on TV. Suicide bombers always wear them under their clothes.'

We all stare at it for a moment.

'Are you sure?' I say.

'Positive,' says Jed.

We're all transfixed. I think about the pictures Lukas showed me on the Internet – of men in white robes with belts just like this strapped underneath.

'Is it live?' I ask.

'Dunno,' says Jed, holding the thing at arm's length.

We all look at each other.

'Then how do you know it won't go off the minute you put it down again?' says Priti.

Jed clearly hasn't thought about this. 'What do you want me to do? Stand here dangling it while you two evacuate the building?'

'That would be the gentlemanly thing to do,' says Priti.

'Go on then!' Jed retorts.

They stare at each other.

'Do you think we should tell Zara so she can evacuate too?' I butt in.

'No one is evacuating,' says Jed. 'I'm just going to put this thing down. One blows, we all blow!'

So we hold our breath as Jed carefully inches the weird-looking contraption back into the drawer where he found it. It's like a scene from a film. As the bomb belt touches the wooden base of the drawer, Priti lets out a little cry.

But there's no explosion. We all look at each other and then Jed gives a loud sigh of relief.

'Shame!' says Priti. 'Would've been a cool way to go.'

'Yeah, blown to a million pieces, just like Ben's dad!' says Jed.

I try to push the image out of my head, imagining bits of Jed flying off in all directions instead.

'Hadn't we better cover it up?' I say to Jed. 'We don't want him to know we've seen it.'

'Perhaps he's got surveillance cameras up here and is giving the order for us all to be assassinated right now!' says Jed.

'Shouldn't we tell someone?' I ask.

'Who?'

'I dunno. The police. It could go off at any time, couldn't it?'

But just then there's a ring at the doorbell and we all freeze. Eventually, Priti peers out of the window. 'It's Ameenah!'

'What do we do now?' asks Jed.

'Come on. We have to get out of here,' says Priti.

We shove things back in roughly the same places we found them then pile quickly out of the room and into the hallway.

Zara's door is closed now and there's music coming from inside the room. The doorbell rings again.

'Who is it?' Zara yells.

'It's Ameenah!' says Priti.

'Oh, God!' Zara curses. There's the sound of hasty movement and then another voice, not Zara's – a male voice.

'Have you got someone in there?' asks Priti.

The door opens and there is Zara pulling her top back on. I look away quickly (Jed doesn't) but not before I've caught a glimpse of Tyreese, topless and grinning, lying on the bed.

'Wow, you're a fast mover!' says Priti.

Jed keeps staring at Zara as she wiggles back into her top.

'Look, Ugli,' Zara says. 'There's a fiver in it for you if you can stall her while I get him out of here.'

'You're on,' says Priti, grinning at Tyreese and then at Zara, who looks genuinely nervous. Perhaps she really is worried about being honour-killed.

The doorbell rings again.

'God, why does the ice maiden have to turn up now?' Zara curses.

'We'll keep her talking while you sneak him out,' says Priti and, for the first time, I get the feeling Priti isn't just in this for the money. 'He can climb the tree house and jump over the fence.'

I glance at Tyreese, who is lying back on the bed now, showing no signs of putting his clothes back on. I imagine him leaping over the fence in just his boxer shorts.

'Come on,' says Priti to Jed and me. 'And don't forget to smile!'

So when the door opens, Ameenah is confronted by all three of us, breathless and barring her entry with our grins.

'Hello, Ameenah!' says Priti brightly.

'Hello, Ameenah!' say Jed and I in unison.

It turns out that Ameenah is stunningly beautiful. Priti only ever talks about how clever she is, and Zara is always saying she's mumsy and middle-aged, so I never expected her to be gorgeous. But she has skin like chocolate peaches, long dark hair and big eyes. She's wearing traditional dress and looks a bit like Princess Jasmine from *Aladdin*. (Blythe is into all that stuff and she's made me sit and watch the DVD with her dozens of times, so that's how I know.) When I look at her, I imagine butterflies dancing around in my stomach.

'Wow!' I hear Jed say under his breath. 'Shakeel is punching way above his weight!'

'Hello, Priti. And Priti's friends,' says Ameenah, ignoring the comment and looking me and Jed over in the way my grandad does to Priti – as if she's not sure she approves. I blush, but I don't look away.

'This is Ben. And this is Jed. They're my friends,' says Priti, still grinning, one hand on the door so Ameenah can't get in.

'I see. Hello, Jed and hello, Ben.'

I open my mouth to respond, but nothing comes out.

'Shakeel said I could drop by and pick up a brochure about the caterers that I need for the wedding plans.'

'I see,' says Priti. 'And how are the plans going?' She sounds like my granny when she says this.

'Very well, thank you.' Ameenah makes a move to come in. Jed and I edge back nervously, but Priti stands firm.

'Would you like a drink?' she asks. 'A cup of tea perhaps? Or a glass of water?'

'No, I'm fine, thank you, Priti. I just need to get that brochure.'

'My mum says you should always offer guests refreshment.'

'Well, you have offered and I have declined. I am sure she would be satisfied with that,' says Ameenah, sounding a bit like a schoolteacher.

'No, she'll be really cross if she hears you were here and we let you leave without something to drink and a bite to eat,' says Priti, trying to out-polite Ameenah. 'She won't believe me if I say you didn't want anything.'

'I'm happy to explain to her if that would help,' says Ameenah in a very sweet voice, but looking slightly impatient. 'It's just that I'm in a bit of a rush.'

'Please, Ameenah!' Priti pleads. Then her face lights up suddenly as a new idea comes to her. 'Besides, I need some help with my homework.'

'I thought school had broken up.'

'It has,' says Jed, who has been unusually silent up to this point. 'Priti's doing this special holiday project. It's a bit like coursework, only for younger kids. It's *dead* important and Priti says you are *really* clever.'

141

'Yeah,' says Priti. 'You are the cleverest person we know.' She gives Ameenah a big grin.

'Who's supposed to be looking after you today, Priti?' asks Ameenah with a sigh.

'Zara, but she's, well, you know what she's like and she's not half as clever as you and she won't even try to help.'

Ameenah sighs and glances at her watch. 'Very well, I'll see what I can do. Five minutes though. What is it you are trying to do?'

Priti glances at me and raises her eyes to the heavens. For once, Jed is quiet. Glancing upstairs, I can see Tyreese on the landing. We have to get Ameenah into the kitchen so he can disappear without her noticing.

'We're trying to build a bomb!' I say quickly.

Jed and Priti both turn to stare at me and so does Ameenah. I feel myself starting to go red. 'It has to be made out of stuff you find in the kitchen,' I add. 'It's a science project. We have to invent something to make an explosion just out of things from around the house.'

Priti and Jed look at Ameenah for her reaction. For a moment, she stares at me and I think I've blown it. Then she starts to smile. 'That sounds interesting,' she says, looking right at me. The butterflies do backflips in my tummy. 'I might have a few ideas. Come on. Let's see what we can find.'

Jed and Priti both grin and as we all troop into the kitchen, Priti whispers, 'That was awesome. How did you know she was into science?'

'I didn't.'

'She was Young Chemist of the Year about twenty years running. That was a stroke of genius.'

'Astro Boy can talk when he needs to!' says Jed, giving me a punch on the arm which hurts more than I let on.

I imagine myself as Astro Boy, taking him out with a well-placed right hook. The thought makes me smile.

Once we're in the kitchen Ameenah starts talking about bicarbonate of soda and vinegar and Coca-Cola, effervescent vitamin tablets and empty film canisters. She's so busy rummaging in the cupboards for stuff to make a big bang that she doesn't hear the front door click as Zara bundles Tyreese out of the house.

A few moments later, Zara appears, wearing her headphones and shuffling in a huge pair of fluffy slippers, like she's just come out from her bedroom.

'Hi, Ameenah,' she says, making her way to the fridge. 'Don't let the rug rats pester you. You'll never escape.'

She's dead cool – she doesn't even look at us. Priti tries not to giggle and Jed pulls kissing faces at her, but she just ignores him. I don't know where to look: Ameenah is butterfly-in-the-tummy beautiful, but Zara, even in her slippers, is something else – something I don't have a word for.

Thankfully, Ameenah doesn't notice anything. She's too busy showing us loads of ways to make explosions. Even Jed seems impressed. And when she leaves, Ameenah says that another day she'll bring us things to make a really big bang.

'Thanks,' I say. 'That'd be dead interesting.'

'My pleasure.'

* * *

'Thanks, that was *soooo* interesting!' says Jed in a soppy voice after she's gone. 'Fancy her, did you, Ben?' And he starts pulling kissy faces again.

'Don't be stupid!'

'You'd better watch out. She's arranged-marriage-engaged to my brother. Her family will be out to honour-kill you, if you're not careful,' says Priti.

'I don't fancy her!' I say.

'*And* she's a terrorist!' says Jed.

'She is not!'

'Don't defend her just because she's your girlfriend. How else did she know all that stuff about explosives?'

'That was just for fun,' I say.

'You heard what she said about making a really big bang!' says Jed.

'I reckon she's the chemist of the group,' says Priti. 'Every terror cell has once. Shakeel makes the detonators. She makes the explosives.'

'Exactly,' says Jed. 'They're probably not even engaged. Just pretending so they can work on

145

the terror plot together without anyone getting suspicious.'

'So you might still be in with a chance, Ben!' says Priti.

'Shut up,' is all I can think of to say.

JULY 23RD

'I've found this website called Tuesdays' Children,'
Priti announces after Jed goes off with Granny for
one of his top-secret appointments. 'It's for 9/11
kids like you.'

'So?' I say. I'm sitting on the floor of my bedroom
with my notebook, doodling pictures of princesses
on flying carpets in giant fluffy slippers. I haven't
seen Priti for a couple of days because she's been
off with her mum and Ameenah doing wedding
stuff. Even Jed said it'd been a bit boring without
her around.

'So there's loads of interesting stuff on there,' she
says. 'There's even a chat room so you could get in
touch with the other bereaved kids.'

'Stop calling me that, will you?'

'Fine, I'll call you a 9/11 orphan.'

'How can I be an orphan? My mum is still alive.'

'If you say so.'

'What's that supposed to mean?'

'It means even Jed talks about his mum more than you do.'

'Just because I don't talk about her doesn't mean she doesn't exist,' I say, putting down my pencil.

'Whatever.'

'My mum will be better soon and then she'll be coming to get me,' I carry on angrily. 'So I'm not an orphan.'

'Look, my point is that there are loads of other kids with 9/11 issues just like yours who are gagging to chat to you online.'

'And what if I don't want to?' I pick up my pencil and try to keep drawing the princesses, but they don't seem to work any more.

'Of course you do. That's just the grief talking,' says Priti.

'I told you, I'm not grieving!' I say, doodling rows of triangles.

'Maybe you feel angry or anxious or lacking hope. They are all forms of grief,' says Priti with a learned expression on her face. I imagine her with a giant pair of glasses and a white doctor's coat several sizes too big for her.

'Have you been learning the website by heart?' I draw a big square, then a smaller one inside it, then a smaller one again: boxes within boxes.

'I reckon I could be a counsellor or something. I'm getting you to talk about your unacknowledged grief here.'

'Aren't you supposed to, like, respect my privacy or something?' I say, my boxes getting smaller and smaller.

'If it's in the patient's best interests, sometimes you have to be cruel to be kind.'

'You just made that up,' I say, abandoning my boxes and trying to doodle Dr Priti.

'Maybe I did, but I still reckon you should be getting in touch with these other kids. They go on camps together and talk about their feelings and build schools for poor kids in Costa Rica and do art therapy and music and meditation and all sorts.'

'Well, I don't want to do any of that, OK?'

'All right! All right! Keep your hair on. There are other things we can do.'

'Like what exactly?'

'Like we make a big poster of your dad and everyone has to write down their memories of him on it and we put it up somewhere everyone can see it. We could do that.'

I look up from my drawing. 'You didn't even know him,' I point out.

'I could pretend I did. I expect he was just like you only grown up and better-looking and a bit less miserable.'

'You can't pretend you knew a dead person if you didn't,' I say, trying to do another Dr Priti, this time with massive glasses perched on the end of a giant Mr Nosey nose.

'Well, you could tell me some of your memories and I could pretend they were mine,' she suggests.

'I don't have many memories of my own,' I say, staring crossly at the cartoon, which looks nothing like Priti. 'I can hardly remember what he looked like.'

But Priti doesn't seem to worry too much about this. 'Well, your granny and grandad must have loads. And Jed says he remembers him and we can ask your uncle Ian. And your mum,' she says pointedly. 'When she gets back again.'

'Granny gets all upset and cries whenever anyone mentions Dad,' I say.

'And your mum?'

I have an image of my mum, lying in a hospital bed.

'She says it's no one else's business,' I say quickly.

'Fine. What about you make a shrine, with his picture and some of his stuff, and you can light a candle there?'

'Granny won't have candles in the house. She reckons they'll set fire to the net curtains and bring down the house on our heads or something.' I draw a little picture of a house with flames coming out of the roof.

'Well, you could have a torch or one of them flameless candles that squirts air-freshener like my mum's got. I'm sure I could nick one.'

But I obviously don't look convinced because then she says, 'Or you can just make a memory box with some of his things and people's memories in it.'

'I really don't want to make a shrine to my dad

or a memory box or whatever.'

'Well, we're going to do something and if you don't decide what then I'll decide for you.'

'Priti, please.' I wish she'd just drop it.

'It's for your own good. You can't just sit around doodling cartoons all day. Hey, is that supposed to be me?'

'No,' I mutter as she makes a grab for my notebook. 'Some doctor you are!' I scribble over the half-finished Dr Priti faces and shove the book under my legs so she can't get it. 'I thought you were supposed to make me feel better, but the thought of doing all this is making me lots worse!'

Priti grins at me. 'See, there you go! You're expressing your emotions at last!'

Eventually, I agree to make a memory box and this shuts Priti up for a bit, mainly because we don't have a box, which means we can't start it today. Priti says she's going to ask her mum for one and meanwhile, I have to start getting stuff together to go in it.

'Don't disappoint me!' she says.

'You sound like someone's mum.'

'I'm going to make a great mum one day,' she says.

'Your kids will never get a word in edgeways.'

'At least I'll be cool. You'll be one of those sad, embarrassing dads. The one who comes to pick the kid up and everyone thinks he's a paedophile.'

'Who says I even want to have kids?' I say.

'Everyone has to. It's punishment for giving your own parents hell, I reckon.'

'Well, I don't.' Without a pencil, I don't know what to do with my hands.

Priti stares at me then says, 'What? You don't want kids or you're one of those freaky kids who don't give their parents a hard time?'

'No,' I say quickly, not sure which bit of the question I'm answering. 'Yes, I mean . . . maybe.'

'I get it,' says Priti. 'I guess with your mum being ill and all you've been forced to grow up before your time.'

'She's nearly better,' I say.

'Did she say that?'

'Sort of.' I look down at my hands.

'Why can't you visit her?'

'Too far away,' I say.

'What's wrong with her anyway?'

I stare at Priti.

'Hey, I figure if you're actually talking about her, I get to ask all the questions I want.'

'She kind of stopped eating,' I say, looking down again.

'That happened to my aunt when she had cancer. Has she got cancer?'

'No.'

'I reckon Jed's got cancer,' says Priti.

'What?' I say, looking up.

'Well, he must have something really serious if he has to go to the hospital every week.'

'Who says he's even going to hospital?'

'All these appointments. What else can it be?'

I shrug.

'I've been looking at my mum's medical book and it's either that or kidney failure.'

'Are you sure?'

'I asked Ameenah about it and she said kids whose

kidneys don't work have to go for this thing once a week to clean all the wee out of their blood. She reckons they look a bit yellow too, with all the wee. Do you reckon he looks yellow?'

'Not really,' I say, imagining Jed with a Simpsons yellow face.

'Me neither. So I reckon it must be cancer which means his hair will fall out, only I can't tell if Jed's is because he always wears that skanky cap. What's it like when he goes to bed?'

'His hair is all right,' I say, thinking of my mum's beautiful hair starting to fall out.

'It might not happen straight away. If he's having chemo, it might take a while.'

'You really think he's sick?' I ask, imagining Jed with a bald head, all his footballer curls lying scattered on the floor around him.

'Must be. No one has appointments twice in a fortnight if they're not sick.'

'I suppose so. But do you really think he might be dying?'

'Might be,' says Priti. 'Guess we'll have to wait and

see. They sure like their secrets in your family.'

'Well, you've got a brother who's a secret terrorist,' I say.

'Yeah, about that, Shakeel was well mad at me for messing around in his room. Wouldn't let me tidy up though, which I reckon is a bit sus!'

'You've also got a sister with a secret boyfriend and another brother who'll kill her if he finds out, so I reckon your family has as many secrets as mine.'

'True,' she says. 'Good job you and me are good at keeping our mouths shut then!'

THINGS I'D LIKE TO KNOW ABOUT MY MUM

1. Why does she have such long hair? None of the other mums I know have hair like hers.

2. Why does she sometimes let me stay up really late and go to bed when I want and eat pizza and not brush my teeth, but at other times she's really strict about bedtime, has no-processed-food-products drives and makes sure I brush my teeth for three whole minutes every time?

3. Why does she always insist on sitting to watch me eat? Just sitting there, watching me, with this weird smile on her face, telling me to tuck in because I'm a growing boy.

4. Why does she have to volunteer for everything? Why doesn't she let some other people volunteer sometimes?

5. Which hospital has she gone to exactly?

6. Why is my granny cross with her for being ill?

7. How can it be that she's so much happier since she's met Gary, but she still got sick again? I know she's happy because she's always singing and dancing and laughing. But she cries more too. And now she's sick again, which doesn't make sense.

8. Why doesn't she like phones? And couldn't she make an exception and call me just once?

9. When is she coming home?

10. Why can't I think of another question? Does that mean I'm forgetting her too?

When Granny and Jed get back from their appointment, Granny seems sad and a bit shaky. She's carrying two plastic shopping bags and a box from the bakery and she says she thinks we all deserve a cup of tea and a little treat. Jed says he doesn't want anything. He just goes straight up to his room, but not before I see that he's wearing a brand-new pair of trainers.

I offer to take Granny's shopping for her and she says, 'Oh, you are a good boy. The arthritis in my fingers is playing up today.'

As I take the bags from her, I notice that her fingers don't uncurl when she lets go: they stay tightly balled up for ages afterwards.

'Did it go OK?' I ask as I take the things out of the bags and put them away in the cupboards: sugar, cereal, milk, jam. Granny is like me; she likes everything to be in its place.

'Oh, yes,' she says sadly. 'At least I hope Jed enjoyed it.'

This seems like an odd thing to say about a hospital appointment, but I don't want Granny to think I'm prying, so I don't ask her any more about it.

'You and I will have to do something nice together soon,' she says, smiling at me.

'I'd like that.'

Then she says, 'You are just like your father. He always used to help me unpack the shopping.' I make a mental note to remember this – I suppose it counts as a memory for Priti's box.

'Do you have a picture of him I could have?' I ask suddenly.

'Of course I do,' she says. 'Why?'

'It's just this idea Priti has. About making a memory box.'

I expect her to ask more about it, but she doesn't, for the same reasons I don't ask her about the appointments, I suppose. I sometimes think Granny and I are quite alike.

'Well, of course I can find you a picture,' she says. 'And if there's anything else that you need, you just come and ask me.'

'Thanks, Granny,' I say. 'I will.'

* * *

'So how was it?' I ask Jed upstairs in our bedroom after I've unpacked the shopping and Granny has gone for a little sit-down. Jed's lying on the bed and staring at the ceiling. He's weirdly still, although his leg is kicking rhythmically as if some part of him has to be moving at all times.

'Boring,' is his reply. 'I don't know why Granny makes me go anyway.'

'I could go with you,' I suggest.

'I don't think that would quite be the point, would it?'

'Point of what?'

'Point of going. Anyway, what have you and your girlfriend been up to while I've been out?'

'She's not my girlfriend!'

'All right. Your girl-mate.'

'She's your mate too.'

'Only cos of you, so it doesn't really count.'

He keeps kicking his foot as if he's aiming it at an imaginary ball. He's in a funny mood – angry and restless – even more so than usual. I pull out my notepad, perch on my bed and start drawing pictures of boxes: shoeboxes and hatboxes and matchboxes – all different shapes and sizes.

'We just hung out. Didn't do much.'

'Find out any more about the suicide bomber?' he asks.

'Not really.' I shrug.

'Some anti-terror squaddie you'll make. When I write a best-seller about shopping the terrorist across the road, I'll be sure to point out how useless you were.'

'Priti did say there were loads of people coming to her house tonight,' I say, trying to draw an eggbox with a dozen spaces for eggs. 'Maybe that's something to do with it.'

'That's brilliant!' Jed sits bolt upright on the bed and grins for the first time all day. 'Right, we have to take pics for the police to ID,' he says, lurching from vegetable to bouncy Tigger in record time, even for him.

'How are we going to do that?'

'On my phone, I reckon,' he says, waving around the state-of-the-art mobile his dad gave him (although he never picks up when Jed rings).

* * *

Granny gets a surprise when Jed agrees to go to bed early – and without arguing. There's normally a good half an hour of negotiation and messing around. As she kisses him goodnight, she says, 'Perhaps today has been good for you,' but Jed just grunts and squirms away from her. Then she looks from one of us to the other and says, 'My two boys!' Only I can't tell if she looks happy or sad.

We listen to her go downstairs and into the sitting room. Our door is ajar and we hear her say to Grandad, 'He's almost like he was before Karen left.'

Jed mutters, 'Yeah, right!'

And I hear Grandad say, 'He's better off without that woman.'

'Yup!' mutters Jed from the bed next to me. I'm not sure if he means me to hear or not.

'I'm just glad to see him settling down a bit, that's all,' says Granny.

'God knows he needs to,' says Grandad.

Jed gets up then and closes the door. 'We don't want anyone eavesdropping on us,' he says. 'The walls are like paper in this house!'

Then he climbs up on to the windowsill.

I don't say anything. I'm not sure if I'm supposed to pretend I didn't hear anything that's just been said.

'Come on!' he says impatiently. 'Have you got the binoculars?'

I get them from under my pillow and clamber up next to him. It's quite late now and visitors are starting to arrive at Priti's house. They're all men, all dressed up in robes, and they are all carrying plastic bags or big packages.

'Bomb-making stuff probably!' says Jed.

He tries to take pictures with his phone, but they're too far away and the pictures come out all dark and blurry.

'No one's going to be able to ID them from these,' says Jed, annoyed.

'Why don't you write down all the car registration numbers?'

'I suppose so,' he says.

'And I'll draw some pictures so we can do one of those photofit things later.'

So this is what we do, but Jed keeps saying things like, 'They all look alike,' and, 'Why do they all have to have the same colour hair? What's wrong with blond or ginger Muslims? Why don't you ever see any of those?' And it's starting to get dark so after a bit we give up because we can't see properly any more.

Anyway, it doesn't really look much like a top-secret meeting of a terror cell to me, or at least if it is, they aren't being very top-secret about it because they're making lots of noise and laughing and there's loud music playing.

The other thing is that Priti's dad seems to be there cos we see him welcoming the guests as they arrive and I don't reckon Shakeel would invite over a load of terrorists while his parents were home. I say this to Jed, but he says that I didn't even notice that Shakeel was a terrorist till he pointed it out, so what do I know about it?

'Anyway,' he says, 'maybe Mr Muhammed is in the cell too. Like father like son.'

'It looks like they're having a party, not planning a bomb attack.'

'That's what makes them so clever, these people,' says Jed. 'They make it all look so innocent until suddenly *boom*!' He mimes a bomb explosion. 'Bang goes the road! Glad I'm not hanging around here for much longer. You'll be the one who gets to do a Ground Zero if your mum doesn't get out of the loony bin soon.'

'She's not in the loony bin!' I say.

'Right, and your dad's living in New Mexico with Elvis, right?'

'They wouldn't blow up the cul-de-sac anyway,' I say.

'You never know with these people. Unpredictability is the key to their success. Like the police are never going to send out the sniffer dogs to a quiet road like this. That's probably why they moved here.'

'Shakeel's hardly going to bomb his own house, is he?'

'What does he care? He'll be living it up in Muslim heaven or whatever with all those virgins. It's not like he's going to miss his widescreen TV.'

'Virgins?'

'Don't tell me you don't know what a virgin is?'

'Course I do,' I say, reddening. 'Just – what've they got to do with him blowing up his house?'

'Suicide bombers get given loads of virgins when they go to Muslim heaven. I read it somewhere. Or my dad told me.'

I have an image of loads of bikini babes dancing on a white fluffy cloud.

'Why?'

'Why do you think?' Jed snorts, looks at me and then a slow grin appears over his face. 'You don't know, do you?'

'Course I do,' I say quickly. 'I meant, why do they get given them? Is it like a reward or what?'

'I knew you didn't understand.'

'Yes, I do.'

'Do you know anything about sex?'

'Yes. Lots,' I say, my face burning.

'Don't worry. My dad'll tell you everything you need to know.'

'No thanks,' I mutter.

'What's that supposed to mean?' he says. 'At least I've got a dad.'

'Who's always having a go at you and never rings you.'

'Like your mum never rings you?'

'That's different.'

'At least my dad isn't the one who went bungee jumping from the Twin Towers without a cable.'

'Shut up,' I say.

'Oops, but we're not allowed to mention that, are we? What *are* we allowed to talk about with you?'

'Shut up,' I say again.

'That's your thing, isn't it? Shut up and put up. Maybe that's what drove your mum to the loony bin. She couldn't stand living with Bennie the mute.'

Something in me snaps. 'She's not in the loony bin!' I shout, launching myself at Jed. We both topple off the windowsill and on to the bed. I'm on top of Jed and I'm punching him. 'Take that back!' I shout.

'Get off, you maniac!'

'Take back what you said about my mum.' I pummel at him with my fists.

Suddenly the door swings opens. 'What is going on in here?'

We both look up to see Grandad standing in the doorway.

For a moment, neither of us says anything.

'Nothing,' says Jed.

'Doesn't sound like nothing to me!' says Grandad. 'I could hear you over the bloody disco across the road.'

'We were just playing,' says Jed.

'Ben?' Grandad looks at me.

I don't say anything.

'We were only messing around,' Jed says again.

Grandad looks at me again, but when I still say nothing, he says, 'Well, stop messing around and get to sleep, do you hear?'

'Yes, Grandad,' we both say.

After he's gone, we both sit totally still for what feels like ages, but is probably only about a minute. 'Thanks for not dobbing me in,' I say eventually.

'Sure,' Jed says.

I climb back into my bed and he climbs into his. I

stare at the stars on the ceiling. 'What did you mean when you said you aren't going to be here for much longer?' I ask.

'What do you think?' he says. 'I'm heading off soon.'

I want to ask him more, but then Granny puts her head round the door.

'Everything OK now, boys?'

'Yes,' says Jed.

I just nod.

'I suppose all the music is keeping you up. Your grandfather is none too pleased about it either. He's going to have a word with Mr Muhammed.'

Then she hands me an envelope. 'The picture you asked for,' she says and kisses me lightly on the forehead before saying, 'Sleep well, my two boys.'

JULY 24TH

According to Priti, the big 'terror cell meeting' last night was actually some kind of pre-wedding drinks party.

'Sorry to disappoint you!' she giggles when she tells us.

The three of us are sitting in the tree house, sharing my dad's binoculars. We're spying on Shakeel again while keeping watch for Zara, but there's not much to see. Shakeel is just sitting at his desk and Zara and Tyreese haven't emerged from the bushes for the last quarter of an hour.

'Seriously, you two are like Dumb and Dumber.'

'Who are they?' I ask, but neither of them is listening.

'Or Scooby-Doo and Shaggy,' Priti goes on. 'In which case, I'm guessing Ben's the dog since he probably doesn't even know what Shaggy means!'

'He stands more chance than you do of ever getting one!' Jed retorts quickly.

They glare at each other.

'How were we supposed to know it was only a drinks party?' I say, trying to change the subject.

'Yeah, I didn't think you Muslims were even allowed to drink,' says Jed. 'Wasn't there that bloke in the newspapers who reckoned he was going to drop dead cos he ate a crisp with, like, one milli-molecule of alcohol in it? Grandad reckons your lot will probably go bombing the crisp factory in revenge.'

'It was a non-alcoholic drinks party,' says Priti. 'And there weren't any crisps either.'

'Yeah, well, my dad reckons you can't be too careful with these terrorists. Even if they were only having Sunny D and pork scratchings.'

'Muslims don't eat pork either!' Priti says.

'Whatever,' says Jed. 'Better to be safe than sorry. I mean, look at him!' We all glance in the direction of Shakeel's window, through which we can see him tapping away at the computer keyboard. 'He could be emailing Al Qaeda as we speak.'

'Do you reckon Bin Laden has an email account?'

I say, imagining a cartoon Osama with his laptop in a cave in the desert.

'He's probably got a picture of your dad jumping out of the tower as his screen saver,' says Jed, grinning.

I look at him. He looks at me.

'All right! Don't go all psycho and start hitting me again,' he says warily.

'I won't.'

'Because I won't go so easy on you next time.'

'Don't then,' I say.

'So what do you remember about Ben's dad?' Priti asks. I know she's thinking about the memory box.

'What like?' asks Jed.

'Like, do you have any particular memories of him?'

'Not really,' says Jed, who is now staring through the binoculars in the direction of the bushes – probably trying to get a glimpse of what Zara's up to.

'You must remember something!' says Priti.

'All right.' He puts down the binoculars. 'I remember this one time we were playing football:

me, Dad, Uncle Andrew and my mum.' He stops for a moment after he mentions his mum. 'Anyway, me and Dad were on one team against Uncle Andrew and Mum: she was rubbish and he couldn't run properly because he had you on his shoulders.'

'Me?'

'Yeah,' says Jed.

'Why don't I remember it then?'

'I dunno. You were only like two or something.'

'Well, you can't have been much older,' I say.

'Don't blame me if you've got a rubbish memory.'

'So what happened?' asks Priti impatiently.

'Ben was on Uncle Andrew's shoulders so he had to hold on to your feet while he ran and you were bouncing up and down and giggling. It was dead funny. Our team kept scoring and my dad kept going on about how good we were and how crap Mum was, and then your dad scored these two amazing goals and then it was time for tea, so it was a draw, and my dad was dead annoyed.'

'That's it?' says Priti, who's been taking notes in a little pad like secretaries or reporters have.

'Yeah. Pretty much. I just remember him saying to my mum, "We can't let them beat us every time, can we, Karen?"'

There's a pause and then Priti says, 'So your mum used to live with you.'

'Yup.' Jed picks up the binoculars.

'When did she stop living with you then?'

'Last year. When she walked out.'

'Just like that? Up and went?'

'She said she was going to come back for me as soon as she was on her feet.' Jed is staring hard at the bushes.

'And did she?'

'Yeah, but my dad said she couldn't just pick and choose when she wants to be a mum.'

'I thought kids always got to stay with their mums when their folks split up,' says Priti.

'Well, I said I didn't want to, didn't I?' says Jed, putting down the binoculars and flicking the hair out of his face.

'Why not?'

'Can't trust her, can I?' he says, not looking at

either of us. 'Like my dad said, she walked out on me once; who's to say she won't do it again? Why do you care anyway?'

'I don't,' says Priti. 'So do you see her?'

'Not if I can help it.' Jed is staring down at the tree trunk, flicking off bits of bark with his finger and thumb.

'Doesn't she want to see you?'

'Course she does.'

'How do you know?'

'She stalks me. Hangs out at the school gates at home time. Comes to parents' evenings where she's not welcome. That sort of thing.'

I didn't know this. 'What do you do?' I ask.

He looks right at me. 'What do you think I do?'

I shrug.

'I ignore her of course.'

'Seriously?' says Priti. 'What does she do then?'

'She calls out and stuff,' he shrugs. 'It's dead embarrassing.'

'Is she allowed to do that?' Priti asks.

'No.' Jed looks away and kicks at the tree trunk so

hard a big chunk of bark comes flying off. 'This one time she was hanging outside the school gates and the headmaster came out and asked her to go away and she started screaming and they had to get the police. She's loopy tunes. A nutcase. Whenever I see her, she's crying. It's pathetic!'

He keeps kicking the tree over and over again and we all fall silent.

Then Priti says, 'I reckon my mum would turn into a screaming banshee if she wasn't allowed to see me. She says I drive her mad, but I reckon she'd be worse if she didn't have me.'

'Yeah, well, all women have a bit of a screw loose,' says Jed.

I doodle Priti with a loose screw twisting its way out of one of her bunches.

'Oh, charming!' says Priti.

'You're halfway there already,' says Jed. 'Just wait till you get older. All women lose their marbles. Look at Ben's mum.'

I look up quickly. 'What about my mum?'

Jed looks right at me. I stare back.

'Has she even bothered to call you since they put her away?' he asks.

'She's in hospital.' I can feel my face getting tight and hot. I can't believe he's going on about this again.

'Whatever,' says Jed.

I don't know whether I want to punch him or burst into tears.

'She's been sending him those cards though,' says Priti.

'How do you know about the cards?' I say, turning away from Jed, shaking my head and blinking to stop myself from crying.

'Jed told me.'

Jed just shrugs.

I blink some more. 'Anyway, she doesn't send the cards,' I say. 'Gary does. It's his handwriting.'

'So she gets Gary to write them for her,' says Priti. 'It doesn't take a detective to work that out. Why would he send you cards saying he loves you like flying pigs? It doesn't make sense.'

I glare at Jed again because he must have been reading the cards.

'They've probably got your mum in a straightjacket in that loony hospital,' says Jed. 'So she can't write them herself.'

I look at them both and I can feel the tears coming. 'You don't know anything about my mum,' I say. 'Either of you.'

'Just don't say I didn't warn you when she buggers off forever like my mum,' says Jed. 'Then you'll have to live with the wrinklies till they die.'

'That'd be cool,' says Priti. Then, seeing the expression on my face, she adds quickly, 'But I'm sure it won't happen.'

I say I'm going back inside to get a drink of water. I hear Priti tell Jed to leave off teasing me.

'It's not my fault he's a crybaby,' Jed replies.

I let myself into the kitchen. Shakeel is there, chopping onions.

'I'm just getting a drink,' I say, turning away so he can't see I've been crying.

'Please, please. Help yourself,' he says. 'Do you want tea? Juice?'

'Just water is fine,' I say. I have my back to him as

178

I fill a cup with water. Looking across the garden, I can see Jed trying to push Priti off the tree house. Priti looks like she's holding her own.

'I was sorry to hear about your father,' Shakeel says.

I hesitate. 'Thanks,' I say, because that's what my mum always says.

'I think I understand now why your grandfather is a little hostile to our family,' Shakeel goes on.

I don't reply. I keep staring at the tree house. Priti is hanging on by her nails, but looks like she's going to bring Jed down with her.

'Please. Don't misunderstand me,' Shakeel goes on. 'He has not been rude, but he is perhaps – and understandably so – ill at ease with us.'

I see Jed looking in the direction of the house, so I turn round.

Shakeel looks at me. He must notice my red eyes because he says, 'I'm sorry, the onions are making you cry?'

'Yes,' I say. I'm pretty sure he knows it's not the onions, but I'm grateful to him for saying it.

Then he asks me something that no one has asked

me before. 'Do you also feel angry towards Muslims because of what happened to your father?'

The thing about having a parent who died in 9/11 is that adults never actually ask you about it. It's the kids who ask all the questions. Adults go out of their way NOT to mention it. Or they mention it and then go silent, like it's a swear word or something. Or sometimes they get really angry and use long words.

'Abomination,' one lady said. 'It's an abomination.' Or they talk about 'terrorism' and 'Islamic fundamentalism'. But they *never* ask me what I think about any of it.

Not that I know what I'd say anyway. Which is why, when Shakeel asks, I just shrug and say, 'I'm not sure.'

Shakeel pauses for a moment. He has finished chopping the onions and he pushes them into a bowl. 'You understand that the men who flew their planes into the towers did so because they believed they were at war. That America and the West are waging a war against Islam?'

'And are they?' I ask. Because I don't want to go

outside. Not just yet. And because I never get to talk about any of this. Not properly.

'That's a good question,' Shakeel says, taking a sweet potato and starting to peel it. 'I suspect the answer depends on who you ask. I don't think that your grandfather and Osama Bin Laden would see eye to eye for example!' he laughs.

'Does it make any difference anyway?' I ask.

'Whether we see 9/11 as an act of war or an act of terrorism? I think so, don't you?'

I shrug again.

'Collateral damage is considered an unavoidable – even a necessary – element of modern war,' says Shakeel, talking like a teacher now. Priti tells me he is always doing this to her. 'Did you know that US drone strikes in Afghanistan kill an average of fifty innocent citizens to every legitimate militant target?'

He turns to me as he asks this. I shake my head.

'No. Very few people do,' says Shakeel. I watch his sharp knife moving swiftly over the sweet potato, revealing the bright orange flesh beneath the muddy brown exterior. 'Why? Because the US is at war in

Afghanistan. These civilian deaths are therefore simply considered unfortunate casualties in a time of war – but whether in reality that label makes the death of civilians any less terrorising is open to debate.'

'I suppose so,' I say.

'So the labels matter, you see.'

Neither of us speaks for a few moments. I watch Shakeel chop the bright orange flesh into cubes, his knife moving rhythmically over the chopping board. Outside, I hear Priti shrieking, Jed shouting something I can't make out.

'So if it *is* a war,' I say, 'then who started it?'

'That is another good question.' Shakeel laughs, looking up from what he's doing. 'I suppose some might say the war started thousands of years ago, when Christians first embarked on the crusades. Others say it started on 9/11.'

'But if the war didn't start till after the planes hit the buildings then it can't have been an act of war, can it?' I say. 'That means it was terrorism.'

'Which is why definitions are so divisive,' he says.

Just then there is a crash from outside, followed by

a lot of shouting. Shakeel looks up. 'I think that an act of terror has just been committed on my sister. Now I suspect there will be out-and-out war.'

He grins. And so do I.

JULY 25TH

Jed has to go to court today because his mum wants to see him and his dad won't let her – or Jed won't let her – I'm not sure which any more. Anyway, Uncle Ian arrives dressed in a suit to take Jed to the hearing. Jed is being really manic and he manages to break Grandad's TV remote control by playing keepy-uppies with it in the kitchen and smashing it into the sink.

Grandad can't get mad with him while Uncle Ian is around, but after they've gone, he's in a foul mood. He refuses to take his de-stress tablets or even eat the biscuits Granny offers him. (She normally won't let him eat snacks between meals as he's supposed to be on a low-cholesterol diet.)

And then Gary turns up at just the wrong time. Apparently, he called and left a message with Grandad to say he was coming, but Grandad didn't pass it on. This means that Granny is all flustered because she hasn't cleaned the kitchen floor and she hasn't got anything in to offer him. (She usually makes cakes and scones and stuff for guests, but today she's only got garibaldi biscuits.)

Gary thinks this is really funny. 'After all I am follicly challenged!' he says, patting the top of his head where the hair is thinning. 'Gary-baldy! I like it!' He laughs. Grandad and I laugh too, but Granny looks mortified.

Gary is sitting on the sofa in the sitting room, with a framed wedding photo of mum and dad on the mantelpiece next to him.

It's good to see him.

'How you doing, mate?' he says when he sees me.

'Good,' I say. I want to give him a hug, but I don't.

'Your mum thought you might be missing some of your things,' he says, indicating a big black hold-all on the floor. 'She gave me a list of things to pick up for you.'

'Thanks,' I say.

I open the bag and inside I can see some more of my manga books and my football boots. There are also lots more clothes, some drawing pencils and a new notebook.

'How is Hannah?' asks Granny.

'She's OK,' says Gary, glancing at me.

'Just OK?' says Grandad.

I pull out the new notebook and get a pencil from my pocket. I start to doodle leaves which quickly turn into slippery fish. I don't look up.

'She's doing her best, but it's hard for her,' says Gary.

'I thought this place she's gone to was the best?' says Grandad.

'It takes time,' says Granny. 'Remember last time.'

The slippery fish turn into birds with sharp, pecking beaks.

'I remember it only too well,' Grandad snaps. 'I just can't believe we're here all over again.'

'I think that it's harder second time round,' says Gary. 'That's what the doctors say. But I'm sure she'll beat it.'

'With all due respect, Gareth –' I'm sure Grandad mispronounces his name on purpose – 'you weren't here the first time. We were the ones who'd just lost our son and then had to pick up the pieces when she couldn't cope.'

'I imagine that was very hard for you,' says Gary. I look up again. He seems uncomfortable, but he's obviously trying his best to be polite. I want to tell him that Grandad can be like this to everyone.

'It wasn't as if she was the only person who lost someone she loved,' says Grandad.

The birds turn into aeroplanes with feathers on their wings.

'I don't think it's something she's done deliberately,' says Gary.

'I mean, aren't there just some drugs they can give her?' asks Grandad.

'I don't think it's quite like that, Barry,' says Granny softly. 'More tea, Gary?' she asks. I realise that their names rhyme and I doodle 'Gary' and 'Barry' in different fonts in the corner of the page, next to the aeroplanes.

Then I realise Gary is looking at me.

'Glad to see you're still drawing.'

I look up and half smile.

'Done any good comic strips?'

'Not really,' I say. 'Just doodles.'

'You should keep going with those strips. You're really good,' he says. I feel myself blushing. 'Blythe misses the cartoons you do of her.'

'How is she?' I ask.

'Having a great time with her mum,' he says.

'Do you miss her?'

'Like mad.' He smiles at me and I smile back. But then I become conscious of my grandparents watching. Do I have to choose – my dad or Gary?

It's only when it's time to go and Gary goes to get his coat that I ask him what I really want to know. 'Will she call, Gary?'

'She wants to,' he replies. 'But she doesn't seem to be able to.'

'Aren't there any phones there?' I say, knowing this isn't really what he means.

'You know how she is, Ben,' says Gary, putting a hand on my shoulder in a way that feels nice, but also makes me want to cry. 'She doesn't want to upset you, and she doesn't think she can speak to you without losing it. And she's never good with phones at the best of times. It's all part of her being ill. But she misses you like mad. You're the reason she wants to get better. Nothing else – not me, not anyone – just you.'

'Then why doesn't she?' I say, trying not to sound like Grandad.

'She's doing her best. We have to hang on in there for her. Here, she asked me to give you this,' he says, handing me another card.

'Thanks,' I say, but I can't even look at it. It makes me think of her in a straightjacket, struggling to hold a pen in her mouth.

I want to ask more questions, but then Granny comes back and he lets go of my shoulder and I have to turn away so that no one can see that I'm starting to cry. I don't wave him off either – I just go up to my room.

I don't look at the card for ages. When I do, I see it has a picture of the village where we live on it. It must have been taken, like, twenty years ago because the people standing on the bridge are wearing really old-fashioned clothes, but otherwise it looks just the same. On the back of the card, still in Gary's handwriting, it says, *Home is where the heart is, so I'm always with you in my heart.*

Perhaps Priti is right about the cards after all.

After Gary leaves, I start to draw a few frames of a new comic strip. It has me and Priti and Jed as undercover agents, hunting down terrorists and suicide bombers. Jed is the maverick (one of Priti's spelling bee words), Priti is the mouthy one and I'm the brains behind the operation. Shakeel is the baddie – of course – and Zara is the girl who gets rescued. I've not decided yet if Ameenah is on our side or not.

Drawing helps to take my mind off the depressing sight of what looked like the entire contents of my wardrobe in the hold-all. One frame shows me karate-kicking down a door. Caption: *Kerpow!*

It doesn't look much like me, but for some reason it makes me feel better.

I haven't decided what to call the strip yet, but I guess I'll think of something.

JULY 30TH

This morning, Jed goes off with Granny to another one of their appointments, and Priti comes over with a shoebox she's nicked from her mum's cupboard and loads of other bits and pieces, like scissors and glue and paper and coloured pens and these plastic jewels that you can stick on things.

'We're going to make the memory box,' she says and I know it's no use trying to talk her out of it.

First we have to wrap the box in hideous wrapping paper. It's pink and gold and covered in bunnies, and I'm sure my dad would have hated it, but when I say this to Priti, she says that we don't have time for me to doodle people with big eyes all over it, so we go with the bunny paper. Then Priti insists we stick the plastic jewels on it which makes it look even worse. I think how, if my dad was around, me and him would have had a laugh about it and that makes me smile.

Then Priti hands me a piece of paper and a pen

and gets one for herself. 'Now we have to write down our memories.'

'But you didn't even know him!' I say.

'You keep saying that, but I've been looking at his picture to work out what sort of person he was. You always can – it's in the eyebrows.'

'So what do my dad's eyebrows say?' I ask. I imagine a bushy pair of talking eyebrows.

'They say he was a nice bloke, but one of those people who tends to be in the wrong place at the wrong time.'

'You can't tell that from his eyebrows!' I scoff.

'Yes, you can.'

'How do you know he was always in the wrong place at the wrong time?'

'I didn't say *always*, did I? You've got to admit that September 11th 2001 definitely wasn't the day to be at the World Trade Center, was it?'

I can't really disagree with that, so I don't try.

'What's your memory then?' she asks.

'I'm not sure yet,' I say.

'Well, you'd better get thinking!'

She insists we both sit in silence and write something. So I do.

Memories of my dad by Ben Andrew Barry Evans

I'm not sure if I can remember my dad or whether I just think I do. Maybe the things I think I remember I just saw in a picture or got told by someone else. I think I remember sitting on his shoulders walking under some trees and the leaves were brushing my face. Another time I was standing on a window sill watching the rubbish truck collect the bins and he was holding me so I didn't fall. I don't think anyone else can have told me about those things. Maybe I saw some other little kid do them with his dad and now I think it must have been me. Or maybe I saw it on the TV?

Under this bit I draw a picture of a TV screen with a little boy and his dad on it.

I wish I remembered more stuff. Why is it that you don't remember things from when you are a little kid? Has anyone ever written a book on that? Is it just too long ago? Even Mum says she forgets things about Dad and that it's OK that I do too, but is it OK to have forgotten everything?

I think I remember him washing my hair one time and me screaming because he got soap in my eyes. I guess that's a memory, isn't it? Hope this stuff all counts — it's a bit pathetic, but it's the best I can do. Sorry, Dad. Love, Ben x

And under that, I draw a little picture of up and down escalators, with him going down one escalator while I go up the other, so we just miss each other.

'Did you realise your initials spell BABE?!' is the first thing Priti says when she's read it.

'My mum thought it'd be sweet.' I feel myself redden.

'Why do parents lumber us with these social handicaps?' Priti muses, sounding more like her mum than ever. 'And as for Barry!'

'It's my grandad's name,' I say.

'That's OK I suppose. Your grandad is cool!'

I wonder what Grandad would think about this.

Then Priti reads out what she wrote:

Memory of Ben's dad by Priti Muhammed.
I never actually met Ben's dad, but I think you should always give dead people the benefit of the doubt, so I reckon he was probably a very nice man (although he did support Villa which counts against him).
Ben's nice and so are his granny and grandad. His grandad can be a bit grumpy, but he's suffed a tragic loss, so that's only to be expected. If he (Ben's dad) was like them, he should be OK.

Anyway, like I said, you should always give dead people the benefit of the doubt. That's if he is dead of course. Because he might just be on a witness protection programme, or abducted by aliens, or so hideously disfigured he has to live like a hermit so that no one ever sees his accursed face   (I got accursed from Shakespeare) Has anyone considered these possibilities?

If he is dead then he must have been nice because only the good die young (I read that somewhere once).

Which means I should live till I'm ninety, and Zara will be around until she's two hundred and wrinkly – which she will hate.

So that's my memory, even though it's not really a memory – Hope you don't mind me making it up, Ben's dad. I'm doing it to help your bereaved son, so I guess you'll forgive it being a bit waggly. He's cool, your son – even though he's miserable and bereaved and that– so you probably were too.

The End

After we read out our memories, we put them in the box. Then Priti puts in Jed's memory that she wrote down the other day and I write down what Granny said about my dad helping her to put the shopping away and liking cricket and we put that in too.

'What do we do now?' I ask.

'We could ask your grandad,' says Priti.

'I don't think he likes stuff like this. Granny says he doesn't like talking about Dad.'

'Don't worry about that,' says Priti. 'I can get anyone talking.'

So we go downstairs. Grandad is watching some programme about people selling antiques from their attic and doesn't seem too pleased about being interrupted.

'What do you two want?' he asks, not glancing up from the TV. The remote control is still broken and he complains all the time about having to get up to change the channel.

'Ben's making a memory box about his dad,' says Priti.

'Your granny will be better at helping you with that sort of thing than me,' says Grandad.

'We just need to ask you a few questions,' says Priti. I think she's trying to sound like one of those polite people off the telly, or like a police officer. (That's what they always say, isn't it? 'We just need you to come down to the station to answer a few questions.') And she gets her reporter's notebook out again, all official, and she even licks the end of her pencil.

'What was the naughtiest thing Ben's dad ever did?' she asks even though Grandad hasn't agreed to help yet.

'What is this memory box anyway?' asks Grandad, looking at Priti and me. 'What's it for?'

'We'll show you it when it's done,' says Priti. 'Now what was the naughtiest thing?'

Grandad looks at her standing there with her pencil poised. Then he leans forward and turns the TV to mute. He sighs then says, 'There was this one time I bought a new stereo. Andrew was about three at the time and for some reason he got a big bag of flour and poured it all over the stereo.'

Priti giggles and Grandad smiles.

'Did it work after that?' I ask.

'Yes, but it was a bit crackly and I was finding white powder in the speakers for ages afterwards. I only threw it out a couple of years ago and I swear there was still flour in there.' He laughs and grins at me and I wonder if he got as grumpy with my dad about the stereo as he did with Jed about the remote control.

'That's great!' says Priti, who is noting things down in her best handwriting. I don't have anything to hold, so I just stand there. 'What was the stupidest thing he ever did?'

'Don't we want to find out nice stuff?' I ask.

Priti looks at me as if to say, *You just don't get it, do you?* Which maybe I don't because I still don't really know why we're doing this. So I shut up and look at Grandad for his answer.

'He sawed a leg off his brother's bed once,' says Grandad. 'And one time he did a poo in the bath because Ian bet him he wouldn't.'

Priti giggles again and I find myself smiling.

'Jed's in that bed now,' says Grandad. 'You can still see where I had to nail the leg back together again!' Grandad laughs and he doesn't seem mad about it at all – I guess he didn't mind kids breaking things so much in the old days. 'Oh, and he stuck a pea up his nose once,' he goes on. 'Your gran will tell you it was my fault because I'd been sticking candy cigarettes up my nostrils and pretending to be a warthog. Only they don't call them candy cigarettes any more, do they?' he says, breaking off – probably because me and Priti were looking confused. 'Nowadays they call them candy sticks or something politically correct like that, just in case kids get muddled up and start eating Malborough Lights, or some other daft nanny state nonsense!' He raises his eyebrows and hmmphs quietly. 'Anyway, I'm sticking these white candy sticks up my nostrils and next minute your dad's crying his eyes out with this massive bulge on the bridge of his nose and it turns out he's stuck a pea up there.' He glances at the picture of Dad in pride of place on the mantelpiece and smiles. 'I had to take him to casualty. Crying all the way, he was. I felt awful.'

'What did they do?' asks Priti.

'They made me blow it out.'

'How did you do that then?'

'A magic kiss, I think they called it. You put your finger over one nostril then blow in the mouth. Pea came flying out and hit me on the nose.'

'Cool!' says Priti.

Grandad glances at me. 'Your dad thought so too. Kept asking me to do magic kisses all the time after that! He looked the spitting image of you back then.' He looks a bit sad and glances back at the framed picture of my dad. Then he leans forward and flicks the sound back on the TV.

'Have you got anything of his that we can put in the box?' Priti asks.

'Your granny has all of that stuff,' he says, but it's like he's not really listening any more.

'But you must have something you can give us.'

The old couple on the TV are now at the auction watching people bid for their possessions, hoping to make a fortune from a snub-nosed pottery bunny and a few toby jugs. 'I think there's still a jar of olives in the cupboard,' Grandad says, a bit distracted. 'Your gran and I won't eat them. Only Andrew liked them. You can have those.'

'Thanks, Ben's grandad,' says Priti.

It doesn't seem very likely to me that Granny would have kept an ancient jar of olives in the cupboard. She's always saying how she doesn't like clutter. But it turns out that Grandad is right. There they are – in the back of the cupboard with a Best Before End Feb 2003 stamp on them.

'Best not eat them, I suppose,' says Priti. 'They've probably grown legs.'

We put the olives in the box and write down the things Grandad said and I put in the binoculars because I remember they used to be Dad's. Then Granny and Jed come back, so we have to hide the box under my bed.

Later on, after Priti has left and when Jed is asleep, I also write out my list of things I want to know about my dad and put it in, along with some of the other stuff I found out about 9/11. Then I put the box carefully back under my bed where no one can find it. I don't want Jed catching sight of the bunny paper and those jewels.

JULY 31ST

'I know what it is with you,' Priti says to Jed.

'What is it with me then?' asks Jed. We've been keeping lookout for Zara in the park all morning, hanging out inside one of the great big concrete pipes that gives us a view of the woods from one end and the alleyway by Priti's house from the other. We're all lying on our backs and me and Jed have our feet on the top of the pipe so the blood is rushing straight to our heads.

Priti is wheeling her shoes up and down the pipe like a hamster on a wheel. 'I looked it up on the Internet,' she says to Jed. 'You've got PAS.'

'What's that?' says Jed.

'Parental Alienation Syndrome,' says Priti authoritatively. 'It's when a kid says he doesn't want to see one of his parents even though actually he does.' (Priti is clearly determined to cure me and Jed of all our 'emotional baggage', as she calls it, before the summer is out.)

'Yeah, but I actually *don't* want to see my mum,' says Jed. 'So I can't have PMT or whatever it's called.'

'No, you don't *think* you do because you've been programmed not to,' says Priti, sounding all school teacherish. (I wonder if she gets this from Shakeel – or maybe her mum.)

'Right. Who by exactly?' says Jed, dead sarcastic.

'Your dad.'

'Actually, my dad's always saying I should see my mum,' says Jed.

'He would do. That's what they do, innit?' says Priti, sounding more like a gangsta now she's getting excited.

'Why would he say that if he's *programming* me?' says Jed. 'He respects my feelings. He says I'm dead brave for telling the truth about how I feel about my mum.'

'If it is the truth.'

'I should know what's the truth and what's not about my own mum, shouldn't I?' says Jed, sitting upright now (which is quite hard to do in a pipe).

'Not according to the stuff on the Internet,' says

205

Priti. 'It starts off with you saying whatever you know will make your dad happy because, no matter what he says, you know he'll actually be dead angry if you say you want to see your mum.'

Jed glares at her and I wish I wasn't sandwiched between the two of them because if Jed takes a swing at Priti, I'm the one who's going to get it.

'You say you don't want to see her and he tells you he's proud of you for "telling the truth",' says Priti. 'You know that's the way to keep him happy. Then you say it so often you forget you're saying it to make him happy and you start to think it really is the truth. Brainwashing complete!' She grins.

'Where are you getting all this crap from?' says Jed, slumping backwards and looking away.

'One of them Parents for Justice websites,' says Priti. 'According to them, PAS is a very effective device for getting custody because the courts nowadays take more account of the child's wishes.' (She's definitely memorised this.) 'I feel dead sorry for your mum,' she says, and as she does so, she wheels her shoes right up to the top of the pipe so she's practically vertical with her feet on the roof and all the blood running to her head, making her face go bright red.

'You don't even know my mum,' says Jed.

'Neither do you,' says Priti and this makes Jed go bright red too – as if he's going to explode.

'If Jed has got PAS, what can his mum do then?' I ask.

'Oh, she's stuffed!' says Priti, coming down quickly so that she's sitting up again, her cheeks flushed. For some reason she's wearing a fluffy sheepskin thing over a velvet, sequinned party dress, topped off with a funny knitted hat with bobbled bits that hang over her ears, even though it's boiling hot outside. 'The UK courts don't recognise PAS, or if they do, they don't do much about it. But they should because it's child abuse you know. Your dad is abusing you.'

'Don't talk about my dad like that!' Jed sits up again and has turned to face Priti. I'm stuck between the two of them as they glare at each other.

'I'm only trying to help you,' says Priti, who doesn't look even a tiny bit frightened of Jed. 'You feel like you've lost one parent and you're frightened of losing the other, so you say anything he wants you to say to make sure that doesn't happen. But he's manipulating you, exploiting you.' (I can't believe how well she's remembered all this.)

'He is not!' says Jed.

'Just because he hates your mum doesn't mean you have to,' says Priti, the bobbles on her hat wobbling as she lectures him. 'Or you should at least be allowed to see her and hate her like normal kids do.'

'I don't want to see her!' says Jed, standing up so suddenly he hits his head on the pipe. For a moment, I think he's going to cry, but he doesn't. 'Don't you get it? I don't want to see her, ever! So stop going on about it, will you?'

And then he storms off.

'That boy has serious anger-management issues,' says Priti.

Just then Zara sticks her head into the pipe.

'Yuk. Have you two rug rats been snogging?' she says.

I go bright red and Priti does a gagging thing. 'If I'm going to be honour-killed, I'd want a better reason for dying than that squirt.'

But Zara doesn't even bother to listen. She's already heading off back to the house so we crawl out of the pipe and follow her. Jed is nowhere to be seen, and neither of us has any ideas about what to do, so we perch on Priti's garden wall. I take out my sketchbook and start doodling a picture of me and Priti and Jed commando-crawling through massive underground pipes, like in *The Great Escape*.

'Here, let me have a look,' says Priti.

She grabs the sketchbook out of my hand. 'It's us!' she says. 'This is well cool.'

'Thanks.'

'What are we supposed to be doing?'

'Catching terrorists and honour killers, that sort of thing,' I say, feeling embarrassed suddenly. I've been working on the comic strip loads since Gary came.

'Cool! So we're like a crack team of elite commandos?'

'Yeah,' I say. 'Sort of.'

'What are we called?'

'I thought maybe the Brummie Bomb Squad?' I say, staring at my feet.

'Lame,' says Priti. 'What about the Bomb-busters?'

'I guess so,' I nod.

'Take my word for it – it's way better. And you should change our names too, make us sound more like superheroes,' she says excitedly. 'Like, Jed could be Jed-eye and you can be – Ben-D! Cool, huh?!'

'What about you?' I ask.

She thinks for a moment. 'I'm tempted by Priti "left eye" Muhammed, but I'm going to go for Lil' Priti – makes me sound hot and funky at the same time. Which of course I am.'

'Yeah, right,' I say.

'So now all we need to do is come up with some cool storylines.'

AUGUST 1ST

Grandad reckons there's enough horrific stuff in the newspapers every day to keep Hollywood in business for a decade. The really bad stories are his favourites: the ones that make out like the country is full of murderers and rapists and on the verge of civil war and anarchy. I sometimes think the worse the news is the happier he is. He says things like, 'This country is going to the dogs!' and, 'I never thought I'd live to see the day,' or, 'It was never like this in my youth!', but all the time he's looking really chuffed about it.

This morning, he's sitting at the breakfast table, tutting over the local paper and looking even more excited than he did when Granny presented him with a new remote control after Jed's last trip to the hospital. By the look on his face I know something *really* bad must have happened.

'Have you read about this young Asian lad that's been stabbed, Rita?' he says.

Granny looks up from buttering her toast. 'It's

the parents I feel sorry for,' she says. 'I wonder if the Muhammed family know them.'

'Bound to. They all know each other, don't they, that lot.' Grandad jabs at the newspaper with his toast. 'You see, this is what annoys me. They're calling it a racist attack just because the boy was Asian.'

'He's fighting for his life, Barry,' says Granny.

'I don't doubt it, but if it was a white boy lying there in hospital, it'd never get this kind of coverage and they sure as heck wouldn't be saying it was racially motivated.'

'Do they know who did it?' asks Granny.

'Newspaper boy reckons they have a couple of lads in for questioning. One of them's called Tyreese – what kind of a name is that? Parents were just looking for trouble calling him Tyreese, if you ask me!'

Jed looks at me and I look at him.

'And do we know if this Tyreese is white?' asks Granny.

'Not yet, but that's not an Asian name.'

'So it *could* be a racist attack,' says Granny, which sounds reasonable enough to me, but Grandad just lets out a big snort and tells Granny she's signed up for the PC Mafia.

When Grandad goes to the kitchen, Jed whispers, 'Do you reckon it's Zara's Tyreese?'

I shrug. 'Dunno, but don't tell Grandad.'

'He'd love that, wouldn't he? Probably give himself a heart attack he'd be so excited.'

But we both want to know, so we bolt down our toast and head over to Priti's straight after breakfast. Granny says it's a bit early, but we tell her we have a special project we're doing with Priti and she lets us go without even brushing our teeth.

Priti answers the door before we even knock and puts a finger to her lips as she beckons us in.

The sound of raised voices is coming from the kitchen. It's Mik and Shakeel. There's no sign of Zara.

'Zara's been in her bedroom crying since yesterday afternoon,' whispers Priti as if she knew what I was thinking.

'Why?' I ask.

'Because her boyfriend has been banged up!'

'So it *is* her Tyreese!' I say.

'Yeah, course it is. Who else do you know with a stupid name like that? I told her he was trouble.'

'What's going to happen to him?' asks Jed.

'They've let him out apparently,' she whispers.

'How do you know?'

'Mik and Shakeel are having a big bust-up about it for a start. It's all going off. You want to hear?'

We both nod, so she ushers us into the dining room which is next to the kitchen and the three of us bundle under the table. Through the half-open door, we can hear what's going on, but can't see much because of the table cloth which hangs down nearly to the floor. Through the tasselled fringe at the edge I can just make out their shoes. 'You can tell a lot from the shoes people wear,' whispers Priti. 'I reckon all shoes have a personality.'

Jed pulls a funny face. 'Told you she was halfway to the nuthouse already!'

'Shut up, you two and listen!' says Priti.

'They put Said in hospital, brother!' It's Mik talking. He's the one wearing funky designer trainers that remind me of Priti's wheelies, only without the wheels.

'You think we should just stand by and do nothing?'

'There's no point in retaliating,' Shakeel replies. 'What can it achieve?' He's wearing brown lace-ups that look like they're from a sensible shop – the sort of place where teachers might go. (Perhaps Priti has a point about footwear.)

'And you don't think it's at all sus that the police let this Tyreese go and two hours later, his little brother walks into the police station, face all mashed up, saying he'd been jumped on by a gang of Asian youths just moments before Said was knifed?'

'Maybe that's what actually happened,' says Shakeel.

'Then why didn't this kid go to the police station yesterday while they had his brother in custody?'

'Maybe he was scared.'

'Like hell. I'll tell you why – because Tyreese went straight home after the police let him go and beat up the poor kid himself! His own brother, just so he could make it look like he stabbed Said in retaliation or whatever.'

'He's trying to turn it into a race issue,' says Shakeel.

'It *is* a race issue, brother. I thought you were supposed to be the clever one!'

'This Tyreese and his gang want it to look like the Asian kids started it,' Shakeel replies. 'You want everyone to think he's right by retaliating?'

'It's a matter of honour.' The white trainers are over by the patio door, the brown shoes by the work surface.

'We don't need any more trouble in this community.'

I imagine a round, black bomb. *Tick, tick, ticking.*

'Said is our cousin, man!' Their feet are right up close now, so that I can imagine they're almost shouting in each other's faces. 'We have to fight to protect our friends, our families, our community. Our right to be here.'

'Yes, but it is not a battle to be fought with fists or knives,' says Shakeel.

'How do you propose to fight it then?'

'It's a battle for acceptance, for hearts and minds.'

'Don't give me that. You dress it up with your fancy words – but in the end you're just a coward.'

'There are different ways of laying down your life for a cause,' says Shakeel. 'Sometimes it means doing nothing even if it hurts your pride to do so. But you prefer Tyreese's way of doing things?'

The flame creeps along the fuse, closer and closer to the round, black bomb.

'You mean, would I beat up my brother to save my own skin?' says Mik. 'Tempting as the offer is, when I take action, I won't be cowering behind you, saying "He started it!"'

'Exactly: personal sacrifice; taking responsibility for your own actions. We make our own bed and we have to lie in it – think about that, little brother.'

The trainers take a step or two backwards then Mik says, 'I can't listen to any more of your bullshit. I'm going out.'

We see Mik's trainers move in our direction and hastily pull in our feet and hold our breath.

'Mik,' calls Shakeel. 'Brother, wait!'

'You're no brother of mine,' says Mik and then we all hold our breath as he storms right past us.

Boom! The bomb goes off.

* * *

We have to wait ages after he's gone before we can get out because Shakeel just stands there in the kitchen for what seems like an hour, his brown shoes not moving.

'What's he doing?' I ask.

Priti shrugs.

'I wish he'd get on with it,' whispers Jed (which can't be easy for someone as loud-mouthed as him). 'I'm dying for a pee!'

Eventually, Shakeel goes upstairs and we all pile out from under the table. My left leg has got pins and needles from staying in the same position for so long. Priti says she can't feel her bottom. Jed offers to give her a kick to wake it up.

'Not likely!' says Priti, thumping him.

'What do you reckon all that was about?' I say quickly.

'You heard what Shakeel said about not using fists and knives,' says Jed. 'He's got something bigger in mind! *Boom!*' He mimes an explosion.

'That's not what hearts and minds means, is it? Blowing their brains out?'

'Guess it must be,' says Priti, rubbing her bum frantically.

'Bet he's gone off to fix up his bomb right now,' says Jed.

'I don't reckon that's what he was saying at all,' I say, unconvinced.

'He can't just admit it right out, can he? Not even to his own brother,' says Jed. 'But you heard what he said about personal sacrifice, laying his life down for the cause, making his own bed and lying in it – making his own bomb and dying in it more like!'

'It's all going to kick off after this,' says Priti, who's still wiggling her bum. 'When Mik gets angry, there's no telling what he'll do.'

'I'm telling you, it's Shakeel we need to keep an eye on,' says Jed. 'If this Said is a friend of theirs, or your cousin or whatever, he's going to want revenge!'

'And when he finds out that Zara is snogging the bloke who knifed Said then there'll be an explosion, I can tell you!' Priti says, patting her pink, velour-covered behind vigorously to try and get rid of the pins and needles.

'She must be bricking it!' says Jed.

'So she should be,' says Priti. 'I'm so going to enjoy saying I told her so.'

WHAT THE INTERNET SAID ABOUT BEING A MUSLIM KID IN BRITAIN AFTER 9/11

Priti and me found this stuff on the *Newsround* site (which is like the *Ten o'clock News* for kids, so it must be right). It's a survey they did a few years ago, but Priti reckons it's still pretty spot on.

1. Six out of ten of all kids interviewed agreed that life for Muslims had got harder since the 2001 terror attacks on New York. ('Can't remember what it was like before,' says Priti.)

2. Four out of every ten Muslim children taking part in the *Newsround* survey thought the news showed Islam in a bad way. ('Too right!' says Priti.)

3. One in three Muslim kids interviewed said they had been bullied, and half of those believed it was because of their religion. (Priti has never been

bullied, but this does not surprise me – who'd take her on?)

4. Seven out of ten Muslim kids identified themselves as Muslim rather than British. ('I'm my own person,' says Priti. 'I object to being put in a box and labelled in this way!')

5. Nine out of ten Muslim children think kids generally need to know more about Islam and almost half of all kids interviewed agreed they wanted to know more about Islam. (I'd like to know more about Islam. Jed doesn't. Priti reckons I need to know more about just about *everything*.)

6. Eighteen per cent of the children interviewed said they associated Muslims with religion, eight per cent said clothes and seven per cent said headscarves. (Jed said curry. Priti said stupid rules. I would have said my dad dying, but neither of them asked.)

AUGUST 2ND

Today is Saturday, but it doesn't really feel like the weekend because it's holidays and there's no school or anything. After breakfast, Uncle Ian turns up out of the blue (like he does) and offers to take me and Jed out in his van.

I don't really want to, but Granny says, 'That'll be nice for you all!' And I can see she's tired and probably needs to have a day off from us.

'Where we going?' says Jed as we get in.

'It's a surprise,' says Uncle Ian.

So we pile into the van, Jed in the middle, next to his dad, and me squashed up by the window. The window is open which means I can't hear most of what they're saying, so after a while, I just stop listening.

I think a bit about my dad and wonder if this is how it would have been if he'd still been alive – me and him going on adventures together, talking about football. But that makes me sad, so instead, I think about the next episode of my Bomb-busters comic strip. (Jed reckons it should be called Bonk-busters and have loads of hot chicks in it.)

We're going slower now, so there's less wind, and that's when I realise they're talking about Shakeel. 'We've been keeping him under surveillance,' says Jed. 'See what he's up to.'

'Good lad!' says Uncle Ian.

This jolts me back to attention. Although we always said we'd pass on the intel to Uncle Ian, I never really expected Jed to do it.

'And you reckon this – whatever his name is – is part of one of these terrorist cells?' says Uncle Ian.

'Yeah, even Priti thinks he's up to something and she's his sister,' says Jed, his feet up on the dashboard.

'You have to watch her though,' says Uncle Ian. 'She could be in on it herself.'

I wait for Jed to say something to defend Priti, but he doesn't.

'I'm just saying, don't trust all she tells you,' says Uncle Ian.

Then Jed tells him about the boy called Said who was stabbed and how he's related to Priti and Shakeel, and his dad says that it could be a trigger for Shakeel to strike, so we need to be vigilant.

'Will you bust him, Dad?' asks Jed.

'All in good time, son,' says Uncle Ian.

I glance at Uncle Ian to try and work out what he's thinking, but he just stares at the road ahead, one hand on the steering wheel, the other hanging on to the van roof through the open window.

'But you said he could strike at any minute,' says Jed. 'Shouldn't you bust him straight away?'

'Just drop it, OK?' says Uncle Ian sharply, slamming his hand on the top of the roof so that it reverberates above our heads. 'And get your mucky feet off my dashboard.' Jed jerks his feet down.

He doesn't talk about it any more after that and we drive in silence for the rest of the journey.

We stop at a pub in the middle of nowhere. It's not like the countryside where I come from – all rolling hills and steep climbs. Here the land is so flat it looks like someone's been over it with an iron. It makes the sky seem huge, like it stretches on forever – a big white tent over our heads.

The pub is what my mum would call 'run down'. One of the windows is boarded up, the pebble-dash is peeling off the brickwork and there's grass growing through the concrete in the car park, which is empty except for a battered, metallic-blue T-reg Golf convertible and a single motorbike leaning up next to the overflowing wheelie bins.

'Go and get lost for a bit, you two,' says Uncle Ian, climbing out of the van.

'Can't we come in with you?' says Jed.

'You can play in the beer garden,' says Uncle Ian, pointing to a square of unmowed grass at the side of the building, with a single pub bench in the middle of it.

'But I thought we were supposed to be spending the day together?' says Jed.

'Yeah? Change of plan. I've got important business to attend to,' says Jed's dad, although he doesn't say what. 'You can have some crisps and Coke, and then I don't want to see or hear either of you for the next two hours. Get it? Now scoot.'

Conversation over, Uncle Ian goes into the pub, leaving Jed and I standing around by the van, not quite sure what we're supposed to be doing. Neither of us says anything. Jed kicks the ground next to the front tyre with his scruffy Vans. He looks as if he'd like to kick the tyre itself, but doesn't dare.

The door to the pub is open. Inside, I can see the bar is shabby and virtually empty. Uncle Ian greets the barman, who barely looks up from his paper to acknowledge him, but inclines his head silently in the direction of a pool table at the back. There are a couple of men standing round the table smoking (even though I thought you weren't supposed to smoke in pubs any more) and not looking like they're playing much pool.

I watch as Uncle Ian makes his way over to the pool men and shakes their hands. Both of the men have closely shaved heads, like Uncle Ian. The younger one is dressed a lot like him too, in a crisp shirt and pressed jeans with a shiny belt and shoes. The older man is a bit scruffier: red-faced and unshaven with a pot belly hanging over tightly belted black jeans and a vest which shows off muscled arms covered in tattoos.

'It's probably all part of an undercover operation they're doing,' says Jed. I turn and see he's looking in the same direction I am. His face is flecked with red and his jaw is tight.

'Who?'

'My dad and his bomb-squad mates in there,' he says, looking down at his feet again. His Vans are covered in dust.

'I thought you said they weren't bomb squad?' I say, glancing at the men again. They're talking and laughing with Uncle Ian.

'Whatever,' says Jed, his face still flushed, almost as if his dad had slapped him when he told him to get lost. 'Bomb squad, counterterrorist unit, it's all the same. Haven't you ever seen any of this stuff on TV?'

'Um, no,' I reply.

'Well, if your mum is still making you go to bed after CBeebies then you won't know anything about how counterterrorism operations work, will you?' he says, kicking the bin lamely, sending dust flying. 'My dad's saving lives. That's why he can't take us out properly today, even though he wants to.'

'I never said he didn't,' I say.

'Yeah, well,' says Jed, reddening again. 'Don't.'

After a few minutes, Uncle Ian re-emerges with Coke and crisps for us both. 'Now scram, the pair of you, OK?'

'Sure, Dad,' says Jed. 'RV here at fourteen hundred hours.'

Uncle Ian laughs. 'That's the spirit, son.'

Then he goes back into the pub, swinging the door shut behind him so we can't see what he and his bomb-squad mates are up to.

Me and Jed spend a bit of time jumping off some old barrels in the beer garden, but Jed soon gets bored and starts looking around for something else to do. That's when he suggests we play Bomb-busters.

The pub backs on to some fields, so we pretend it's a war and crawl through the maize, which is nearly as tall as I am, moving along on our bellies, holding imaginary rifles. The aim is not to disturb a stalk and not to be seen while we pretend to kill terrorists.

'Why did you tell your dad about Shakeel?' I

whisper as we crouch in the long grass, awaiting enemy incursions.

'Had no choice, did I?' says Jed matter-of-factly, looking around all the time as if the enemy might approach any minute. 'Can't sit on that kind of information. It's a matter of national security.'

'Will your dad tell his bomb-squad mates?' I whisper, staring through the maize, imagining cartoon terrorists hidden behind the stalks.

'Bound to,' says Jed.

I turn to him, still staring intently forward as he's fixed on an invisible target. 'And what will they do if they find out he really *is* building a bomb?'

'Kill him,' hisses Jed quickly. Then he raises his imaginary machine gun at an invisible target and lets out a splutter of bullets through his teeth. *T-t-t-t-t-t-t-t-t-t-t-t-t-t-t-t!* 'Got him!' he grins.

We must have been in the field for longer than we realised because when we get back, Uncle Ian is well mad at us.

'Where the hell have you been?' he shouts as we

walk towards him, dusty and covered with bits of straw. 'I've been doing my nut here!'

'We were just messing around,' says Jed.

'I've been trying to ring you on that piggin' phone for about half an hour.'

'I left it in the van,' said Jed, looking down at his feet.

'What the –!' Uncle Ian is standing with the two bomb-squad men in the car park. They're both a lot bigger than him. He has a pint of beer in one hand and his face is red. I wonder if he's drunk. 'Don't know why I even bothered getting you a phone if you're gonna piss around with it.'

'I'm sorry,' says Jed. And all his cool is gone as he stands in front of his dad, head down, red-faced.

'You will be!' Uncle Ian says, slapping Jed round the head. And though he says this to both of us, I know it's Jed he's really mad at.

'You could have been kidnapped by piggin' Muslims for all I knew,' he says.

The bomb-squad man with all the tattoos seems to think this is funny. 'Some bleedin' white kid nabbed by Mussies!' he laughs. His arms are so thickly covered with ink that if it weren't for his face, you wouldn't be able to tell what colour his skin was. 'That'd make a great headline. Really help kick-start the civil war on terror!' He laughs again and I imagine the ink running off his arms and forming black liquid patterns in the air around him.

Then Uncle Ian laughs too. 'Maybe it's a shame they didn't take you, eh!' he says, grabbing Jed and rubbing his knuckles over his hair even harder than usual. 'Could have been your contribution to the war effort!'

Jed tries to grin, but I can see he's got tears in his eyes. He turns his head away so Uncle Ian can't see he's upset.

'Gonna be a soldier like your dad, kid?' asks the younger of Uncle Ian's mates, who's leaning against the battered T-reg Golf. It matches him somehow – flash but slightly dated.

'You'll need to get rid of that nancy-boy haircut if you want to sign up!' says Tattoo Man, laughing again.

I glance at Jed. He tosses his head slightly as if to show he doesn't care.

'Nah, he's too much of a mummy's boy for the army, aren't you, son?' says Uncle Ian.

'No,' says Jed, looking down at his feet. I notice his fists are tightly balled by his sides.

All three men laugh.

'So who's the play date?' says Tattoo Man, nodding at me.

'My brother's lad,' says Uncle Ian.

'The 9/11 kid?' asks T-reg.

Uncle Ian nods.

'That right?' says Tattoo Man, looking at me properly now. I feel myself redden. 'What would you do if Osama Bin Laden walked in this car park right now?'

I shrug, more blood rushing to my face.

'Sure you do. Say I had a gun right here,' says Tattoo Man. 'What would you do?'

'Dunno,' I say.

'Pretend your long-haired sissy cousin is a suicide bomber, explosives strapped to his chest,' says the other man. 'Watcha gonna do now, huh?'

I stare at Jed. I try to imagine for a moment that

he's a terrorist. The terrorists who killed my dad. I imagine pulling the trigger and sending off a round of gunfire – sending the evil terrorist twitching into the air, blood spurting everywhere. But all I can really see is Jed standing there, covered in dust, with bits of straw in his hair.

'So you gonna shoot, 9/11 boy?' says Tattoo Man.

I just stand there, no idea what to say, so hot I feel like I'm going to explode. Or wet myself. The silence stretches out, flat and white like the sky. The men are staring at me with sneering looks on their faces. Jed is looking down at his feet.

Eventually, Uncle Ian breaks the silence. 'You're a gutless wonder. Just like your dad, eh, kid!' Then he cuffs me round the head like he does to Jed. It hurts more than you might think. 'Probably why he jumped,' he says. 'Never could face up to stuff.' Then he laughs and tells me and Jed to get into the van.

In my head I pull the trigger and send the three men twitching and screaming into the air.

* * *

On the way home in the van nobody talks much. It seems like Uncle Ian has had too much to drink because he's driving too fast and he keeps swearing at other drivers.

After we've been going for a while, Jed asks if he can do a wee and Uncle Ian says no, he'll have to wait till we get home.

Then he says, 'Sorry I shouted at you, kid,' although he doesn't sound that sorry.

'That's OK,' says Jed. 'I know you were just worried about me.'

Then Uncle Ian says, 'Your mum's been at it again. It's rattled me.'

'What did she do now?' Jed asks.

'She's making you go to see some new shrink on Thursday.'

'Why?'

'She reckons I'm brainwashing you or something.'

And I think of what Priti said earlier.

'What if I don't want to go?' Jed says – too quickly, I think. Maybe he's remembering what Priti said too.

'Try telling that to your mum!' says Uncle Ian,

which seems a weird thing to say since Jed never gets to talk to his mum. But Jed doesn't reply or say anything more after that and he doesn't even ask about going to the loo again, which is a shame because I really want to go as well, but I'm too scared to ask Uncle Ian.

As we turn into the cul-de-sac at last (the journey seems much longer on the way back) Jed turns to his dad and says, 'Those men in the pub – they were the counterterrorism team, weren't they?'

'Summat like that,' says Uncle Ian.

'And you told them about Shakeel?'

'Don't worry, son. He'll get what's coming to him,' says Uncle Ian before pulling up outside the house and turning to both of us. 'Now no telling your gran what happened today, boys. Just our secret, eh?'

So we have to pretend we've been to the zoo, which Jed thinks is funny, but I don't like it as I'm not a very good liar and I feel bad lying to Granny.

And it's only later, after he's gone, that I realise Uncle Ian hasn't asked Jed one thing about his appointments or how he's feeling.

THINGS I'D LIKE TO KNOW ABOUT UNCLE IAN

1. Why doesn't he want Granny to know about the meeting in the pub?

2. Is he really a member of the bomb squad or the counterterrorism intelligence unit or is that just a load of rubbish Jed's come up with as an excuse for all the times his dad lets him down?

3. Why did he bother taking us on a day out if he was just going to leave us hanging around outside all afternoon?

4. Why doesn't he ever ring ahead to tell Granny he's coming?

5. Why did he leave the army? Or is he really undercover now?

6. Did he tell his bomb-squad buddies about Shakeel? (Assuming he even believed us.)

7. Why doesn't he ever say anything nice about my dad?

8. Why does he hate Jed's mum so much?

9. Why does he always seem like he's lying? (Like Priti says, it's all in the eyebrows.)

10. Why does Jed think he's so great?

AUGUST 4TH

Little Stevie and her family are back from their holiday. I hadn't even noticed they'd been away, to be honest. We don't have much to do with Stevie because Priti refuses to play with her. But now she's out on her bike again – the pink one with tassels on the handlebars – cycling round her driveway in a little sunhat and shorts, looking nearly as brown as Priti. I once saw a programme about little girls in America who dressed up as beauty queens with lots of make-up and big hair and she reminds me of one of those.

Me and Priti are sitting on the wall outside Priti's house and Jed's gone to see the court psychiatrist (or 'nutjob doctor' as he calls her – Granny told him off for swearing). I've been telling Priti all about the trip to the pub and the undercover counterterrorist agents.

'Do you think Jed's dad just fancied a beer?' asks Priti. 'Cos I can't say I'd blame him if he couldn't face the idea of spending any more time with you two.'

'He said he had important business,' I say.

'Yeah, well, you'll believe anything, you,' says Priti. Then she says, 'I wish baby Barbie would stop staring at us!' I glance over at Stevie, who has stopped cycling round and keeps looking over at us all the time, like she really wants to join in.

'We could see if she wants to play,' I say.

'Only little kids play,' says Priti. 'We are hanging out.'

'We could see if she wants to hang out then.'

'I'm not hanging out with someone who still has Disney princesses on her underwear,' says Priti.

'But you've got a *Princess Diaries* poster on your wall,' I point out.

Priti looks at me and raises her eyebrows. 'If you don't understand the vast cultural difference between the Disney anti-feminist-merchandising machine crap and an Anne Hathaway classic, you're not going to make it far in the world of animation,' she says.

'She just looks a bit lonely.'

'Then she needs to find some friends her own size,' says Priti finally. 'Now tell me more what happened at the RV.'

'RV?'

'You really don't watch any TV, do you? It means rendezvous in undercover speak.'

So I tell her all about it. Well, not quite all. I miss out the stuff Jed told his dad about Shakeel and about how gutted Jed looked when his dad told him to get lost. Priti is still unconvinced. 'Why would the bomb squad recruit Jed's dad? That's what I don't buy,' she says.

'Maybe because his brother died in 9/11?' I suggest.

'That's exactly why they wouldn't though!' says Priti. 'I've watched enough US cop shows to know that a team member who makes it too personal can jeopardise the whole operation.'

'Maybe it's different in real life,' I say.

'Never underestimate the wisdom of TV,' says Priti. 'I've learned more from watching teen drama than I did in the whole of Key Stage Three. No kidding.'

Stevie is back on her bike again, riding round and round, her circles getting wider and wider, so that with each circuit she cycles closer to where we're sitting.

'Look at me!' she says as she whizzes past, pigtails

239

flying, tassels rustling in the breeze. I just wave. Priti doesn't even look up.

'So d'you reckon your uncle Ian told his bomb-squad buddies about Shakeel?' she says.

'I'm not sure,' I say. I can feel my cheeks colouring.

'Cos we'll be in loads of trouble if they find we were making it all up.'

'Not as much as Shakeel will be in if it's true,' I say. 'They'll send him to jail.'

'Or worse,' says Priti.

'What do you mean?'

'Haven't you heard about lynchings?'

I shrug.

'Like in cowboy movies, when people take the law into their own hands and string the baddies up or shoot them through the head and put their heads on sticks.'

I start pretending to doodle a picture of Shakeel dressed as a cowboy.

'Can I play with you?' We both look up and there is Stevie, right in front of us astride her pink bike, smiling and looking like one of those plastic kids from a breakfast-cereal advert.

'Can you count up to a hundred?' asks Priti.

'No,' says Stevie.

'Can you spell supercalifragilisticexpialidocious?'

'Um . . . no.'

'Can you stand on your head for ten seconds or hold your breath underwater for a minute?'

Stevie looks as if she might be about to cry as she shakes her head.

'Then you can't play with us,' says Priti. 'Now go away because we have important business to discuss and a silly baby like you wouldn't understand.'

Priti turns away and studies the chipped varnish on her nails so she doesn't see the tears welling up in Stevie's big blue eyes.

Stevie looks at me. I go bright red and stare at the pavement. After what seems like a very long moment, I see her little feet in a pair of jewel-encrusted pumps pedalling away. I think of Blythe and I feel really mean.

I'm just about to risk making Priti mad by calling Stevie back when Priti says, 'So, like I was saying, Shakeel could be the victim of a lynching if anyone finds out.'

'Who exactly is going to lynch him?' I ask, glancing over to the Sanders' weed-ridden driveway, to which Stevie has retreated.

'I dunno. Irate locals? The bomb squad?' She shrugs then looks at me, suddenly serious. 'What will they do to him if he gets arrested?'

'There's no way they're real bomb squad,' I say.

'I just wish Jed could've kept quiet until we had all the evidence,' Priti goes on. 'Then we could have confronted Shakeel ourselves and made him change his ways. Now who knows what your uncle Ian will do.'

'I suppose so,' I say, but I'm still thinking about Stevie.

Just then Stevie's mum comes out and calls her in for her tea. My grandad reckons only common people say tea. Anyone with any upbringing calls it dinner or supper, he says. I don't get the feeling he approves of the Sanders much.

Mrs Sanders is pregnant and she has this huge belly full of baby, but the rest of her is scrawny and her skin is blotchy red and peeling. She stands at the top of the driveway and yells Stevie's name again dead loud, even though she's only ten metres in front of her (something else my grandad hates). Stevie doesn't much look like she wants to go in. She drags her sparkly shoes along the tarmac as she trails off after her mum and we hear her saying, 'The big kids won't play with me!'

Mrs Sanders turns and looks over at me and Priti. 'Why not?' she snaps.

'That Priti says I'm a silly baby.'

'Well, that Priti is a mean cow,' Stevie's mum says loudly, looking back in our direction again to check we've heard and giving us a stare that is as sour as lemons. Then she slams the front door behind her.

'And you wonder why I don't associate with people like that!' says Priti. 'Come on. Let's go to your house and get on with the project. We don't need that scraggy-armed hippo giving us dirty looks!'

So we go inside and Priti soon cheers up. Today Granny is in charge of us because all of Priti's siblings are busy doing things for Shakeel's wedding and Grandad has taken Jed to see the shrink. And Granny being in charge seems to make Priti behave all prissy and princessy, like some kid from an advert. 'Yes, please, Mrs Evans,' and, 'That's *sooo* kind of you, Mrs Evans.' When I ask her why she's pretending to be so nice, she says, 'Are you trying to say I'm *not* nice?'

'No, it's just you're not normally so girlie.'

'So you're saying that I behave like a boy?'

'Sometimes.' I hesitate because she looks really cross. 'A bit.'

She purses her lips like I've really offended her. 'Come on,' she says primly. 'Let's just get on with your stupid box.'

So we go upstairs to my bedroom and look at the things we've got so far.

'What else do we need?' she says.

'Didn't it say an item of clothing?'

'Yeah, how are we going to get hold of that? Is there any old stuff hanging around in the wardrobe?' asks Priti.

'No, I looked.'

'Only one thing for it then.'

'What's that?'

'Got to ask your granny.'

I don't really want to, but Priti is already off down the stairs. 'Mrs Evans,' she says, and she's being so posh she sounds like the Queen.

'Yes, dear?' Granny emerges from the kitchen.

'We were wondering – well, Ben was wondering if you could help us with something? It's for this sort of project we're doing.' She stands on the tips of her toes as she speaks as if she's trying to be a ballerina or something.

'What do you need, dear?'

'The thing is that we need something – a piece of clothing that belonged to Ben's dad.'

That's how she says it – just like that – no hesitation as if she was asking for a glass of water or something.

Granny's cheeks go pink and she glances at me, but I can feel myself colouring too and I can't say anything.

'The thing is that Ben's doing this thing,' Priti goes on, hopping from foot to foot, which is something she does when she's nervous. 'Well, we both are. It was my idea, but it's Ben's box, so I suppose it's a joint project. It's about his dad, you see. A memory box.

On the website we found it said it was a good idea for grieving kids. Therapeutic was the word they used.'

'I see,' says Granny. Her eyes are pink at the edges now and a bit watery-looking. I've got an awful feeling that she's going to cry.

But she doesn't. Instead, she asks, 'Can I see it?'

'Of course,' says Priti.

This is just what I was dreading.

But it's too late. So we take Granny up to my bedroom and she sits down on the bed and looks at all the things in the box. And I think even Priti is starting to wonder if this was such a good idea after all because she keeps hopping from one leg to the other. She doesn't look at me and I don't look at her. We both just watch my granny as she takes out each thing slowly, one by one, looking at them carefully before laying them down neatly on the duvet next to her. She doesn't say anything and neither do we.

The last thing Granny takes out is my list of 'Things I'd like to know'. She looks at this for ages. Then she puts everything back in the box carefully and closes the lid. Everything except the list which she keeps folded on her lap.

When she looks up, her eyes are sparkling and the little pink spots in her cheeks are brighter now.

'Can I keep this?' she says quietly.

We both nod.

'I'm sure I can get you something your dad wore,' Granny says, standing up. 'I'll look something out for you.'

But she doesn't say anything about the box or what she thinks of it.

It's four o'clock by the time Jed and Grandad get back and Priti has gone home. Jed says he wants to go to bed and then goes straight up to our room and closes the door. I knock, but he just tells me to go away.

I start to go downstairs, but Granny and Grandad are talking in the kitchen and I don't want to disturb them, so I sit on the stairs with my notebook, but I don't draw anything.

Through the banisters, I can see my grandad leaning against the sink. He's staring out into the hall, but he doesn't seem to register that I'm there. He's a big tall man and still has all his hair, so even though he's pretty ancient, he still looks quite young. (I wonder if Uncle Ian gets mad that he didn't inherit the tall genes?). Today he seems sad though and that shrinks him somehow.

Granny asks Grandad how it went and he says, 'Awful really.'

'What did they ask?' says Granny.

'Just why he didn't want to see his mum. Why he thought he hated her. Just what you'd expect really.' Grandad looks down at his feet. 'He got terribly upset though.'

'Poor boy,' says Granny and I'm not sure if she means Jed or Grandad.

'I didn't know what to do.' Grandad looks up. His face is all crumpled and there are tears in his eyes.

Granny goes up to him and puts an arm round him, which looks funny because she's so much smaller than he is. 'It's not your fault, Barry,' she says in a soft voice.

'It's that woman's fault,' says Grandad. He sounds

angry now, not sad any more. 'If she cared for him as much as she says she does, she'd just drop all this and leave him be.'

'I don't think she can,' says Granny. 'She's his mother.'

'Are you saying this is all Ian's fault?' Grandad shrugs Granny off and looks like he's cross with her.

'No, of course not,' says Granny.

'Because that's what that psychiatrist was trying to get Jed to say,' says Grandad. 'I promise you. She was implying that his dad put him up to it. That he's being brainwashed.'

'I'm sure that's not what they were thinking,' says Granny.

'I'm telling you it was!' He sighs. 'I just can't see an end to it all, Rita.'

'I want an end to this as much as you do,' says Granny. She's holding a tea towel in one hand. I can't see her face, just her fingers fiddling with the towel. 'But until then we just have to love him through it. We have to love them both through it.'

'I hope you're right,' says Grandad and he reaches

for Granny's hand, the one not holding the tea towel, and he holds it in his own big hairy one.

And the two of them stand like that for nearly a whole minute, not saying anything, holding hands by the kitchen sink.

Then Grandad says, 'Has Hannah called?'

I don't hear Granny say anything, so I guess she shakes her head.

'These women call themselves mothers,' says Grandad, 'but between the two of them there's precious little mothering going on.'

AUGUST 5TH

Mik is a really bad babysitter, which means we think he's a really *good* babysitter. He's supposed to be in charge, but he just sits at his PlayStation and tells us not to bother him or he'll kill us. So we basically get to do whatever we want.

The problem is that there's not actually much to do. After we've raided the biscuit barrel and jumped on the sofas with our shoes on and watched trashy TV (which is actually pretty dull) we get bored, so Mik tells us to 'bugger off and play in the park'.

I ask, 'Are you going to sit in the tree house so you can keep an eye on us?'

'And why the hell would I want to do that?' Mik replies. 'It's only the other side of the fence, not the red-light district!'

I go bright red.

'Just don't get yourselves kidnapped, OK?' Mik says. And I remember the thing Uncle Ian's tattooed bomb-squad buddy said about white kids being kidnapped and kick-starting the civil war. 'Cos if you do, I'm not paying the ransom!'

It's probably because of my mum, but I'm no good at doing stuff I'm not supposed to. All the time in the park, I keep expecting Granny or Priti's dad to turn up and start shouting, or one of the neighbours to catch us and snitch on us.

'You know if we get caught, Mik will say he told us to stay in the garden,' says Priti.

'And even if he doesn't, they'll say that we should have known better,' I say.

'Yeah, but when was the last time Granny pitched up to play on the swings?' Jed points out. 'Or your dad for that matter? Don't sweat it!'

I imagine Granny and Mr Muhammed dressed as little kids, flying high on the swings.

Priti pretends she's not bothered but I reckon she's a bit worried about getting caught too because she suggests we play in the woods where we're less likely to be seen. So we all trail off in the direction of the copse. Jed thinks we should be looking for condoms

252

to see if Zara and Tyreese are 'doing it', but Priti says that's gross. So we play Bomb-busters – which involves Jed-eye and Lil' Priti nuking terrorist-cell bases – and we end up going miles further into the woods than we meant to.

The park is actually massive. Beyond the swings is a field big enough to fit three football pitches in and all round the edge is this woody bit that stretches right down to the main road. Turns out there's even a gate I never knew about leading to the shops on the Peacock Parade.

This is where we bump into Tyreese's gang. They're all hanging out by the gate, sitting on their bikes, smoking and knocking back cans of lager, and by the time we see them it's too late to turn back because they've already clocked us. I'm about to run for it anyway, but Priti has other ideas. She shouts, 'Hey, Tyreese – how's your kid brother?' She's got her hands on her hips and a funny look on her face.

Tyreese looks at the others. Sitting on his bike he's about twice as tall as Priti and he's got this big grin on his face. 'Why, do you fancy a piece of him?'

'No thanks, I don't go for white trash,' she says, taking another few steps towards him. 'Not like my sister!'

She grins and Tyreese glares. I realise that his gang probably don't know about him and Zara.

'Oh, yeah, I remember your sister – what was her name? Nice bit of brown sugar!' He puts up his hand for a high five and the gang roar with laughter.

'But, hey!' Tyreese goes on. 'I haven't seen her sweet little tush for a few days now. Your peeps packed her off to Pakistan or something? Married her to some fat, oily, middle-aged Paki?'

The gang laugh again.

Priti starts the hopping from foot to foot thing, but then stops herself. 'Well, from what Zara told me, even "Paki" OAPs have bigger willies than you,' she says boldly.

I hear Jed whistle gently through his teeth.

'Yeah?' Tyreese says. 'That why she couldn't get enough of me?' He revs his motorbike and thrusts his hips, making the other bikers laugh.

'Perhaps that was before you stabbed her cousin,'

says Priti. Her eyes have narrowed and she's glaring at Tyreese.

'Don't know anything about no stabbing, me.' Tyreese grins at the gang, who all laugh. 'But then, you all look the same 'sfar as I'm concerned.' This gets another laugh.

'And all you white-trash thugs look the same to us too,' says Priti, starting to hop nervously again. 'So I expect Zara's moved on to the next bit of rough. But don't worry, I'll be sure to give her your love.'

The bikers laugh, but this time Tyreese looks well mad.

'Come on,' Priti hisses. Me and Jed don't need telling twice. Priti turns round and starts to walk off and we follow her.

'As if I'd ever fall in love with one of you!' Tyreese shouts. But Priti just keeps on walking, so fast me and Jed have to trot to keep up with her.

'Keep walking,' Priti hisses.

'You rocked back there,' Jed whispers.

'Thanks,' says Priti.

'What if they follow us?' I ask.

'I don't know,' she says. 'Just don't look back.' Glancing at her I can see she's trembling although she keeps her head high and her shoulders back. 'Zara always says if you talk the talk you gotta walk the walk,' she says.

So we all keep walking. I try really hard not to turn my head, but Jed takes a little peek. Tyreese shouts after us, 'You tell that sister of yours I'll be waiting for her.'

We go back across the football pitches, rather than through the woods. I think we all reckon Tyreese is less likely to knife us out in the open. It feels like a long way back to the swings and when we finally get there, Jed turns to Priti. 'For a little kid, that was pretty cool. Have you got a death wish or something?'

'Live fast, die young: that's my motto,' says Priti, with a little flick of her head.

'What was all that about then?' says Jed.

'He just annoys me, that's all,' says Priti as she clambers over the fence at the end of her garden and up into the tree house.

'So has Zara really dumped him?' asks Jed, jumping up after her.

'You'd like that, wouldn't you?' says Priti. She looks a bit rattled, her skin pale beneath the green sparkly eyeshadow and circles of Barbie-pink blusher she's wearing today.

'I just don't get what she sees in that loser, that's all.'

'It's the bad boy thing,' says Priti. 'Makes her feel like a rebel!'

'Why did you tell Tyreese she'd dumped him if she hasn't?' I say, forcing myself into the tiny gap they've left for me on the platform.

'Wishful thinking!' Priti replies.

'Didn't the whole stabbing-her-cousin thing put her off him then?' says Jed.

'Zara reckons Tyreese didn't attack Said,' says Priti. 'She thinks he's being framed.'

'What do you think?' I ask.

'I said he was trouble from the start,' she says, sounding a bit more like the old Priti now that we're all safely back in the tree house. 'But when I told her

that, she just threw things at me. Sisters!' She sighs.
'What can you do?'

THINGS I'D LIKE TO KNOW ABOUT PRITI

1. Is she really cleverer than me and Jed (like she says she is) or does she just talk more?

2. How can such a cool person wear such stupid clothes?

3. What's the difference between a 'student of human nature' (Priti's phrase) and someone who's just plain nosy? And which category does Priti fall into?

4. Does she really believe in the whole honour-killing thing or is it just an excuse to get Zara to give her stuff?

5. Does she fancy Jed? (I hope not, but girls are funny like that.)

6. Why doesn't she have to wear a headscarf if she's a Muslim?

7. Why doesn't she hate all white people like Grandad says all Muslims do or is she just pretending to like me and Jed?

8. *Does* she actually like me and Jed? Maybe I'm just her holiday project.

9. Why does she dislike Stevie Sanders so much?

10. Are there actually any words she *doesn't* know the meaning of?

AUGUST 6TH

Today Granny and Jed have another of their secret appointments, only this time I get to go with them because Grandad has hurt his back and says he needs some decent peace and quiet and Priti's whole family are busy doing wedding stuff. Jed really doesn't want me to come and he gets this weird look on his face when Granny tells him I am and then he locks himself in our room all morning and won't talk to me. So I go and join Priti, who's sitting on the wall outside her house, waiting for her mum and sister to get ready for this bride-painting ceremony they're going to at Ameenah's house.

'All the bride's friends get to paint tattoos on her hands and feet and then she can't go out afterwards till she gets married,' Priti explains to me, kicking her feet against the tarmac. She's wearing traditional dress and her hair is tied up all neat. She looks really different – not quite herself somehow.

'I thought tattoos were dead painful,' I say,

thinking about the ink-stained arms of Uncle Ian's bomb-squad buddy.

'Not real tattoos, dumbo. Just henna – it's like this brown gunk that comes off after a bit.'

I imagine a bride in a white dress, her arms and neckline covered in dark, swirling images.

'Zara doesn't want to come, but Mum's making her,' says Priti, kicking her pretty beaded shoes again like she wants to ruin them or something – maybe she'd rather be wearing her wheelies. 'She's well grumpy at the moment.'

'Why?' I ask.

'Tyreese won't see her cos I told the gang they were getting it on. She's well mad at me.' Priti raises her eyebrows, but she's not looking that cheerful herself. 'If he wasn't such an idiot, I'd almost wish they'd get back together. At least then she'd get off my case and I'd start earning protection money again!'

I tell her that Granny is taking me along to Jed's appointment.

'Oooh!' she says, perking up immediately and starting to talk like a gangsta rapper again. 'Now we gonna find out how long he gotta live!' she says. 'Then we can plan stuff like taking him to Disneyland!'

'Why Disneyland?' I ask.

'They always take kids who are dying to Disneyland,' she says, dropping her rapster speak. 'If we get everyone to give loads of money, we can go too.'

I must look a bit dubious because she says, 'Don't you want to know what his mystery illness is?'

'Yeah, but maybe he doesn't want *us* to know.'

'Of course he does,' says Priti. 'He wants us all to make a big fuss over him and tell him how wonderful he is just cos he's dying. He'd love that.'

'I suppose so,' I say.

'What are you drawing?' she asks, peering over my shoulder. 'Is it another Bomb-buster strip?'

'Maybe,' I reply, closing my notebook.

'Can I see it?'

'Not till it's finished.'

'What happens in this one?'

'Lil' Priti gets kidnapped,' I say.

'Who by?'

'A gang called Da Hona Killaz,' I say.

'And I suppose you and Jed-eye rescue me in a typical hero-rescues-damsel-in-distress patriarchal narrative?'

'Maybe,' I say because I can't be bothered to ask what patriarchal means. 'Maybe not. I haven't decided yet.'

'Fine,' she says. 'Lil' Priti will just rescue herself then. What am I wearing in this one?'

On the way to the appointment, Jed walks several paces ahead of me and Granny and refuses to sit with us when we get on the bus.

So Granny and I sit together and she tells me all about the places we see along the route and how they've changed in the time since she and Grandad first moved here. She shows me the school my dad went to and where he went to Cub Scouts and a few other things which are really interesting. I want to ask her more, but Jed is sitting in front of us snorting at everything she says, so I don't.

I take out my notebook and do a few more frames of my cartoon instead. I draw Jed getting nuked by a stun gun, trying to rescue Priti from Da Hona Killaz. He ends up with a bald head which makes him look like one of those cancer kids.

I don't ask where we're going, although I'm dying to know. (Perhaps I shouldn't say 'dying' in case Jed is?) I don't even say anything when we go past the stop for the hospital. The bus keeps on going in the direction of the city centre, but it's not until we turn into a busy shopping street that Granny says to me, 'Jed hasn't actually got an appointment at the hospital today.'

I glance at Jed who just glares at me.

'I'm sorry we lied to you,' Granny goes on. 'It's just that your grandad doesn't know, you see.'

But there's no time to ask questions because the bus stops. Jed gets up and starts to make his way down the aisle towards the exit, without waiting for us. Wherever it is we're going, Jed has obviously been there before. Flustered, Granny hastily picks up her handbag and starts to get up and follow him. The doors of the bus begin to shut and Granny has to call out to the bus driver to keep them open. By the time we emerge in the middle of the busy high street, filled with people carrying big bags, she's in a complete tizz. She seems really tiny: I remember her once saying that she doesn't like coming into the city any more because the crowds make her nervous and all the tall buildings make her think of Dad and she worries about them falling down on top of her.

And Jed must know this – especially if this isn't the first time they've come here – but he's rushing ahead without even looking back. Granny calls to him to stay close, but he pretends not to hear. I can see she's anxious, so I tuck my arm in hers as we follow Jed into a large department store.

Inside the revolving doors the store is packed full of people and stuff and weird bright yellow lights and, for a moment, neither of us can see Jed. We make our way through all the make-up counters with the brightly painted ladies behind them, and past the racks of gloves and scarves and handbags, and cases full of jewellery. Then Granny sees Jed over by the lifts. He's standing there, his finger jammed on the call button, pressing it over and over again. He doesn't look up as we approach. I expect Granny to tell him off for running ahead, but she doesn't. She just pats his arm. He shifts awkwardly, shrugging away from the contact.

When the lift opens and we all get in, Granny says, 'Can I tell Ben where we're going, Jed?'

Jed just grunts, which Granny obviously interprets as a 'yes' because she turns to me and says, 'We're going to have tea with Jed's other grandma. She's called Brenda.'

'Oh,' I say. I can't decide if this is more or less of a shock than hearing that Jed is dying of a terrible disease.

Jed looks at his feet and scowls. Granny tucks her hand into mine and I can feel that it's trembling.

The lift goes up.

Jed's other grandma – his mum's mum – is already waiting for us when we get to the café on the top floor of the department store. I've never heard Jed talk about her and I'm not sure if I've ever met her. But she seems nice. More round and cuddly than my granny (who's still very slim and pretty for her age)

266

but perhaps a bit younger. She must have looked just like Auntie Karen once upon a time because she has the same eyes and smile and I wonder if that is weird for Jed.

Granny Brenda looks pleased, but maybe a little frightened when she sees Jed. He doesn't even look at her, but just throws himself down into a chair.

'Hello, Jed,' she says nervously.

Jed just grunts.

She looks at him and smiles then turns to my granny. 'Hello, Rita.'

'Hello again, Brenda.'

'I can't tell you how grateful I am that you came,' says Granny Brenda.

'Jed's been looking forward to it,' says my granny, although looking at Jed, it's obvious this is a lie. 'Haven't you, Jed?'

Jed just grunts again and gets out his games console. I've never seen him quite like this.

'You must be Ben?' says Granny Brenda, still looking nervous. 'I don't suppose you remember me. You've grown up a lot since I last saw you!' She smiles.

'How long *is* it since you saw Ben?' asks Granny, trying to jolly things along.

Brenda glances nervously at Jed, who has pulled the hood of his sweatshirt over his head like it's an invisibility cloak. 'It was at Andrew's funer–' She breaks off suddenly, turns to my granny and goes bright red. 'I'm sorry. I shouldn't have . . .'

The red spots have appeared in Granny's cheeks, but she says, 'Don't apologise.' And she gives a funny little laugh. 'I expect you hardly recognise Ben if it's been so long.' She pauses, blinking a little. 'Although he looks so like Andrew, don't you think?'

'Yes,' says Brenda quietly. 'He's the image of him.'

Jed throws down his game in disgust, folds his arms and stares at the ceiling.

'And Jed has told me such a lot about you, Ben,' says Granny Brenda.

If Jed is always like this when Granny Brenda is around, I find this hard to imagine.

Granny Brenda gives Jed a new game for his console (suddenly the other new stuff makes sense!) and my granny has to prompt him to say thank you.

Then Granny Brenda asks him what he's been up to and he says, 'Not much.'

My granny tells Granny Brenda about us building the tree house and the day out to the zoo with Uncle Ian. Granny Brenda says, 'Oh, I bet you enjoyed that. What was your favourite animal, Jed?'

Jed snorts and says, 'Dunno.'

So Granny Brenda asks me what mine was and I say, 'Giraffe,' and Jed gives me a look that says, *We both know we never went to the zoo, you pathetic liar!* and then I go all red and stop talking, so the two grannies have to talk to each other.

Granny Brenda orders cake for all of us, tea for her and my granny and Cokes for me and Jed. She tries a few more times to get Jed to talk but he just fiddles with his cake and blows bubbles into his Coke, which is weird because he normally gobbles everything in sight in two seconds flat (unless it's brown bread or vegetables) and he's always complaining that Granny doesn't let him have fizzy drinks. I glance at him from time to time to try and work out what he's thinking, but he avoids my eye.

Granny Brenda and my granny start talking about women's stuff, so I have a go at trying to talk to Jed.

'You're not ill then,' I whisper.

'No, why should I be?' he says loudly.

'You had all those appointments. I thought there must be something wrong with you.'

'Granny told Grandad I had to see the kiddie-shrink so he wouldn't get suspicious,' says Jed. 'Why, did you think I was dying?' He laughs.

'No,' I say quickly. Then, 'I dunno. Maybe.'

'Well, sorry to disappoint you.'

'Priti thought you had cancer,' I say. 'We were going to take you to Disneyland.'

'Well it's a good job I'm not about to kick the bucket because I hate all that Mickey Mouse crap,' he says.

'Right,' I say.

Then he slides down his seat so he's practically horizontal and starts fiddling with the top of his hood, pulling it down over his forehead till it touches his chin.

'Can I look at your game?' I ask.

'If you want to.' He passes it over and starts mashing his fork into his cake till it's a squishy mess. His head is only just level with the table by now and I notice that people on the other tables are staring at him.

'It looks cool,' I say.

'She always brings presents. Adults reckon they can buy you.' He says this really loud again, but Granny and Brenda are talking about Jed's mum now and I guess they don't hear because I reckon Granny would have told him off otherwise.

'How is Karen?' Granny is saying.

Jed squishes his cake even harder and pretends not to listen.

'She always enjoys hearing about our little get-togethers,' says Granny Brenda, which doesn't seem to me to be exactly answering the question. 'I tell her all about what we get up to, pass on all the news.' She pauses. 'You know she'd love to see him.'

'Yes,' says my granny quietly.

'Perhaps one time she could – I don't know – perhaps she could join us for a minute or two?' says

Granny Brenda. 'She misses him so desperately.'

'You know I can't do that,' says my granny.

'Just five minutes would mean the world to her.'

'I know, but Ian would go mad if he found out,' says my granny. 'I'm frightened of what he'll do if he finds out about this.'

'I really appreciate what you're doing for me,' says Granny Brenda. Then she glances at Jed. 'Although I'm not sure Jed feels the same way.'

Jed grunts. Granny Brenda smiles, a bit sadly.

'You are his grandma. You have a right to see him,' says my granny.

'So does Karen,' says Granny Brenda. 'She's his mother.'

'I can't go against the court ruling,' says my granny.

Granny Brenda pauses, glances at Jed. Then she says softly, 'You do know that the court granted her contact time?'

Jed looks up.

My granny looks confused for a minute. 'Ian told me the judge said she couldn't see him.'

Jed looks from one granny to the other.

'I didn't like to say anything before now because you've been so kind.' Granny Brenda glances at Jed, but he just looks down. 'But I'm afraid that's just not true.'

Granny falters, 'But Ian said . . .' She stops.

'If you don't believe me then ask Jed,' says Granny Brenda. 'He was there when they gave out the contact order, weren't you, Jed?'

Jed says nothing.

'That's what this new hearing is about – Karen wants to get the contact order enforced, to make your son comply with the schedule of access to Jed that was agreed in court.'

My granny looks at Jed. She seems really upset now. 'Perhaps we should agree not to talk about this,' she says.

'Karen just wants to see her son,' says Granny Brenda.

'But I don't want to see her!' Jed's voice sounds very loud in this funny department store café where little old men and ladies sit drinking tea and eating scones with their coats on.

'I'm sure you don't mean that,' says Granny Brenda.

'I do and no one can make me see her if I don't want to!'

'This is just your father talking,' Granny Brenda says.

'Please don't say things like that,' says my granny.

'All she ever does is let me down,' insists Jed. The people on the neighbouring tables are looking over now to see what all the fuss is about.

'She loves you, Jed. She misses you,' says Granny Brenda.

'No, she doesn't. She just wants to win the battle with Dad.' His voice is even louder than usual (and that's saying something). I think he's doing it on purpose, like he's trying to make a scene. Even the waitresses have stopped work to watch what's going on – it's like something out of a daytime soap opera.

'It's not about winning or losing, Jed,' says my granny.

'It's about your right to have a mum in your life,' says Granny Brenda, who is nearly crying now.

'Is this being filmed?' I hear one old lady whisper loudly.

'I don't want my mum!' shouts Jed, standing up suddenly and knocking over his chair with a great clatter. 'I don't even want to see you. I only come because Granny makes me.'

Granny Brenda's face crumples, but Jed doesn't seem to care – he just storms off in the direction of the lifts. Everyone watches him go.

'What a horrid boy,' I hear a lady on a table nearby say.

'He's not horrid,' I say. 'He's just upset.'

My granny goes after Jed and when they come back, she makes him apologise to Granny Brenda. He does, but I don't think he really means it. Granny Brenda pretends everything is OK, but she looks like she's going to burst into tears again as soon as we're gone. She hugs my granny, who says that they had best agree not to talk about this again, but let the young people work it out themselves. They make a plan to meet again the next week. Then my granny tells the old people on the other tables that the show is over and they all stare at their teapots and pretend not to have been eavesdropping at all.

Jed is like a thundercloud in the lift and all the way home on the bus. Granny tells me not to worry, that he always gets like this after he sees Granny Brenda. She buys us both a Cadbury Creme Egg, but Jed says he isn't hungry, so I get to eat his too and then feel sick afterwards.

When we get home, Granny tells Grandad the counsellor is pleased with Jed's progress and I'm impressed with how good she is at lying. I wonder what else she's keeping secret.

I ask Grandad if my mum has called, but he says no.

AUGUST 7TH

Today Jed's acting like nothing happened and I'm playing along. He's even nuttier than usual though: crashing around the house, swinging off the banisters and jumping down the stairs six at a time. I hear Grandad saying to Granny, 'What do you do in those sessions? He always comes back worse than he was before.'

Another card has arrived for me. This one has a picture of the Aston Villa squad on it. On the back, Gary has written, *To my star player, with a great big team hug!* Jed says it's rubbish (because he supports Liverpool) but it cheers me up loads because Gary supports City. Villa is my mum's team.

We go over to see Priti (who's bound to ask him loads of questions, so it's not like I need to anyway). We're all sitting in the tree house, but before Priti gets a chance to start the interrogation, Zara comes storming out looking mad as anything. Normally, she spends most of her time in her bedroom talking on the phone to her mates or Tyreese, so we're surprised to see her striding down the garden – especially with her big pink fluffy slippers on.

'Uh-oh,' says Priti. 'Here comes trouble!'

Zara marches up, hands on hips, and I can tell she's really angry. 'What are you doing meddling in my love life, you little brat?' she says. She doesn't shout – I suppose she doesn't want the neighbours to hear – so she's kind of hiss-whispering.

'What are you doing going out with a criminal?' Priti retorts. She also has her hands on her hips and they look like little and large mirror images of each other.

'Nice slippers by the way,' says Jed, leaning over the platform of the tree house and grinning at Zara.

Zara just glares at him.

'Zara still reckons it's OK to shag the brains out of the guy who knifed her cousin,' says Priti. I notice she's hiss-whispering too. She might be mad at Zara, but she's still protecting her secret.

'Tyreese did not do it!' says Zara.

'You sure about that?'

'If he's supposed to have done it, why would the police release him?' says Zara.

'They haven't got enough evidence yet, that's why!' says Priti.

'Because there *is* no evidence, little sister!'

'Yes there is and we're going to find it and prove it to you.'

'Yeah, right.'

'If we can prove he did it, will you dump him?' asks Priti.

She stares at Zara. Zara stares back.

'I thought he already dumped her?' says Jed.

'Like you understand anything about relationships,' says Zara.

'They got it back on,' says Priti. 'Worst luck.'

'And my darling sister was so narked about it she decided to send him a text with a picture of me in my wedding gear – headscarf and all!' says Zara.

'Sexy!' says Jed.

'Not!' says Priti, snorting.

'Actually, he thought it was,' says Zara with a little toss of her head.

'Which is just plain weird, if you ask me,' says Priti.

'What is your problem? Do you fancy him yourself? Is that it?'

'I don't go for criminals!' says Priti. 'So will you?'

'Will I what!'

'Dump him if we can prove he did it?'

I look from Zara in her fluffy slippers and miniskirt to Priti, who's wearing a polka-dot playsuit that Zara gave her as a hush payment, with striped leggings and a Hello Kitty visor and matching leg warmers. Neither of them looks as if they're going to budge.

'Like I'm going to make a bargain with you,' says Zara.

'Fine!' says Priti. 'I'll just tell Mum and Dad about you and Tyreese then, shall I?'

'You can if you like, but you'll be in just as much trouble as me. And if they're up for an honour killing, they might as well kill two birds with one stone. They can probably get a discount.'

Zara turns to go. 'Just keep out of my love life!' she snaps.

'It's been nice looking down your top,' Jed calls

after her. 'Do I get to cop a feel if I keep schtum about your boyfriend?'

Zara swings round and glares. 'You say a word about him and I'll make sure you never get a girlfriend for the rest of your life, you little pervert.'

Then she storms off, tripping up on her slippers as she goes, which spoils the effect a bit.

'Just wait till we get the incriminating evidence!' Priti shouts after her. Zara doesn't even bother to look back.

'What evidence?' I ask after she's gone.

'No idea,' says Priti. 'But I can't let her get the last word in, can I?'

AUGUST 8TH

It turns out it's not that easy finding evidence. We don't have any leads, none of us knows how to do DNA analysis, we can't talk to any witnesses (even if there were any) because we're not allowed to go out on our own, and we can't interrogate Tyreese and force a confession out of him because he's hardly going to spill his guts unless we know how to do some of that proper torture stuff, and we don't.

Jed reckons our best bet is to wait till Mik is babysitting again and then sneak out to the park and hope we bump into him, but we've got Shakeel today, so we'll never get away with it.

It starts raining and we discover that the roof on the tree house leaks so we abandon our lookout and hang out in Priti's room and talk about how they solve crimes on TV. When we get bored of that, Priti tells us about the party that happens the day after the wedding – the one everyone on the road has been invited to. I reckon it sounds fun, but Priti says it won't be and that by then she'll probably have died of wedding boredom anyway.

'I'm going to agree to an arranged marriage with the elephant man, so long as I can sneak off and do it without all the fuss,' she says. 'Mind you, the bride does get loads of new outfits. Maybe I could put up with it for the wardrobe!'

'So what does Ameenah see in a loser like Shakeel?' Jed asks. We haven't been in Priti's room much because Zara says she doesn't want smelly boys in there, so I'm having fun looking at all the weird things she has – like fluffy pens with feet and loads of little plastic animals and a collection of cacti with woolly hats on.

'Dunno,' says Priti. 'They've just known each other forever.'

'She's probably in it for the money,' says Jed, who's been checking out all the girlie stuff. Priti won't let him look in Zara's underwear drawer, but he's messing with all her make-up and flicking through her magazines. 'She knows he's going to top himself, so she gets a great payout when he carks it,' he says.

'I hadn't thought of that,' says Priti, who is sitting

by the window spying into the neighbours' houses with my dad's binoculars, which I've taken to carrying round with me for some reason.

Jed gets up and joins her and says he can see Stevie's mum taking off her bra in her bedroom. 'That bump is massive!' he says, 'What's she got in there? A baby hippo or something?'

'Give me back the binoculars,' says Priti, grabbing them from him and training them on the upstairs window of Stevie's house. She can't see anything and, when I have a look, neither can I, so I reckon Jed just made it up about seeing her topless. But he keeps going on about Mrs Sanders' boobs, and the thought of it makes me feel a bit odd. I can't stop glancing over at her house in case she decides to do another striptease.

Through the binoculars, we can see Stevie watching TV in the sitting room. Jed reckons it's the show with the talking flowers, but I say it's the one with all the fluffy night-time creatures and then he laughs at me because I know the difference.

'You watch baby TV with your mum!' he says.

Although he's pretending to be all normal, he's still in a funny mood.

'No I do not!' I say.

'Yeah. You do. You and your mum all cuddled up on the sofa, watching the dancing daisies and drinking beddy-byes milk. You're probably still breastfeeding.'

'I am not!'

'That's why you miss her so much.' Jed laughs and Priti does too.

I stand up. My fists are tingling. I don't know what I'd have done if Priti hadn't suddenly said, 'Shut up, you two! Look.' She points out of the window. 'Who's that?'

I look where she's pointing and see a woman knocking on Granny and Grandad's door. She looks like she's been knocking for a while and getting no answer because she's really banging.

'Can't she tell they're out?' says Priti, but Jed and I don't say anything because we both recognise the person.

I haven't seen my Auntie Karen for a couple of years, but I glance at Jed, who's gone all pale and his mouth is in a straight line, and then I know it's definitely her – Jed's mum.

'What do your reckon she wants?' asks Priti, who has no idea and is just enjoying the drama of it. Jed's mum is shouting something now. 'I'm going to open the window, so we can hear what she's on about.'

Before either of us can stop her, Priti props open the window and leans out. Jed's mum's not at the front door any more – she's moved back a few metres down the drive so that she can shout up at the house.

'Let me see him!' she's shouting. 'I need to see him!'

'This is great!' says Priti. 'The most exciting thing that ever happens on this street is the supermarket delivery van. Hey, do you reckon your grandad is having a steamy affair?'

'Shut up,' says Jed.

'No need to be ageist! Old people have girlfriends too, you know,' she says.

'Shut up,' I say.

'What?' Priti turns round and looks at us both. 'What's up with you?' she says to Jed. 'You look well weird.'

The woman is shouting louder now: half screaming, half crying. 'I have a right to see him. I've got a court order to prove it. Please let me see him.'

'What's she on about now?' asks Priti.

'Just close the window,' says Jed.

'Why? This is class! Do you reckon I should shout out and tell her they aren't in?'

'Shut the window,' says Jed again. His face is so pale it's like all the blood has gone out of him.

'Please! Please! Have pity!' Jed's mum shouts again. 'I need to see him. I need him to know how much I love him.'

'Who'd have thought anyone would fancy your grandad? She's pretty too, and way younger than him! Dirty dog!'

'Shut the window, Priti,' I say, but she's still leaning out of it making it impossible for either me or Jed to reach the handle.

'What is with you two today?'

Then Jed lunges for her and, for a second, I think she's going to fall out of the window. But he pushes her to one side, grabs the handle and slams the window shut. Priti is sent flying on to the bed below.

'What the hell are you doing? Trying to kill me and break the window at the same time?' she shouts.

'Just close the curtains,' says Jed. I notice that his hands are shaking. I jump up and pull the curtains shut.

'Why do we need to close the curtains?' says Priti. 'What's going on?'

'Because I don't want her to see me.'

'Why? What's going on? Who is she?'

'Just how thick are you?' says Jed.

Priti looks at me with a confused expression.

'That's Auntie Karen,' I say quietly. 'She's Jed's mum.'

'Oh!' says Priti, eyes as wide as saucers. 'I see.'

None of us says anything for a moment.

'She doesn't look much like you,' Priti blurts out. 'I guess your dad cut your mum out of your gene pool as well as your life.'

Jed doesn't reply.

I peek through the curtains. Auntie Karen has stopped shouting. She sits on the wall and cries. I wonder if she knows all the neighbours are watching her and how that makes her feel.

'She looks all right to me,' says Priti, peering out from behind me. 'Nice shoes.'

'What would you know?' says Jed, who is sitting on the bed, refusing to look out.

'She looks well upset too. Can't say I'd be that gutted if I never got to see you again.'

'I wish,' says Jed.

'If you want to go out and see her, I'll go with you,' I say.

'No thanks,' says Jed.

'We wouldn't tell anyone,' says Priti. 'I could run down and tell her to go meet us in the park then keep lookout in case your granny and grandad come back. Like with Zara and Tyreese.'

'I said, no thanks,' says Jed again.

'But don't you want to see her even a little bit?' she asks.

'No.'

Priti doesn't seem like she's going to drop it even though Jed is getting really annoyed, but then I spot Granny and Grandad's car turning into the cul-de-sac.

'Shh!' I say. 'Granny and Grandad are back.'

Priti turns her attention to what's happening outside and even Jed comes to see what's going on.

The little car turns into the drive and I'm not sure if they've seen Auntie Karen because they get straight out of the car and then there she is, standing right in front of them.

The funny thing is that Granny and Auntie Karen look quite alike. Granny's older, obviously, and her hair is grey and white while Auntie Karen's is gold and brown, but they're both short and petite and have sweet faces.

Jed draws the curtains and opens the window a little bit to try and hear what's going on.

Granny is trying to say something, but Auntie Karen is talking over her. She takes Granny's hand and holds it in hers.

'Just get rid of her,' I hear Jed mutter under his breath.

But Granny can't get her hand free and Grandad is coming round from the other side of the car and he is waving his arms and shouting something. But still

290

Auntie Karen is holding Granny's hand and she seems to be pleading with her. Granny looks like she wants to cry.

Grandad is shouting at Auntie Karen and then he tries to push her away, but it's Granny who trips and falls. Auntie Karen goes to help her, but Grandad blocks her way.

He's really shouting now and we can make out the words, 'Now look what you've done!' and, 'Haven't you done enough damage to this family already?'

Auntie Karen steps aside as Grandad helps Granny indoors. 'I'm sorry!' she's saying, or I think that's what she's saying.

'Just go away and leave this family alone!' shouts Grandad, slamming the door in her face.

Jed winces.

'Wow!' says Priti. 'Your grandad does *not* like her!'

'He's just looking out for me,' says Jed.

'What do you reckon she'll do now?' says Priti, still watching Auntie Karen. 'Bet she falls down on the grass and starts crying. Or maybe she'll chain herself to something so the police have to come and cut her free. That would be cool! Well, not cool, but . . .' She glances at Jed, who is still staring at the floor. 'I mean, it's dead sad and I feel totally sorry for her – and for you – but . . .'

'Well, don't,' says Jed.

'I just reckon if I were her, I wouldn't go down without a fight,' says Priti.

But Auntie Karen doesn't fall down weeping or chain herself to anything. She just picks up her bag and takes something out of it – something small and white – an envelope maybe. Then she glances up at Priti's house. Right up at the window from where we're watching. We all dart down quickly beneath the windowsill.

'Did she see us?' asks Jed.

'I don't know.' I peek over the windowsill then duck down again quickly. 'She's still looking up here.'

'What's she doing now?' asks Jed.

I lift my head a little and watch as Jed's mum bends down and places the envelope beneath a bush, where it can only be seen from our vantage point – not from Granny and Grandad's house. She keeps glancing up at the window. Jed has raised his head a bit so he's watching her too and as she turns to go, she blows a kiss up at him.

'She saw us then,' says Priti as we watch Auntie Karen walk off down the cul-de-sac.

I nod. Jed doesn't say anything. He's watching his mum walk away. At one point she glances back at the house. Me and Priti duck, but Jed stays standing, watching her. For a moment, I almost think he's going to wave. But he doesn't.

He does go and get the letter though. Or rather he sends me to go and get it. Priti wants him to open it there and then, but he won't. He says he's not going to open it at all; he's just going to bin it, and the only reason he wants to get it is to stop someone else snooping into his business.

We go back home and Grandad makes the lunch because Granny has hurt her hand in the fall. Grandad doesn't make us food very often, and he tells me and Jed we have to help too. For once, Jed is really helpful, clearing the table and doing the washing-up without moaning. Nobody mentions Auntie Karen, but everything is weird and different.

After lunch, I go upstairs to our bedroom to draw. I'm sitting on my bed, trying to come up with the next frame for the Bomb-busters cartoon, but for some reason I can't think of anything. I stare out across the room, and that's when I notice something peeking out from under Jed's pillow. It's the letter from his mum – he hasn't thrown it away after all. I wonder if he's read it.

It makes me think about my mum, and the cards, and her not calling, and all that other stuff that I try not to think about most of the time.

THINGS I'VE BEEN THINKING ABOUT MY MUM

1. What's it like – the hospital she's in? Is it like a hospital with beds or more like a hotel only with nurses? Does she lie in bed all day or can she walk around and read and draw and do stuff (she hates having nothing to do)? She's not really wearing a straightjacket is she?

2. Does everyone there have the same thing as her or is it full of people with other sorts of problems? Are

any of the other people scary or dangerous?

3. Who is making sure she eats? And how do they do it? Do they force her to eat? Because I don't think she'd like that. Or do they let her do it the way she needs to?

4. Why isn't she desperate to see me, like Jed's mum is with him? Is that part of her being ill? And will it ever change?

5. What if she never gets better?

6. Where will I go if she dies?

7. Can I catch her illness? I think I read somewhere that kids are more likely to get it if their parents have had it.

8. Is her hair still falling out?

9. Why can't I remember her face properly? Does that mean I've stopped loving her enough?

10. Why doesn't she write the cards herself?

When I go back downstairs, Granny has gone for a lie-down and Grandad sends me and Jed to the parade with money for ice creams. Nobody mentions what happened this morning, but then I suppose Grandad doesn't even know that we saw.

When we get back from the parade, I see a white van in the driveway.

'Your dad's here then,' I say to Jed.

'No shit, Sherlock' says Jed irritably.

Uncle Ian is chatting to Grandad in the sitting room.

'Go and tell your gran her son is here,' is the first thing he says to Jed.

But Granny must have heard him arrive because she comes downstairs in her slippers, still looking pale and shaken.

'You all right?' says Uncle Ian. 'You don't look it.'

'Just one of my headaches,' says Granny, glancing at Grandad, who just shrugs. 'I'll make us all some tea. If I'd known you were coming, Ian dear, I'd have made some of your favourite lemon cake.'

I help Granny make the tea, but it's like she doesn't even notice me. She lays the tray in silence and it's only when it's all done that she seems to see me. 'I'm sorry, Ben. I was miles away,' she says. 'Thank you.'

'That's OK, Granny.'

'I'm sorry we have to keep things secret,' she says. 'About Jed seeing his grandmother. I mean, I know a mother shouldn't keep secrets from her children, but I think it's for the best. Or at least I hope so.'

She looks at me and I feel like I should say something, but I can't think what. She picks up the tray and carries it into the sitting room.

'What's all this about extra appointments with the counsellor?' says Uncle Ian, turning round as she comes in.

Jed looks at Granny and so do I.

'She suggested we fit in some extra sessions over the holiday period,' says Granny, putting the tray down on the stacking tables, little pink spots appearing on her cheeks.

Last time she talked about the counsellor she said it was a man, but Grandad doesn't seem to notice.

Jed, who is sitting astride the sofa fiddling with an elastic band, goes bright red and starts stretching the band more ferociously.

'I never got a letter about it,' says Uncle Ian.

'We sorted it all out at the appointment. I made a note of all the times,' says Granny, handing him a cup of tea. 'She probably didn't think she needed to write.'

'You might have mentioned it,' says Ian.

Jed pulls the elastic band over his nose so that his features are all distorted.

'I'm sorry,' says Granny, her hands fluttering a little as she speaks. 'I thought I had mentioned it actually, but I must be getting forgetful in my old age.'

Jed pulls the band so taut it looks like it's going to break.

'Do you remember when you had to go to the hospital to have your verruca burned off?' says Granny, sitting down on a pouffe which makes her look even smaller than usual. 'What a fuss you made!' She laughs softly and Jed releases the tension in the band for a moment.

'That was Andrew, not me,' says Uncle Ian flatly.

Granny looks as if she's about to disagree with him, but then doesn't. 'Why don't I get some biscuits,' she says, getting up.

'I don't want some counsellor sending him the same way as his loopy mother,' Uncle Ian calls after her.

Jed's elastic band goes flying across the room, landing on Grandad's paper. Grandad looks up and glares. 'That Paki lad getting stabbed has stirred things up a bit round here,' he says.

'I bet it has, Dad,' says Uncle Ian.

'I was at the parade the other day and I thought there was going to be a fight.' (Grandad's told us this story about seventeen times already, but he's obviously glad to have a new audience.) 'Boys on bikes and Asian lads in their robes shouting at each other. Not sure which is worse.'

'At least the yobs are British!' says Uncle Ian.

'That young lad from across the road was there,' says Grandad.

I look up. So does Jed. Grandad hasn't mentioned this before.

'He was shouting at the lads on bikes about how they'd get what was coming to them for stabbing his cousin.'

'Which brother?' I ask.

'Can't say as I recall,' says Grandad. 'I get their names muddled up.'

'Even if you could tell one from the other!' Uncle Ian laughs and so does Grandad and, for a moment, they look a lot alike.

'Are you going to meet your army friends again?' Jed asks suddenly.

Uncle Ian nods.

'Can I come?' asks Jed.

'Isn't he a bit young for that?' says Grandad and I wonder for a moment if Ian has told him about the bomb squad.

'Never too young to start learning to be a man,' says Ian. 'Sure you can, son! Just don't tell your gran, eh!'

Jed smiles, but he doesn't actually look that happy.

'I hear Karen's been making a nuisance of herself again,' says Uncle Ian when Granny returns with the biscuits.

Granny glances at Grandad, who just shrugs as if to say, *Of course I told him. What did you expect?*

I glance at Jed, who has ducked down behind the

sofa to retrieve the elastic band. He emerges red-faced, pulling angrily on it.

'I'm glad you didn't have to see that, son,' Uncle Ian says to Jed.

Jed just shrugs and pulls the band so tight it looks as if it'll break.

'And I'm sorry you got hurt, Mum,' he says, turning to Granny. 'Dad told me about the fall.'

'Oh, it was nothing,' says Granny quickly. 'And it was my own silly fault anyway.'

'You have to remember that she's not well,' says Ian. 'It's an illness. I'm not saying she can't help herself because she could go and get help and she won't, but she's sick – that's why she is how she is.'

'And that's why the court won't let her see Jed?' asks Granny, offering him a biscuit.

'That and the fact he doesn't want to,' says Uncle Ian, taking a biscuit and dropping it into his mouth whole. 'The courts take into account kids' views these days, which is a good thing, if you ask me.'

'So if he wanted to see her, he could?' asks Granny.

'In theory, yes, but he doesn't, do you, son?'

'No,' says Jed, colouring a little.

'And what about you, Ian?' asks Granny. 'What do you think?' She's looking at him with an odd expression on her face.

'If it was down to me, he'd see her on a regular basis,' says Ian, helping himself to another biscuit. 'But I'm not going to force the lad. It's his decision and I think we have to respect that.'

'Of course,' says Granny, although she still sounds uncertain. 'We have to respect his decision.'

'Don't let her get to you, Granny,' says Jed. 'She does that. She makes you feel sorry for her. You just have to ignore her. That's what I do.'

Granny looks at Jed and she seems really sad. 'Is that what you do, love?' she asks.

'The lad's right,' says Uncle Ian. 'Don't let her get to you.'

'I'll try not to,' says Granny.

AUGUST 9TH

Last night, after we went to bed, Gary called and talked to Granny for ages. She spoke in a soft voice, so that I couldn't make out what they were saying.

When we're eating breakfast, I try to ask her about it, but she just says, 'It's nothing for you to worry about,' and then she stands up and starts clearing up the breakfast stuff.

I sit there, finishing my boiled egg. Granny and I are slow eaters – Granny because of her sore fingers and me because – well, just because. I'm always the last to finish and normally Granny sits with me long after Jed and Grandad have left and then we tidy away and wash up together. But today she doesn't wait for me, so I can tell something is wrong.

'Jed's mum really misses him, doesn't she?' I say.

Granny stops what she's doing and looks at me. 'I imagine she does, yes.'

'Do *you* think she should be allowed to see him?' I ask.

After a moment, she says, 'That's not for us to decide. We have courts and judges who are better placed to make those decisions.'

'But you think he'd be happier if she was, don't you?'

She stands very still and she doesn't look away. 'Possibly,' she says. 'I don't know.'

'I do,' I say.

Then I turn back round so I don't have to look at her as I ask my next question. 'You still miss my dad, don't you?'

She stays very still as she answers. 'Every day. Yes.'

'Mums don't . . . forget . . . do they?' I say.

'No,' she answers quietly. 'No, they don't.'

And she stands there, waiting for another question, but I don't ask one so eventually she says, 'Is there anything else you wanted to ask?'

'No,' I say.

So I get on with eating my breakfast and she gets on with the washing-up and nothing more is said.

THINGS I'D LIKE TO KNOW ABOUT GRANNY

1. Why doesn't she like my mum? I once read somewhere that mothers never like the girls their sons marry because they take them away, but my dad's gone anyway. Does Granny blame my mum for him dying then? And if so, why? Or is it because my mum's got a new boyfriend? Or is it because she thinks my mum has forgotten about me?

2. If my dad was still alive and he split up from Mum, would she tell him that I should be allowed to see her?

3. I was going to say, does she ever visit my dad's grave, but he doesn't have a grave. I think his name may be on a plaque at Ground Zero but I'm not sure and anyway, I know she's never been to America because she doesn't like aeroplanes. (Is that because of what happened to Dad or was she always that way?)

4. Did she have a favourite child and who was it – my dad or Uncle Ian?

5. Did she like Auntie Karen before she split up with Uncle Ian?

6. Would she have let Auntie Karen in yesterday if Grandad hadn't been around?

7. What will she say if Uncle Ian finds out about her taking Jed to see Granny Brenda? (Priti says it's not *if* but *when*; she watches a lot of soap operas.)

8. If Uncle Ian is in the bomb squad, does she know about it?

9. Why does she let Grandad watch TV all the time and not do any of the cooking or cleaning, even though she's the one with bad hands?

10. Does she ever wish she had more grandchildren?

11. (I reckon I can have another one because No. 3 wasn't really a question.) Why won't she tell me what Gary said on the phone last night?

* * *

Shakeel and Ameenah are getting married today. It's the main wedding ceremony and then they have a big dinner and the newly wedded couple sit together for the first time, but they can only see each other through mirrors (according to Priti). We all watch from the front window as Shakeel goes off in a big limo dressed like a prince from *Aladdin*. There aren't any drums or musicians though, or a horse for that matter. Priti says the groom has to arrive on an elephant or a horse with music and banging drums, but they're going in a car and meeting up with the music men nearer the venue because it would be too far for them to walk.

Priti looks weird wearing a sari and with her hair all neat and tidy. I half expect to see her wheelie shoes peeping out from the bottom of the folds of silk. She sees us watching from the window and waves wildly till her mum tells her to stop and get in the car.

'I never thought I'd live to see the day!' says Grandad, who's watching with us from the sitting-room window.

'Nor should you have to, Dad. Nor should you have to!' says Uncle Ian, who stayed the night and is now sitting in Grandad's chair, reading the newspaper and refusing to watch. 'We're in Birmingham, not Bombay.'

I take out my notebook. I've started a new Bomb-busters strip with Jed-eye, Ben-D and Lil' Priti hunting down the person who attacked Lil' Priti's cousin. I draw Priti in her tutu skirt and an oversize pair of wheelies, karate-kicking a skinhead on a giant motorbike.

Grandad tells Uncle Ian about the party that's going to happen tomorrow in the road.

'You gonna have a load of Muslims throwing a party in the cul-de-sac?' says Uncle Ian.

'It's some kind of thing they do,' Grandad says. 'A custom or whatever.'

'To build a bond between the two families,' adds Granny.

'And they've got to take over the road to do that?'

'They want to extend their hospitality to all their neighbours,' says Granny.

'They don't do things by halves,' says Grandad. 'Pre-wedding parties. Post-wedding parties. Must be costing a fortune.'

'Who do they think they are?' asks Uncle Ian. 'Lords of the manor throwing a party for all the poor white locals?'

'It's tradition,' says Granny. 'I'm actually quite looking forward to it!'

'Maybe it's tradition where they come from, but not round here it's not. They want to be British, they should do things like the Brits. What's wrong with a white dress and a knees-up at a posh hotel?'

'I rather like all the colourful dresses,' says Granny. 'And the food is supposed to be wonderful at an Indian wedding.'

'That's as may be, but let's not forget one thing,' says Uncle Ian. 'Those people killed your son.'

I stop drawing. Granny goes pale and her hands flutter by her side.

'So before you get all "love thy neighbour", just remember they are the people who flew aeroplanes into tower blocks, yeah?' he goes on.

I see paper aeroplanes, tumbling towers of bricks, men falling like leaves.

'And all so they can eat curry on their wedding day and wear bleedin' red saris. Heaven forbid their daughters should wear a white meringue like English girls. They make no effort to fit in with the traditions

309

of the country that keeps them in silks and spices and you're happy to let them take over the street you live in and fill it with the stench of Bombay spice!'

Granny looks really upset. 'The Muhammeds weren't responsible for what happened to Andrew,' she says quietly, holding her hands still now.

'You can think that if you like,' says Uncle Ian. 'But from where I'm sitting every Muslim in the world is accountable for what happened to my brother.'

'It's only one day,' says Granny, who has turned away from the window now and looks close to tears.

'It's the thin end of the wedge,' says Uncle Ian.

'That's enough, Ian,' says Grandad. 'You're upsetting your mother.' It's the first time I've ever seen anyone stand up to Uncle Ian and by the look on his face, I don't think he likes it one bit.

But he doesn't say a word.

Uncle Ian takes Jed with him to meet his bomb-squad buddies. Granny thinks they're going tenpin bowling. Grandad is watching some chat show with lie-detector tests.

Granny suggests we have a special mid-morning hot chocolate. She looks tired, so I make the hot chocolate while she sits at the table.

'I've found you another photo of your dad when he was about your age,' she says, reaching into her cardigan pocket then passing me an envelope which I don't open. 'You do look awfully like him.'

'Thanks,' I say. I place the mugs of hot chocolate on the table, sit down and look at the envelope. I don't open it.

'I've been giving some thought to the other things too,' she says. 'The things on your list that you wanted to know about your dad. I can help you with them if you want. Do you?' Without her make-up on she looks more like an old lady than usual.

I nod.

'Then let me see,' she says, taking my list out of her pocket and unfolding it in front of her. Then she takes out another piece of paper on which she's written some notes.

'Who was his favourite *Star Wars* character?' she reads then looks up and smiles, although her eyes look

311

a bit teary. 'I had a think about this one and was there a chap with a dark helmet who breathed a bit funny? Darth something? Wait there, I've written it down. Your grandfather reminded me.'

'Darth Vader?' I say.

'That's the one. I think he was the one your dad liked most.'

I imagine Darth Vader lifting off his helmet to reveal my dad's smiling face.

'So he liked the Dark Side too!'

'I think all little boys do,' says Granny, 'for a while anyway.' Then she peers at the paper again (she has reading glasses, but she refuses to wear them). 'Now the football one was a bit easier because I know he always got so excited when England were playing. I remember him and your grandfather watching one match where England beat Germany by five goals to something.'

'Five–one,' I say. 'World Cup Qualifier. Summer 2001.'

'That was the one!' she says. 'Your dad got so excited, even Grandad got into the spirit of it. Andrew used to say he was an England supporter before anything else.'

'Me too!' I say.

'Well, there you go then.' She pauses, seems to think of something. 'That match must have been only a week or two before he died. I never thought about that before.'

Then she is quiet for a moment and I look at my mug of hot chocolate, so that I won't have to see if she starts to cry.

Then she coughs and says, 'Now I'm afraid I can't tell you who he thought was the best ever Sports Personality of the Year, but I did find this.' She passes me a plastic bag. Inside is a glossy book of photos called *British Sporting Heroes*. 'Your father was very fond of this book,' says Granny. 'I thought perhaps you might like it? Maybe you can tell which were his favourites by seeing which page it falls open on.'

I smile and run my hands over the pages, thinking of my dad's hands doing the same.

'As for the other things . . .' She peers at the list

again. 'I know he and Ian used to like making little bonfires, but I think they used matches.'

'Oh,' I say.

I try to picture my dad and Uncle Ian as small boys, making a bonfire in the garden.

'And by "keepy-uppies" do you mean the thing that Jed does when he bounces the ball off himself over and over again?'

I nod.

'Well, he wasn't very good at those. Not as good as Ian – or Jed for that matter.'

Me neither, I think.

'But I do know that he was a morning person,' Granny goes on, smiling now. 'And that he'd definitely have been good cop because he would let you get away with murder he loved you so much.' Then she adds, a fraction too late, 'As I'm sure your mum does too.'

She peers closely at the paper again, scanning down the page to the last few questions.

'What did he smell like and what did it feel like to hug him? I liked this one.' She smiles again. 'And it's really two questions, you know, so you did come up with ten things to ask about your dad after all.'

She looks at me and I nod, because I guess she's right.

'So, what did he smell like? Well, for the first year or so, I remember him smelling of baby sick and milky poo.' I giggle and so does she. 'Then later he smelt of farts as all little boys do! Then there was that horrid teenage deodorant he wore and VO5 hair gel and spot cream.'

'And when he was grown up?' I ask.

'He had some aftershave – I don't know what it was called, but when I smell it, I always think of him. And then he went back to smelling of baby sick again after you were born because you kept throwing up everywhere. He always had a milky blob on his shoulder, but he never did mind.'

I imagine my dad with baby sick all over his shoulder and the thought makes me smile, but when I look at Granny, she has a faraway look in her eyes, like she's trying to remember something – or perhaps forget.

'I kept a jumper of his that he left here once,' she says a little distractedly. 'I used to think I could smell him on it, but I'm not sure now. But here it is anyway. If you want to put it in your box or just keep it, that's fine.' She passes me another bag from under the table, but I don't open this one. I just sit with it there on my lap – Dad's jumper, still with the scent of Dad in it. I daren't open it in case I don't recognise the smell.

'What did it feel like to hug him?' she reads and I can see tears in her eyes now. 'That really is a good question. These are very good. She smiles, but doesn't look at me. Her voice is crackly as she says, 'Let me see. As a baby, he was such a one for hugs. I felt as if I could hold on to him forever.' She hesitates and I can tell she's trying not to cry. 'And when he grew up, he still gave wonderful bear hugs. He seemed so big – my tiny boy all grown into a man.'

She stops for a long while after saying this. I sip my hot chocolate and try to think of Priti in her sari hitting the wedding guests with flowers (which is what they do apparently). They're celebrating a wedding while me and Granny are here: an old lady and a boy sitting at the kitchen table talking about someone who is never coming back.

Granny is properly crying now so I get up and put my arm round her shoulder, which is what I always do when my mum cries. Granny looks up and wipes her eyes. 'Sorry – silly old Granny,' she says. 'Now what's the last question? What did he think of you, little man?' She looks up at me and puts a hand to my face. 'He thought the same as me,' she says, smiling through tears. 'He thought you were the best boy in the world.'

We finish our hot chocolates (Granny's must have been stone cold by the time she drank it), and Granny goes to get changed and put her face on. I sit at the kitchen table, but I don't take my notebook out. I look at Dad's book, but not at the picture or the jumper.

When Granny comes down again, we get the chess set out. Since Jed's been here we haven't had much chance to play.

'Dad played chess, didn't he?' I say, thinking of the chess trophy in the little bedroom.

'He did,' says Granny. 'He was school chess champion two years running!' She looks dead proud when she says this, just like Mum does when I do something good.

'Mum can't play,' I say, starting to set out all the little pieces on the board. 'So I'm glad you do.'

And then Granny says, 'Your mum is coming home this weekend.'

I look up quickly as an electric pulse shoots through my stomach.

'She's just going to see how she is on her own for a bit,' Granny continues.

Another pulse. This one makes me feel sick. The good feeling from all the stuff about my dad drains away.

'If she's up to it, perhaps you can join her before school starts.'

But the word 'if' hangs in the air between us, big and resonant.

'And if she's not?' I say, looking down again.

'We'll see,' says Granny.

'Will Gary be there?' I ask, still not looking up.

'Yes,' says Granny. 'He's going to pick her up tomorrow.'

'So she won't be on her own. Gary will look after her.'

'Yes,' says Granny.

I can't think about my mum, going home without me. So instead, I try to think about Shakeel's wedding: the groom drinking sherbert; the newly-weds looking at each other through mirrors. I even try to imagine Shakeel blowing himself to smithereens in the middle of the party, an eruption of colour as guests and banquet explode into the air.

'That's good news,' I say.

One time, when we were looking on the Internet, Priti found this thing about bereaved kids who blame themselves for the death of a loved one. *'Sometimes you blame yourself. Did you cause the person to die?'* it said. *'Was it because of something you thought? Was it because you argued, stayed out late or were untidy or noisy? Feeling this can make you angry with yourself and everyone around you. But you did not cause the death, however naughty or badly behaved you think you have been. Death has many causes, but is never a result of the way you think or behave.'*

Priti asked if I thought it was my fault my dad died. Did I do something really bad that caused his death? 'No, of course not,' I said at the time. But I've been thinking about it a lot since and, despite what that website said, I've been wondering if maybe I did.

Mum says when I was a toddler, I once pulled nine keys off her laptop keyboard (she only got her thing about computers after dad died) and threw them down a crack in the floorboards. My dad was away working at the time and she had to send him an email without using the 'e' 'f' 's' 't' 'a' 'r' 'l' 'o' or 'd' buttons, which was hard work as there aren't that many words you can make without using at least one of those. Try it sometime and you'll see.

Another time I dug up all the bulbs dad had spent hours planting in the garden (he was into gardening – that's one thing I know about him, I guess) and scattered them all over the lawn. And another time I took a bite out of the washing machine – the rubbery bit round the door that stops the water coming out – and it leaked all over the kitchen floor. I also did a poo on the floor then trampled it all over the carpet before putting my hands in it and smearing it all over my clothes and my face and hair. I was only a toddler and I guess I wasn't such a clean freak back then.

So I was naughty, but then all toddlers are naughty, aren't they? That's what they're supposed to be like. That's why they call it the terrible twos, isn't it? And the things I did, although they must have been pretty annoying, don't sound bad enough to have killed my dad. Do they?

But my mum told me once that Dad had resigned from his job just before he was killed. He handed in his resignation in August and was just working out his notice period. He didn't want to work away from home so much, she said. He wanted to spend more time with his family. With me.

So maybe if I'd been a nicer baby, and more fun to be around, he'd have handed in his resignation a month earlier and then he'd never have been in New York at all that day. He'd have been at home with us.

Perhaps it's like a football match, when your team is playing and you don't want to go to the loo in case the other side scores while you aren't looking. Maybe it was like that with my dad: I didn't keep my eye on the ball, didn't will him to stay alive enough. Because if I had, he wouldn't have died.

When it comes to my mum, I've always tried to be extra, extra careful. I've tried to look out for her: make sure she eats even when it means sitting at the table with her for over an hour; tell her I love her at least once a day; tell her she looks beautiful, that she's a great mum.

And I've always tried to be good, never get in trouble, never break the rules. Because I don't want to lose another parent.

Only maybe I already have.

AUGUST 10TH

Despite what Uncle Ian said about Asian weddings he stays overnight again and hangs around today to go to the street party. And for some reason he's in a really good mood. Jed, on the other hand, is acting even weirder than usual. I ask him what it was like meeting his dad's bomb-squad buddies and if they talked about any of the terror suspects they'd apprehended. But he just said, 'It's confidential. Need-to-know basis, OK?'

'So they really are bomb squad?'

'I told you they were, didn't I?'

'Um – sort of,' I say. 'So what did they talk about?'

'Well, I can't say, can I? It's classified.'

'Just tell me if it's to do with Shakeel,' I say.

'I'm afraid you need higher security clearance for that sort of information,' he says smugly. And then he refuses to talk about it any more.

So we help Priti and her brothers get things ready for the party. We set up long tables at the end of the cul-de-sac, in the bit where people normally turn their cars, and we hang bunting from the lamp posts. Mik helps us set up a huge pair of speakers which blare out tinny music with a lady wailing (which is really cool in Pakistan apparently). Then a white van – like a fish-and-chip van – turns up to serve everyone curry from big steaming saucepans, the biggest you've ever seen, like witches' cauldrons.

Then loads of people turn up – old grannies and little kids too, all dressed up for the wedding. More Asian people than I've ever seen in my life. Zara is there with a bunch of girls wearing saris. Her sari is sky blue and it makes her look so beautiful I can hardly look at her. Mik – who looks totally different in a robe, like one of Shakeel's – hovers close to the sari girls, trying to talk to them, until Zara tells him to get lost.

And then the neighbours come out of their houses, wearing a funny assortment of clothes like none of them could decide quite what to wear to an Asian wedding. Granny (who's wearing her Sunday best, but not a hat, on Grandad's advice) says it's just like a royal-wedding street party. Grandad (who always wears a shirt and tie and isn't about to change for a load of 'foreigners') just goes '*Hmmph*!' although I reckon he's impressed too.

Uncle Ian (wearing jeans and a polo shirt) goes to stand with Stevie's mum and dad (strappy sundress; shirt and shorts combo) who've set up deckchairs on their drive and are drinking beer. The rest of the neighbours (in a mix of church clothes and stuff you might wear to the beach) all hang around the edges, hovering on their driveways and not mingling with the guests around the tables.

But then the curry is served and it's a free-for-all because it smells so good and that's when the colours start to mix up a bit. I even see my grandad chatting with Ameenah (who's wearing a red sari, the colour of poppies and the lipstick my mum wore the day she left for the hospital), while Granny chats to the ladies who made the curry about the ingredients they used.

The good thing about it is that there are so many people that nobody's really looking out for me and Jed and Priti, so we can do whatever we want. We skip curry and just eat bowlfuls of pudding, then we crawl under the tables to play Bomb-busters and Priti's beautiful sari gets covered in dirt. We make a base under the largest table and check out people's legs for a bit. (I remember what Priti said about shoes having a personality and I imagine them with faces, wigs, accessories.) Then Jed suggests we go mine-sweeping.

'What's that?' I ask.

'It's when you swipe the dregs of all the beers that the grown-ups leave around,' he explains. 'It's great. You can get really pissed.'

'Right,' I say.

'Bet you've never even had lager before,' says Jed.

'I have,' I lie.

'What does it taste like then?'

'It's nice,' I say, trying desperately to seem more convincing. 'And it makes you feel like laughing.'

'Liar,' says Jed.

'No alcohol at a Muslim wedding,' says Priti. Her face is smudged with pudding and her hair is coming loose from the tight plaits her mum put in this morning. She's persuaded her mum to let her wear her wheelies today, so, all in all, she looks a bit more like her normal self.

'My dad's drinking,' says Jed. 'And so are some of the neighbours.'

Jed's right. Uncle Ian has brought along a couple of six packs and is drinking straight from a can. Stevie's mum and dad are drinking too, although I'm sure my mum told me once that you're not meant to have alcohol when you're pregnant.

'I thought you weren't supposed to drink when you're having a baby,' I say.

'Maybe by the time you're that fat it doesn't matter any more,' suggests Jed.

Stevie's dad has taken his shirt off and his chest looks red from the sun. He and Uncle Ian are laughing loudly about something. They sound like they've drunk quite a lot already.

'What's your dad doing here anyway?' says Priti. 'Shouldn't he be off catching some terrorists or something?'

Jed glares at her then says, 'Maybe he thinks something's going to go down right here.'

'Is that what he said?' I ask.

'Can't give you that level of clearance,' says Jed.

'Jed reckons he's got some inside information he's not telling us,' I say.

'From his dad and his imaginary anti-terror squad?' Priti laughs.

'What's that supposed to mean?' says Jed.

'It means, I reckon your dad's more nine-to-five than MI5,' says Priti.

'Oh, yeah?' says Jed. 'Come on then. Let's go over and check out what's going down.'

'If you say so,' says Priti. 'We can nick some of their lager while we're at it.'

Uncle Ian is adding his cans of lager to those already floating in Mr Sanders' bucket of ice water.

'Is he allowed to drink on duty?' I ask.

'He's got to blend in, hasn't he?' says Jed.

'An ex-squaddie necking beer at a Muslim wedding,' says Priti. 'Oh, yeah, he really blends in.'

So we sneak out from under the table and hide out behind a bush that divides the Sanders' driveway from Granny and Grandad's.

Jed wants to start mine-sweeping straight away, but Priti's more interested in checking out his dad's bomb-squad credentials.

'For a spook, he's not exactly good-looking,' Priti whispers, peering round the bush then pulling her head back in quickly.

'He's supposed to be catching terrorists, not entering a beauty pageant,' Jed whispers, trying to nab a half-finished can of beer by Uncle Ian's feet.

Just then his dad turns around and catches him red-handed. Uncle Ian grabs Jed's arm and yanks him to his feet so hard it looks like he's going to dislocate his shoulder. 'If you take even one sniff of my beer, I'll break your neck, kid.'

We all freeze.

There's a long moment before Uncle Ian starts to laugh. 'Only kidding, son. Never too young to start learning to hold your beer.'

He pulls Jed's head to his chest in a rough embrace that looks like it hurts and all the other adults laugh.

'Where have you stashed your Paki mate and that deaf mute cousin of yours?' says Uncle Ian.

'They're just . . .' Jed tails off, waving in the

direction of the bush that me and Priti are crouching behind.

Rumbled, we stand up and step forward, trying to make it look like we weren't hiding, but not really succeeding.

'Been fumbling around in the bushes with your girlfriend, have you, Ben?' says Uncle Ian. I feel myself reddening to the very roots of my hair. I try to answer, but nothing comes out. 'So come on, who's your Bombay babe?'

Jed looks at his feet and mutters something.

'Speak up, son. Don't mumble!' barks Uncle Ian.

'Priti,' Jed says quietly.

'I asked you what her name was, not if you thought she was fit!' says Uncle Ian, knocking back a mouthful of beer and laughing. The others all join in, even Stevie's mum.

'That *is* my name,' says Priti. 'Are you deaf or something?'

I tense, waiting for Uncle Ian's response.

'No, but your mother must have been blind to have given you a name like that,' he says quietly. Then he laughs, too loud, too quickly. 'But I guess even the elephant man's mama thought he was beautiful, eh!'

Everyone laughs again. Priti looks furious.

'So which one is the suicide bomber then, kid?' says Uncle Ian. 'Sorry, little lady. I hope that doesn't cause you offence?'

'Don't mind me,' says Priti.

'My son reckons one of your neighbours is part of a terror cell,' Uncle Ian says, turning to Stevie's dad and releasing Jed from the headlock with a shove that sends him flying.

Stevie's dad laughs and says, 'Oh, yeah? Which one should I steer clear of then?'

'That one,' says Jed, picking himself up and pointing to Shakeel.

'So much for keeping it to ourselves,' Priti hisses.

Jed doesn't even look at her. He's rubbing his neck, but I reckon his pride is hurt more than anything else.

'Yeah, he looks like the type,' says Stevie's dad, his face red with alcohol.

'They all look the type,' says Uncle Ian. He takes a swig of his beer. 'I'm surprised you can stand to see your street overrun with this lot. Can't stand the sight of them, me, and I've heard the stink of curry brings the house prices down by ten per cent.'

He grins like what he's said is really funny.

'There's no way he's actually bomb squad,' Priti whispers in my direction. 'I mean, he's not exactly deep cover, is he?'

'Do you reckon he's going to blow us all up today?' Jed says. Priti snorts. Jed ignores her. 'With all these people here?'

I glance at Priti, who just rolls her eyes.

'It'd be all too easy to hide a bomb under that poncy robe,' says Stevie's mum, pulling on a cigarette and glaring at Priti.

'Yeah, I thought the bride was supposed to be the one in the white dress!' says Mr Sanders, winking at me.

'Nah, it won't be today. There are too many of his own kind here,' says Uncle Ian in a serious tone now. 'It's good, honest white folks he wants to kill.'

'Not you then!' whispers Priti under her breath.

'You got something to say, little memsahib?' says Uncle Ian.

'No,' says Priti, who has her hands on her hips and a defiant look on her face.

'Cos the terrorist – he's your brother, right?'

'One man's terrorist, another man's freedom fighter!' says Priti.

'You say tomato and I say . . .' He hesitates. 'I say, shut your little black mouth or I'll . . .'

'What exactly *will* you do to me in full view of two hundred of my closest friends and family?' Priti cuts in. 'Or perhaps *you'll* just blow us all up? That's what you ethnic minorities do, isn't it?'

Stevie's dad laughs at this, but none of the others join in.

I feel as if I should say or do something, but I don't. Instead, I imagine Uncle Ian blowing himself to smithereens.

Boom!

'She's got a right gob on her that one,' I hear Mrs Sanders mutter.

'I'd love to blow up the piggin' lot of you!' says Uncle Ian.

'Dad!' says Jed quietly.

333

'I'm sure my brother can lend you some explosives,' says Priti. 'I can ask him if you like?'

'Smart-arse little Muslim, aren't you?' says Uncle Ian. 'Just make sure you don't get your clever little butt kicked when your curry-house friends aren't around to take care of you, you know what I'm saying, kid?'

'Are you threatening me, mister?' says Priti.

'I'm not Supernanny. I don't bother with warnings. Just remember that.'

Then he turns to Jed whose face is flecked red and white, puts an arm round him and says, 'You've done good work here, kid! Get in with the natives to keep an eye on the terror suspect – nice tactic. I like it.'

Then he shoves his can of beer into my hand. 'Here, have this, daddy's boy. I'm dying for a slash.'

I feel my fist forming into a ball by my side. I imagine a giant boxing glove knocking him out cold.

Thwack!

But I don't say anything. Uncle Ian laughs and slaps me hard on the shoulder so that the beer spills all over the front of my trousers. Then he staggers off in the direction of our house. I watch him go, and in that moment, I can't decide who I hate more: him or me.

'Come on!' says Jed.

For once Priti doesn't argue and I'm too angry to. So, armed with what turns out to be nearly a full can of beer, which Jed grabs off me and hides not very successfully under his T-shirt, the three of us head off in the direction of the tree house for 'a bender'.

'Thanks for standing up for me, you two,' says Priti crossly.

'Sorry,' I mutter. Jed says nothing.

'Is your dad always so delightful?' Priti asks.

'He's only doing his job,' says Jed, not looking at her.

'So did he miss out on the Charm Offensive section of his James Bond training?' says Priti. 'Or is harassing little girls part of the MI6 handbook these days?'

'You shouldn't have answered him back,' says Jed. 'He hates that.'

'Oh, yeah. Cos what happened back there was definitely my fault!'

But Jed doesn't have a chance to answer because

suddenly there's a deafening roar of engines and the screech of brakes. A biker gang are at the bottom of the road, blocking the entrance to the cul-de-sac: five or six of them on gleaming motorbikes, red and black and silver, glistening in the sun.

All the people at the party turn around to look at them and the talk and laughter fade away until all that can be heard is the tinny sound of the singer over the speakers and the hum of the bikes' engines. Then the biker in the middle takes off his helmet and we can all see that it's Tyreese.

I glance over to where Mik and Shakeel are standing, next to the curry van. Mik makes an angry movement like he's about to go and confront them, but Shakeel puts a restraining hand on his arm.

The bikers only stay a minute, less than that probably, although it feels like loads more. Then they rev up their bikes, turn around and leave.

Uncle Ian is the first person to say anything. Emerging from our house, he gives a cheer and shouts like he's at a football match. 'Come on, England!'

From the Sanders' drive comes an answering cry of,

'Eng-er-land! Eng-er-land!' from Mr Sanders.

Everyone else is frozen, like a game of musical statues.

I think everyone is hoping it won't all kick off.

And it doesn't. Less than a minute after the bikers have gone, the Sanders and Uncle Ian start laughing and someone turns the music up and people start talking again, but it's not the happy buzz of chat it was previously.

'So much for keeping a low profile!' Priti hisses at Jed.

'What the hell do you know about counter-intelligence anyway?' says Jed.

'More than your dad, I reckon,' says Priti.

Just then Zara appears and grabs Priti.

'Keep lookout for me, will you?' she hisses, looking around her nervously.

'Please tell me you're only hooking up with that idiot to tell him he's dumped?'

'Will you keep a lookout or what?' she says, not answering the question.

'What's it worth?'

'Same as usual.'

'You'll have to make it worth our while if we're going to be stuck up a tree while there's a party going on!' says Priti.

'What do you want then?' Zara says impatiently, glancing at her phone.

Priti thinks for a moment. 'I want your pink ankle bracelet and that new toe ring. AND I want your old handset – with a new top-up card.'

'And who are *you* gonna call?' says Zara. 'Ghostbusters?'

'Close,' Priti grins.

'You haven't got any mates apart from these two losers!' She smirks at Jed, who can't come up with a quick enough comeback.

'Then it's no deal,' says Priti, crossing her arms to show she's not budging (although we all know she's dead easy to bribe).

Zara looks well cross. Her mobile beeps and she glances at it. 'OK, fine,' she says quickly.

'What do *we* get?' Jed asks.

'A slap in the gob!' is Zara's response.

'Then we'll just go and tell your mum and dad, shall we?'

'If you're after another snog, you can have one,' says Zara. Jed grins. 'But if you think I'm kissing you here in front of everyone, you are off your rocker.'

The smile fades on Jed's face. 'When then?' he asks.

'Later, all right?'

'You'd better not be messing because I've got pictures on my phone that your parents would love to see,' says Jed.

Me and Priti exchange glances, not sure if he's bluffing.

Zara isn't sure either, but she says, 'Yeah, right!'

'Don't believe me then,' says Jed with a big grin on his face, hand still stuffed up his T-shirt holding the beer, so he looks a bit lopsided. 'But what if I'm telling the truth?'

'Just get up that tree, you little perv,' says Zara. 'You'll get what's coming to you later.'

Jed seems happy enough with this response and he blows Zara a kiss as we head off in the direction of the garden. She just holds her fingers up to her forehead in a 'W' sign, which Jed reckons means 'Whatever!' although Priti says she thinks it's something else!

So the three of us end up in the tree house drinking warm beer while everyone else is partying in the cul-de-sac.

'Have you really got pictures of Zara and Tyreese?' I ask.

'Wouldn't you like to know!' says Jed.

'I bet he has too,' says Priti. 'He's a peeping Tom!'

'I like to think I'm more like the paparazzi,' Jed grins.

From our vantage point we can see the bikers in the park, their motorcycles parked up against the swings. When Zara appears, they all start to whistle and catcall, but she just stands, hands on hips, and stares them down and that makes them shut up.

Then she goes right up to Tyreese, whispers something to him then turns and walks off in the direction of the woods. Her hips are swinging and she doesn't look back. Tyreese hesitates for a moment before getting off his bike to follow her. The other lads call after him, but he just ignores them. He looks a bit sheepish and it occurs to me for the first time that he might actually really like Zara.

While he and Zara are off in the woods doing whatever they do (Jed reckons they've made up – Priti doesn't, and she also refuses to discuss what they might be doing if they *have* made up) we take turns to sip the beer, which tastes warm and bitter. Jed says it's called 'wife beater', 'Cos it makes you want to beat up your wife!' He laughs.

'Is that why your dad likes it then?' asks Priti.

'What you trying to say?'

'I'm just wondering if he ever hit your mum,' Priti shrugs. 'Maybe that's why she left him?'

'Don't be soft. My dad never did anything to her.'

'Which is exactly what you would say,' says Priti.

'You don't get it, do you?' says Jed, his face red, just like his dad's when he was shouting at Priti. 'My mum is the evil cow, not my dad.'

'If you say so,' says Priti.

'I do,' says Jed. 'So just shut up, all right.'

Priti just grins and that makes Jed all the more angry, but he doesn't say anything after that and neither does

Priti. We all sit and watch in silence as bikers hang off the climbing frame and try to do headstands on the swings. They look like big overgrown kids or monkeys – far less frightening mucking around off their bikes than on them.

'Do you reckon they really did knife that boy?' I ask after a bit.

'Probably,' says Priti. 'Tyreese hates Asians.'

'So does my dad, but he doesn't go around stabbing them, does he?' Jed says. 'But then he doesn't go round *doing* them either!'

'No, it's just you who wants to do that!' Priti retorts.

'I don't want to *do* any Paki,' says Jed.

'Yeah, you do. You want to do my sister. Don't try to deny it – it's obvious.' Then Priti starts to do an impression of Jed. 'Can I have a kiss, Zara? I'll keep quiet if you let me, Zara.' She flops her head around just like Jed does. Jed looks as if he might explode.

Fortunately, he doesn't get a chance to because just then a gang of kids come running along the alleyway below, shouting and screaming as they emerge into the park. Young kids from the wedding, playing a game of tag. Little Stevie is with them, running at the back, her arms outstretched like she's flying, a broad grin on her face.

'Looks like that kid has finally found some friends,' says Priti.

'What if their parents come looking for them?' I say. 'We need to warn Zara.'

'Good point,' says Priti, suddenly serious.

We all start scrambling down the tree and Priti sticks two fingers in her mouth and gives out a high-pitched whistle intended for Zara.

'D'you reckon she heard that?' she asks. 'Can't have the mosque gossips catch her snogging a racist thug on her brother's wedding day.'

'D'you reckon that's what they're doing?' says Jed.

'Whatever she's doing, we'd better go get her.'

But just then a couple of the little kids' mums appear, looking for their children.

The kids are running around the playground now, oblivious to the bikers, who for some reason don't seem to scare them. But the women in their saris are scared and they hang back, calling to the children. The bikers start to shout and jeer at them, but the kids take no notice and keep running around.

Me and Jed and Priti jump down over the fence into the park, but we can't go running off to the woods without one of the women noticing, so we just stand there, watching, hoping Zara won't choose this particular moment to re-emerge.

Priti whistles again, twice this time. 'I hope she knows that means "stay where you are",' she says.

The mothers keep calling to the children, but they take no notice. Eventually, two of the women have to go into the playground to get them and the bikers crowd close to them, jostling and heckling, laughing loud like hyenas.

With the bikers following them, the women hurriedly round up the kids – all except Stevie whose mum is probably still drinking with Uncle Ian. Now the children are starting to look a bit frightened too. The bikers don't actually touch them, but they kick up dust and take turns in blocking their way out.

A bottle smashes and one of the children lets off a scream as glass shards fly.

'We should go,' says Jed.

'We can't. We promised Zara,' hisses Priti.

The women and children head for the exit, the bikers still following them. More flying glass as another bottle is thrown on to the tarmac path, right in front of the women. The glass shards explode like a bomb, narrowly missing the kids' faces. A third bottle shatters against the fence. The bikers laugh. A couple of the children have started crying.

One of women sees us and says something to Priti in Punjabi. She replies in English. 'It's OK. My mum lets me come here!'

The woman says something else. Priti mutters something then raises an eyebrow at us. 'OK, let's go,' she says.

'But Zara . . .' I say, glancing in the direction of the trees.

'We've got no choice,' says Priti. 'They're going to tell Shakeel if we don't come.'

As the women crowd hastily into the alleyway, the

bikers fall back, laughing and whooping and throwing more bottles. We get dragged along with the kids and the mums and the last thing I see as I turn to leave is little Stevie. She's been left behind – I guess her mum and dad don't mind her being in the park, or at least they haven't come looking for her – and she's standing in the middle of the tarmac bit with her arms aloft spinning round and round and round. She hardly seems to have noticed the bikers at all.

'Do you think we should get her to come with us?' I say.

Priti shrugs and Jed says, 'Nah. She'll be OK. They won't bother with a white kid.'

Still, I feel a bit bad about leaving Stevie, but the bikers are jeering louder than ever, catcalling and smashing glass, and Priti is dragging us away.

As we head down the alleyway, I glance back and see little Stevie, still spinning windmills on the tarmac.

Uncle Ian is in the alleyway. He's arguing with someone – we can hear raised voices – but the mums and kids are pushing past him, so we can't see who it is at first. It's only when we're nearly upon them that we see it's Auntie Karen.

She turns to look at us at about the same time we spot her.

'Jed,' she says, stretching her arms out to him. 'Baby!'

But the minute he sees her, Jed turns on his heels and runs back down the alley, in the direction of the park. Back towards the bikers.

'Please, baby, come back!' shouts Auntie Karen. 'Jed – darling. I just needed to see you!' Her eyes are red and puffy and her make-up is smudged like she's been crying. Uncle Ian grabs hold of her so she can't run after him. Me and Priti stand frozen to the spot, not sure what to do.

'You see!' Uncle Ian is shouting at her. 'He wants nothing to do with you. Stop stalking him.'

'I only came to look at him, Ian.' She's turning to him now, pleading. Even with black streaks down her face she's still very pretty. 'I need him to know that I still care, that I haven't given up on him even if he's given up on me.'

'You're stalking him. That's what the police will say. Harassing him.'

'I wasn't even going to talk to him. I was just going to stay here and watch. Ian, please. A son needs his mother.' She looks desperate, but not mad – I half expected her to seem crazy, but she doesn't. Just sad, that's all.

'Not a mother like you.' Uncle Ian still has hold of her even though she's stopped struggling.

'What did I ever do to him?' she asks. 'I know I hurt you, but I never hurt him.'

He shoves her away when she says this – like she's spat on him or something. 'Just get out of here before I call the police.'

'And say what?' She's calmer now and it's Uncle Ian who looks mad. 'That I turned up for a rendezvous with my son on the day specified by the court? That you are flouting a contact order? That you are indoctrinating our son? Emotional abuse they call it – in the US people have lost custody over it. I know what you're doing and soon the judges will too, and then you'll be the one begging *me* for contact.'

'Just get out of here, you twisted old witch,' says Uncle Ian quietly, but with a dangerous look in his eye. 'I'm going to find *my* son. If you're still here when I get back, I'll call the police.'

Then he pushes past her and goes off towards the park.

Me and Priti are left standing there with Auntie Karen, not knowing what to say or do.

After a moment, she says to us, 'I'm sorry you had to hear that.'

'It's OK, Auntie Karen,' I say.

'I expect your mothers would fight to see you too,' she says with a little smile.

Just then Mik comes running down the alleyway, going in the direction of the park. He pushes past Auntie Karen and ignores me and Priti. He looks angry as hell.

'Oh, boy!' says Priti. 'We're really in trouble now. Come on, let's get out of here.'

She grabs my hand and drags me back in to the party. We leave Auntie Karen standing there, staring towards the park where Jed has gone.

* * *

Me and Priti sit under one of the tables, watching the entrance to the alleyway from under the long red and gold papery cloth and sipping at a can of cider that Priti's managed to swipe from Mrs Sanders. It's warm and I think it tastes pretty disgusting, only I don't say so.

It's ages before Jed reappears – without his dad – and he looks really upset. More upset than I've ever seen him in fact. More than the time in the pub, or when Auntie Karen was screaming outside Granny's house, or even when we went to see Granny Brenda.

Priti sticks her head out from under the table and whistles through her fingers. Jed clambers under the table then pulls the cloth right down like he doesn't want to be found and sits hunched up and shivering (although it's not even cold). When we ask him what's up, he says, 'Nothing!'

'Doesn't seem like nothing,' says Priti. 'What happened?'

'Nothing's happened,' says Jed.

'Fine,' says Priti. 'You don't have to tell us if you don't want to.'

'There's nothing to tell.'

'If you say so.'

We all take turns to swig on the cider and I start to feel sick. Jed stares at the alleyway, but Mik doesn't reappear and neither does Uncle Ian or Zara. Priti reckons Mik and Zara might have got back into the house over the garden fence. 'Unless Mik caught Romeo and Juliet in the act, in which case – *hasta la vista*, Zara,' she says, grinning.

'My dad had to go home,' Jed says after a bit.

'Why didn't you say so?' asks Priti.

The mood of the party has changed and the Asian music has been replaced by English pop music. Some of the younger people are dancing while the older guests start to make their way home. Zara reappears from the house and starts dancing with a group of other Asian girls. She's got really bright lipstick and a new sari on – green and gold this time – and she has a big grin on her face like nothing is the matter, but she's wearing sunglasses, even though it's not sunny any more. And there's still no sign of Mik.

I don't know what time it is that people start clearing up. I suppose it must be quite late because it's starting to get dark. We crawl out from our cider den. (I feel all dizzy and sick and the sky looks really bright somehow, although it's nearly night.) And then I hear Stevie's mum calling for her.

Mrs Sanders does that thing at first that always makes my granny tut and get cross when she hears women do it in the supermarket. She starts to scream at Stevie to stop messing around – 'You little madam, where the bloody hell are you!' and, 'You get back here now or I'll give you one!' – that sort of thing. I can see Granny blanching because she hates hearing adults yelling like that at children.

But after a while Mrs Sanders starts saying, 'Where the hell is she?' and then, 'Has anyone seen my daughter?' and she starts sounding really worried and soon people are looking everywhere for Stevie – and no one can find her.

'She's probably fallen asleep somewhere,' says Granny and then someone suggests that she might have climbed into a car or garage and got trapped there, so we check all those places. And all the time it's getting darker and Stevie is nowhere to be found.

Someone asks the three of us if we know where she could be. I say that she was in the park earlier, but Priti glares at me and says we haven't seen her and Jed doesn't say anything. So some men, including Grandad and Stevie's dad, go and check out the park and Grandad comes back moaning about smashed beer bottles and more graffiti, but says there's no sign of Stevie.

Granny is comforting Stevie's mum, who's crying big fat tears (they must taste of cider, I reckon) and even Stevie's dad, who's a big man, looks smaller and not so drunk any more and no one knows where else to look.

Then someone suggests calling the police (which makes Stevie's mum cry even more) and Granny tells me and Jed to go inside. She doesn't want anything happening to us, she says.

Suddenly I realise that something might have happened to Stevie. Up till now I'd thought she was just hiding somewhere and had fallen asleep or got lost and she'd be found snoozing on a neighbour's sofa or something. I was too busy thinking about Zara and Mik and Tyreese, and what happened with Jed's mum and dad, so the idea that Stevie might be in some kind of danger hadn't crossed my mind. I think it had crossed Jed's though because he seems even more worried and upset than before.

Me and Jed go inside, but we keep watching from our window as the grown-ups keep looking in all the places they've already checked. And then the police turn up. Across the road we can see Priti and Zara watching from their window. Zara looks loads younger with her hair down and wearing her pyjamas. We wave and they wave back – even Zara. And it's hard to tell because of the light, but I could swear she's got a black eye.

Then Granny comes in and tells us to get into bed and I guess we fall asleep at some point because all night long I dream of Lil' Priti and Jed-eye and Ben-D trying to find a little girl who's gone missing. Only in my dream it's Blythe, not Stevie, who can't be found, and at some point she turns into my mum and I'm looking all over for her, but I can't find her anywhere.

I wake up in the middle of the night with a hangover (or at least I think it's a hangover because my head hurts a lot and I feel sick). When I look outside, the police car is still there, so I know Stevie is still missing.

AUGUST 11TH

It's a weird thing when a kid goes missing because everyone suddenly starts acting differently. All the neighbours are pretending to be friends with Stevie's mum and dad, even though Granny says they've been moaning about the state of their front garden and their gaudy Christmas lights for years. And first thing in the morning they come out of their houses, in their slippers and their dressing gowns, and they talk to each other in low voices in the middle of the street – neighbours who've barely said hello to each other for years, Grandad says – suddenly all matey with each other.

The other thing I notice is that everyone is looking at their watches all the time. Jed says this is because cases like this are time critical.

But other than the police car permanently parked outside Stevie's house, and the fact that neighbours in their slippers are talking to each other over the privet hedges, you'd never know anything had happened here yesterday. Grandad said that the cul-de-sac would be covered in litter and all the flower beds trampled after the party, but actually everything's been tidied up just like new, so I'm guessing the Muhammeds were up late last night clearing things away. 'So much for Shakeel's wedding night,' says Jed, earning him a look from Granny.

This morning, Mr Muhammed is out with a can of paint going over the new graffiti which has been painted along the fence down the alleyway, and we hear him telling old Mrs Underwood from No. 21 that his sons cleared the park of broken glass to make it safe for the kiddies.

We don't go over to Priti's. Granny says me and Jed aren't allowed out – just in case we go missing too, like there's suddenly a black hole or Bermuda Triangle in the cul-de-sac. So Jed and I hang around the house. I draw cartoons while Jed comes up with theories on Stevie's disappearance.

'Perhaps she's been abducted by aliens or transported back through a time vortex to another millennium,' says Jed.

I draw a spaceship hovering over the cul-de-sac, Stevie Sanders being beamed up on her pink bike with the tassels on the handlebars.

Granny says he's been watching too much *Dr Who*. Then she sighs and says that Stevie's mum and dad would probably welcome the appearance of a tardis with Stevie in it right now.

I draw a picture of Stee-V (I figured Stevie can be in the Bomb-busters strips too) being kidnapped by little green men while Jed-eye and Ben-D attack the spaceship with swords. Lil' Priti just stands by, eating a toffee apple.

About ten o'clock in the morning another police car arrives. Two officers get out and go round to all the houses in the cul-de-sac.

'Will they come here?' Jed asks.

'I should think they'll want to talk to everyone,' says Granny.

'Right,' says Jed, and he stops going on about UFOs and time travel after that.

Eventually, they come to our house – a policeman and a young policewoman with a ponytail, who

Grandad says doesn't look old enough to be out of school. Granny makes them a cup of tea and then they talk to Granny and Grandad first in the sitting room while me and Jed wait outside in the hallway. Although he keeps making jokes, Jed's in another of his weird moods.

'Do you reckon they'll talk to your dad too?' I ask.

'Why would they want to do that?' he snaps.

'I don't know,' I say. 'I just wondered.'

'He doesn't know anything, just like we don't,' says Jed, staring down at his shoe and kicking it against the banister.

'But we *were* nearly the last people to see her,' I say.

'No, we weren't,' he says quickly.

'How do you figure that then?'

'What about the bikers and Zara and Mik? They all saw her. They're just not saying so, that's all.'

'So was she still there when you went back to the park?'

No answer.

'What about your dad? Did he see her?'

But I don't get to hear his answer because just then

the policewoman comes out and says she wants to talk to us.

So me and Jed have to sit on the sofa side by side while the policewoman sits on the pouffe in front of us. It's too low, so her knees are nearly up to her chin as she asks us questions in a soft nursery-rhyme voice, as if we're about three years old. The other officer stands by the window, pretending to look out, but I know he's listening to everything we're saying: the old bad cop, good cop routine.

When did we last see Stevie? lady cop asks.

'In the park,' I reply.

'What time was that?'

'Not sure. Before it got dark,' I say.

'Who else was there?'

'The bikers,' I say. For some reason Jed is letting me do all the talking.

I glance at Granny and Grandad, who are standing in front of the fireplace, next to the picture of my dad and Uncle Ian, watching us anxiously.

'Do you know their names?'

'No,' I say, although this is a lie because I know

360

Tyreese's name. I'm not sure why I don't tell her.

'How many of them were there?'

'Four maybe.'

'Are you sure?' The policewoman looks up from her notepad. 'It's just that some other people said they saw five men on bikes ride into the cul-de-sac.'

'There were only four,' I say.

She notes it down. 'Anyone else?'

I suddenly wish I'd spoken to Priti about what to say. I shake my head which feels like less of a lie than actually saying 'No.'

'Did you see anyone else going in the direction of the park after you left?'

'Mik,' I say and it occurs to me that I haven't seen Mik at all since then.

'Mikaeel Muhammed?'

I nod.

'Do you know why he was going to the park?'

'No.'

'Could you tell what sort of mood he seemed to be in?'

'No.'

'Anyone else?'

I turn to Jed, but he doesn't say anything, just stares at his feet. It's like we've switched identities – today he's the mute and I'm the big mouth.

'Ben,' says the policewoman. 'Did you see anyone else going into the park after you left?'

I pause then say quietly, 'I think Jed and Uncle Ian might have gone back for a bit.'

'No, we didn't!' Jed's head shoots up as if he's suddenly woken up.

'You ran off after we saw . . .' I stop, remembering that Granny and Grandad don't know about Jed's mum.

'I didn't go to the park, stupid!' Jed's staring at me and his face is red with anger.

'OK, you didn't then,' I say.

'Where did you and your dad go then, Jed?' the policewoman asks.

'Just . . . about.'

'Where?'

'Does it matter? We didn't go to the park, OK.'

'OK,' says the policewoman, glancing at the

policeman standing by the window who hasn't said anything up to this point.

'Several people told us that when they were searching for Stevie in the park last night, it looked like a fight had gone on and other people say they heard shouting – but this morning, the place has been cleaned up.' The policeman stares at me and Jed. 'Did either of you hear or see a fight?'

'No,' I say.

'No!' Jed repeats it a fraction of a second after I do.

'And did either of you see anyone hanging around, acting suspiciously, perhaps someone who hadn't been invited to the party? Did anyone approach you maybe, try to talk to you?'

This time Jed and I both say 'No' at exactly the same time.

The police officers go after that, although I hear them say to Granny, 'We'll need contact details for the boy's father. We want to talk to him too.'

'Of course,' says Granny.

'I'm afraid he was rather drunk,' we hear Granny say as she ushers them out into the hall.

'He misses the routine of army life, you know?'

I turn to Jed and whisper, 'Why didn't you tell them that you went back to the park?'

'Because I didn't,' says Jed.

I'm not sure if he means he didn't go back to the park or just that he didn't tell them. But he looks so angry I know there's no point in asking him again, so I drop it.

At lunchtime we hear them talking on the radio about the 'disappearance of local girl, Stevie Sanders'. Then a bit later, a van pulls up outside and some people with big cameras and microphones and stuff get out.

'Here comes the media circus,' says Grandad, who seems to be enjoying this. He hasn't even bothered to switch on the TV this morning – he told Granny that the soap opera unfolding outside is far more interesting.

'I expect they'll do one of those TV appeals,' says Grandad. 'I wonder if the Sanders know that the police psychologists study the footage to see if any of the family members did it.'

'Did what?' I ask.

'Nothing,' says Granny, glaring at Grandad.

'He means killed her,' says Jed, who's hardly looked at me since the police left.

'I'm sure nobody has killed Stevie,' says Granny quickly. 'Soon enough the police will find her safe and well.'

'So long as she's not *dead*,' says Jed.

Grandad was right. Stevie's mum and dad are on the news tonight. They're sitting in their lounge, holding a picture of Stevie which must have been taken quite recently as she's brown as a nut. Stevie's mum cries quite a lot and doesn't say much. Her dad says, 'If anyone knows anything that can help us find our angel, please, please contact the police.'

'We just want you back, baby girl!' says her mum at the end.

Then her dad says, 'Wherever you are, if you're watching this, Stevie, we love you.'

'What do you reckon?' says Grandad, flicking the switch to mute after it's finished so we can just see the silent, crying face of Mrs Sanders. 'Guilty?'

'Don't put ideas in the boys' heads, please,' says Granny.

'Think about it, Rita,' says Grandad. 'If we're living next to a child-killer, where will he turn next?'

'Darling, please!' She only ever calls him darling when she's really mad.

'After everything that's happened to this family, we don't need any more tragedy,' Grandad says.

On the TV they've gone live to a reporter who's standing outside Stevie's house. Me and Jed jump up to look out of the window and, sure enough, there he is, standing on the driveway, just like he is on the TV.

'Turn the sound back on, Grandad,' says Jed.

Grandad flicks the remote. 'In cases like this the first forty-eight hours are crucial, so police are redoubling their efforts,' we hear the reporter saying. It's weird watching him through the window and hearing his voice come out of the TV at the same time.

'It really is live,' says Jed. 'Watch his lips – you can tell.'

We both watch. There's a very slight delay as the

reporter's lips aren't quite synched with the voice-over. 'Tomorrow, local volunteers will comb the park area where Stevie was last seen.'

'Are you going to volunteer?' Jed asks Granny and Grandad.

'We probably should, Barry,' says Granny.

Grandad just nods and I don't know if that's a yes or a no.

'Do you reckon we should tell the reporter about Shakeel's bomb?' whispers Jed. We're both still watching the reporter who has stopped filming and is drinking coffee from a flask.

'Why?'

'It might be connected, you know.'

'I don't think we should tell them anything until we're completely sure,' I say, nervously glancing round to make sure Granny and Grandad can't hear what we're saying.

'I suppose so,' says Jed. 'We don't want to jeopardise the investigation. And it might all be linked.'

'What?'

'Stevie's disappearance and the bomb plot.'

'Really?' I say dubiously.

'I bet you it is,' says Jed. 'You just wait and see.'

THINGS I'D LIKE TO KNOW ABOUT GRANDAD

1. Has he really hurt his back or does he just say that so he doesn't have to do jobs like hoovering and washing-up? And did he help Granny more when their boys were younger? Is it just since my dad died that he stopped wanting to do anything much?

2. Why does such a clever man spend so much time watching TV and why doesn't it rot his brain like my mum says it does? (It can't have because he's still amazing at Scrabble, if he can be bothered to play.)

3. Did he always dislike Muslims or is it just since 9/11?

4. What does he think of Uncle Ian?

5. Does he like having me and Jed staying or will he be glad when we've gone?

6. Were he and Granny madly in love when they were younger and do they still love each other?

7. Does he miss my dad as much as Granny does?

8. Why is he mad at my mum?

9. Why is bad news the only thing that seems to make him smile?

10. Why does he sign up to help with the search even though he tells Granny they won't find anything and it will be a waste of time?

After lunch, I do some drawing. Granny lets me sit in the posh dining room – the one that only gets used when they have visitors. She tells me not to worry about the washing-up today: she and Jed will do it. Jed complains for a bit, but Granny shoos him off and tells him to get started.

I think she's being extra nice to me because my mum is going home today. I've spent all morning trying not to think about it. The police coming was kind of good because it was a distraction, only then I felt bad because a kid going missing is not exactly the sort of thing you should be glad about. And perhaps

I shouldn't be trying so hard to forget about my own mum either.

In any case, when I sit down at Granny's best dining table with my notebook in front of me, I can't think of anything else. I thought drawing would take my mind off it, but I can't seem to think of anything to draw. I just sit and stare at the crochet doily thing in the middle of the table with the silver salt and pepper pots on it.

In the front of my sketchbook is another card from my mum, which arrived this morning. This one doesn't have a picture, just a message spelt out in letters cut from magazines – like a ransom note in a film. It says, *Roses are red, violets are blue. Home is home, but not sweet without you.*

I glance around the room at the glass-fronted cabinet with Granny's best wedding china in it, the grandfather clock that actually did come from her grandfather, and the pictures on the wall of me and Jed, and Dad and Uncle Ian as babies. Everything in here is neat as a pin – Granny dusts and polishes every day – but it still has that untouched feeling that rooms get when no one has been in them for ages.

I wonder if that's how our house felt when Mum walked into it today. Is my stuff still where I left it: my school bag and PE kit by the back door, my maths textbook sitting on the side in the kitchen, a dirty pair of football socks on my bedroom floor? Just like it was that morning when she left. Just as if nothing had changed.

But *she* must have changed, mustn't she? I don't remember the last time she went away, so I don't know if she was different when she came back. I want her to be better, but what if she doesn't seem like my mum any more? What if she doesn't need me now she's OK?

I stare out through the patio doors to the garden, where Grandad is watering the Busy Lizzies. He told me once that he hates them, and he only plants them because they're Granny's favourite. I flick to the back of my sketchbook and I start to draw. I draw Grandad watering the flowers; I draw Granny in the kitchen, washing up; I draw Jed scowling with a drying-up cloth.

And I draw my mum, holding up a ransom note. Wearing dark black lipstick and not so skinny any more.

They still haven't found Stevie by the time we go to bed.

'Do you reckon they'll let us help with the search?' I say to Jed, who's still being weird with me about what I said to the police.

'I doubt it,' he says. 'There's no point anyway. She's most probably dead by now.'

'Why do you say that?'

'You heard what they said: the first forty-eight hours are crucial. That's because if kids go missing for longer than that then odds on they're dead.'

'But if the kidnappers kill her then they won't get the ransom money,' I say.

'They don't just nick kids for the money, stupid!' says Jed.

'What do you mean?' I say.

'If you don't know then I'm not going to tell you,' he says. 'It'll give you nightmares.'

I can't get to sleep anyway. I think about Stevie's mum saying, 'We just want you back, baby girl!' and Jed's mum, hanging around the party just to catch a glimpse of him. Then I think about my mum again. Does she know about Stevie? About what's happened? If she hasn't turned on the TV or the radio then maybe she still hasn't heard. If she has, I know she'll be worrying about me. Because she's like that. Or at least she used to be.

I'm still awake when Uncle Ian turns up and by then it's nearly midnight.

AUGUST 12TH

Uncle Ian takes Jed off for a 'boys' breakfast'. Jed says he doesn't want to go, but Uncle Ian just starts shouting at him and Grandad says Jed needs to be taught some manners, which just makes Uncle Ian even crosser.

Uncle Ian doesn't look like he's slept or washed since the wedding-party day. His face is all stubbly and he's acting like Jed does when he's in one of his weird moods. None of us says so, but we all breathe a sigh of relief when they've gone.

When the post comes, there's another card for me. This one has a picture from the film *Ghostbusters* on the front and on the back it says, *Still stronger than the ghosts and the monsters under the bed! Times two! Love you!*

It makes me smile because it reminds me of a song my mum used to say was our song. I try to sing the rest of the words to myself under my breath, but I can't remember them all. I wonder if she knows what's going on yet. I wonder if she'll call.

I ask Granny if I can go over to Priti's.

'OK then, but go straight there – no detours. Your mum won't forgive me if anything happens to you.'

'Really?'

'Of course not,' she says, but she doesn't look at me as she says it.

So I go straight across the cul-de-sac, which is now full of TV crews and reporters. One of the reporters shouts, 'Hey, kid! Were you friends with Stevie Sanders? When did you last see her? Were you with her on the day of her disappearance?'

But I just say, 'No comment.' I've always wanted to say that, but it sounds weird when I do somehow.

Priti must have seen me coming because she answers the door before I've even rung the bell. She's still in her pyjamas and she ushers me in quickly. 'Don't want them taking pics of me in my jimmy-jams. Look what that did to Cherie Blair!' she says. I have no idea what she's talking about, but this is nothing new.

'Wicked, isn't it? Having reporters on your doorstep!' She giggles. 'My mum says you can't even go out to get a pint of milk without one of them accosting you. This must be what it's like to be famous!'

According to Priti, Zara is skulking in the bedroom, so we go to the dining room and hang out under the table again.

'Have the police been here?' I ask in a whisper.

'Yeah. They wanted to know all about when we saw Stevie and who was in the park and stuff. Did you tell them that Zara was there?'

I shake my head.

'Cool! I nearly texted to tell you not to, but then I remembered you didn't have a phone, so I just tried to use ESP instead.'

'ES – what?'

'ESP. Telepathy. Mind-reading, whatever. You know, you seriously need to extend your vocabulary.'

'Right,' I say. 'And . . .?'

'And you obviously got the message.'

'If you say so. Anyway, I didn't tell them Zara was there, if that's what you mean. Or Tyreese,' I add.

'Oh, I said he was hanging with the others.' She

scrunches up her face. 'Shouldn't think it matters though. So long as you didn't mention Zara that's OK. Or Mik,' she adds quickly.

'Why not Mik?' I say, colouring.

She ducks her head quickly out from under the tablecloth to check no one is around then leans in close and whispers, 'Mik got beaten up.'

'When?'

'The night of the party.'

'Was it the bikers?' I ask.

'He won't say, but it must have been.'

I fiddle with the hem on the tablecloth. 'Jed lied about him and his dad going back to the park.'

'What did he want to do that for?'

I shrug. 'Dunno.'

'He's been acting weirder than ever since his crackpot mum showed up,' says Priti. 'My mum says he's a troubled boy. Which I suppose is only to be expected, since he's dying and that.' (Jed made me promise not to tell Priti about Granny Brenda, so she still thinks he's terminally ill.) 'Hey! You don't reckon she did it?'

'Who did what?'

'Jed's mum – stole Stevie?' Priti looks excited.

'Why would she do that?'

Priti's all fired up and starts talking in this deep voice, like she's doing a movie voice-over. 'She can't have her own child so, crazed with desperation and vengeance, she steals someone else's.' Priti grins. 'Perhaps she'll hold Stevie to ransom until she gets Jed back.'

I imagine a crazed Auntie Karen with wild eyes, holding Stevie Sanders bound and gagged in a cave.

'Auntie Karen's not that bad,' I say.

'She's a loon.'

'She's just upset because she's lost her son. Granny's hair went grey when my dad died and my mum . . . My mum got thinner.'

'Yeah, and look what happened to you.'

'I haven't got grey hair and I don't go screaming outside people's houses or stalking people or stop eating – or whatever.'

'No, but you do reckon everyone's parents are basically good, nice human beings, just as long as they're alive.'

'No, I don't.'

'Go on then, name one person's mum or dad who you don't like.'

'Jed's dad,' I say quickly, triumphantly.

'You're right,' says Priti. 'He's a creep!' She pauses for a second as she puts on her psychiatrist hat. 'OK, you've just got a mother complex then. You think all mums are saints.'

'No, I don't,' I say, trying to think of an example of a mum I don't like. 'What about Britney Spears?' I say eventually.

'Well, that's just crap! Britney would be just the best mum ever!' Priti exclaims. 'She and I would have SO much fun shopping together!'

We're not allowed to join in when they search the park for clues and Jed and his dad still aren't back, so me and Priti just sit in the tree house and watch.

Loads of people come to help and the police make them stand in a big long line while they shout instructions to them. There are people I recognise from the wedding (although they look really different

379

in jeans and stuff) and all the neighbours are there, and some people I recognise from the shops at the parade, as well as a lot of people I've never seen before. Granny and Grandad turn up, and Stevie's dad and mum (even though the reporter on the radio said her baby is due any day now and she should have her feet up rather than putting herself through this ordeal).

Priti's got a little portable radio that belongs to Shakeel, so we listen to the reporters talking about the search while it's going on. They say things like, 'The strain on Stevie's parents is showing,' and, 'As each day passes, the chances of finding their daughter alive are diminishing.' Meanwhile, the TV cameras film Mr and Mrs Sanders holding hands and walking across to the park to join in the search. I reckon reporters like the doom-and-gloom stuff almost as much as my grandad does.

Even Tyreese and the other bikers are there. Priti says it's probably the first time they've ever cooperated with a police enquiry in their lives.

The police officers make everyone stand in a long line with their backs against the perimeter fence and then tell them to shuffle forward, dead slowly, eyes to the ground, looking for clues.

'I've seen this on *CSI*,' says Priti.

'What do you reckon they're looking for?' I ask.

'Footprints or blood or bullet casings or something,' she replies.

'Why would there be bullet casings?'

'I dunno, do I? Maybe there was a shoot-out!'

'Wouldn't we have heard gunshots?'

She thinks for a moment. 'I suppose so. I'm not sure how loud guns are though.'

I'm amazed to hear Priti admitting she doesn't know something. 'I thought guns were illegal in this country anyway?' I say.

'Doesn't mean to say no one's got one,' says Priti. 'Gun crime is a growing problem in Britain's cities,' she says, sounding like she's quoting something she's read again.

The park is pretty big, so the general public are combing the play area and the football pitches, while the police search the wooded bit. They've got big dogs with them.

'Sniffer dogs,' says Priti. 'They're bound to work out Zara's been in there.'

'What will happen then?' I ask.

'Dunno,' says Priti, who's picking a bit of bright pink nail varnish off her fingernail and doesn't seem that interested in what will happen to her sister. She's dressed as an emo goth today – which means loads of black and jeans that are too big for her – 'out of respect for Stevie'. (I want to point out that she always said she didn't like the kid, but I don't.)

'What are you drawing?' she asks, peering over my shoulder.

I hand over the latest Bomb-busters strip.

'Jed-eye gets held hostage by crazy Big Momma terrorist,' says Priti. 'I like it! Bagsie Lil' Priti gets to rescue him.'

'Jed will hate that,' I say.

'Exactly.' She grins. The black top she is wearing is covered in little pink CND symbols with a sparkly pink *Ban the Bomb* logo – the same colour as her peeling nail varnish. I wonder what Shakeel makes of it.

'How's Mik?' I ask.

'The doctor reckons he may have cracked ribs,' says Priti, flicking bits of peeled-off varnish on to the bare wooden slats.

'Really?'

'And his face is pretty messed up.' She pulls a scrunched-up face which I guess is meant to be Mik.

'Do you know what happened?'

'He won't talk to anyone except Zara. So did you hear from your mum?'

I look down at the wooden slats, dusted with pink flakes that look like dead skin. 'Why would I?'

'Jed said she got out of hospital.'

How does Jed know? Did Granny tell him?

'Yeah, yesterday,' I reply, blowing away the pink varnish flakes and tracing my finger along a pattern in the bare wood.

'So?'

'So what?' I keep my finger following the swirls of the wood. I can make out a face, a hand.

'So when do you get to go home?'

'I dunno.' I don't look up.

'That's a bummer,' says Priti, standing up and

sending a shower of pink off her jeans and on to the grass below.

'You gonna stop gossiping and let me up or what?' shouts a voice from below.

Looking down, I can see Jed standing in the alleyway beneath. He scrambles up the fence and grabs hold of the trunk of the tree then me and Priti haul him up to the platform.

'Where've you been?' asks Priti.

'Just out for breakfast with my old man,' says Jed, shrugging his shoulders like it's no big deal.

'What's he come back for anyway?' asks Priti. 'I thought he only came at weekends.'

'Figure he's worried about me with a kiddy-fiddler on the loose.'

'Does he reckon the kidnapper will try and nab one of us too?' asks Priti, interested suddenly – even if it is Uncle Ian's idea.

'Not you,' says Jed. 'My dad reckons it's white kids they're after.'

'Your dad would say that,' says Priti. 'But what he doesn't realise is that colour is about genes not skin.'

She sounds like she's quoting a book again.

'Colour is about *colour*, stupid,' says Jed.

'Anyway, we reckon it was your mum who nicked Stevie,' Priti goes on, like it's so obvious she's right she can't be bothered to argue with him. 'Because she misses you so much.'

'Yeah, right!' says Jed.

'She was there, stalking you. Nobody saw her but us. None of us saw her leave.'

'My mum did not do it,' says Jed, angry suddenly.

'It's all right. I never told the police she was there. Reckoned you wouldn't want me to.'

'Tell them what you like. My mum wouldn't do a thing like that!'

'I thought you said she was an evil witch capable of anything?' says Priti.

'No, my dad said that.'

'Same thing, isn't it?' says Priti, looking him straight in the eye.

'No,' says Jed. 'It's not.'

* * *

Just then we hear Uncle Ian's voice coming from the other end of the alleyway. 'I don't want my name to be included, you understand?' he's saying. 'Just say I'm a friend of the family.'

We crowd over to the edge of the tree house to see what's going on. Uncle Ian has his back to us, talking to a pretty lady reporter.

'Here's the thing,' he's saying. 'Apart from my boy and my nephew, Ben, Stevie Sanders was the only white kid there that afternoon. Not many white kids left around here these days, more's the pity!'

'So you believe her disappearance is racially linked?' the reporter lady is asking.

'Oh, that's real helpful that is,' Priti whispers.

'I'm not saying it is, and I'm not saying it isn't,' says Uncle Ian. 'But they reckon we dress our kids inappropriately, don't they? And there were all these Asian girls covered from head to toe in their burkhas or saris or whatever, and there's little Stevie wearing an itty-bitty vest and shorts. Maybe in their culture that means she's asking for it, but it doesn't in mine.'

I glance at Jed. He has the same pink spots in his

cheeks that Granny gets when she's upset.

Priti lets out a long breath and I'm sure she's about to say something bad about Uncle Ian so I butt in quickly. 'Jed, you don't look too good,' I say. Which he actually doesn't, but that's not really the point. 'We should get you home.' I give Priti a significant look because, after all, she still thinks he's dying.

Jed doesn't even bother to disagree. He clambers down the tree and I follow him although he doesn't look grateful or anything.

'See you later?' I say to Priti.

'Whatever,' she replies.

Then me and Jed troop across the road. Uncle Ian has gone and the pretty lady reporter follows us. 'Has anyone ever approached you? Are you made to feel welcome by the Asian families who live around here?' But we just keep walking in silence.

When we get through the front door, Jed turns to me straight away and says fiercely, 'It's just because my dad cares about me, you know!'

And he looks like he really needs me to agree with him, so I say, 'Yeah, I know.'

AUGUST 13TH

Uncle Ian's comments were on the news last night and in all the papers today (not that his name appears – the reporter kept her word on that). And what he said seems to have started something cos suddenly all the newspapers are talking about racial tensions in the area and the reporters start asking questions about Priti's family and the people who were at the wedding. More reporters turn up and they bring up the story about Said being stabbed and Tyreese's brother being beaten up, and the fight at the parade. And somehow or other they seem to know that Mik was in a fight that night – although I don't know how they can have found this out.

Stevie's mum and dad are on the TV again, doing another press conference. And this time it's Stevie's mum who does all the talking. She looks right at the camera and she has her hand on her bump the whole time she's talking and she reads from a piece of paper where she must have written down what she wants to say.

'We appeal to the Asian community to help us find our child,' she says as camera flashes go off all around her, making her look blotchy red and yellow. 'If one of you knows where my angel is, I beg you to not close your ears to our pleas for help just because of the colour of her skin.' (I can't help thinking how Stevie is almost as brown as Priti at the moment – perhaps Priti was right when she said that colour is not about skin at all.)

'Relations between the Asians and the whites around here may not have been too good in the past,' she goes on, 'but this is a child's life here. We appeal to all the Asian people to help us – if any of you knows something, please come forward. Cos Stevie is only a kid, no matter what colour her skin is.'

'Well, that's done it,' says Grandad.

'They'll be making speeches in parliament now,' laughs Uncle Ian, who's watching it with us. 'Good on her! Somebody needed to say what we're all thinking.'

'But there's no proof that the abductor was Asian,' says Granny.

'Bound to be,' says Uncle Ian. 'That's what those men go for, isn't it? They want their own wives all wrapped up like mummies and a nice little blonde bit on the side.'

'She's a child, Ian!' says Granny.

'So do you really think Stevie was taken by one of the Asians?' asks Jed.

'Think about it, son. You start moving these people into a neighbourhood and the crime rates soar. It's a fact, innit?' says Uncle Ian. 'The detectives know that same as us. They'll find whoever did it soon enough.'

'Don't be so sure,' says Grandad. 'What about that little girl who went missing abroad? Couple of years ago now. They never found out who got her.'

'Reckon the British police are a bit better than the foreign lot, don't you?' says Uncle Ian. 'They'll find her.'

'Really?' says Jed.

'Course, son,' says Uncle Ian. 'And when they do, they'll find some piggin' Asian behind it all. I'd put money on it.'

* * *

After Uncle Ian leaves, I find Jed sitting in Grandad's gardening shed, listening to his iPod.

'Your dad's gone,' I say.

He takes his earphones out and stares at me. 'Has he?'

'Didn't you want to say bye to him?'

He shrugs.

'My mum reckons you should always say goodbye.'

'She probably never said goodbye to your dad properly or something, that's why.'

I stare at him and imagine doodling a black rain cloud over his head.

'Did your dad say that?' I ask.

'Maybe.'

'And you believe him.'

'Course. We always tell each other the truth.'

'Why didn't you tell him you've been seeing your other gran then?' I say.

He looks up. 'Why don't *you* tell Granny you don't want to go home?'

'Because I do want to,' I reply.

'Yeah? I reckon if you did, you'd have called your mum by now.'

'Not everyone hates their mum like you do!' I say.

'Look, your dad got to die and be the hero. Lucky him. Cos it's a lot easier not to mess up when you're dead.'

And he puts his earphones back in and I just stand there, staring into the shed filled with Grandad's gardening stuff – stuff he never uses. Then I kick the shed door and walk away.

At bedtime I ask Granny if I can ring Mum now she's home. 'Of course you can,' she said.

But I don't.

AUGUST 14TH

There's going to be big service in the city cathedral on Sunday to say prayers for the family of Stevie Sanders. Granny asks if we want to go, but me and Jed both say no. Granny and Grandad agree to stay at home and watch 'The Service for Stevie' on the twenty-four-hour news channel instead. 'It'll be heaving and I'm not one for crowds,' says Granny. Grandad just says, '*Hmmph!*'

We're all in the sitting room, watching the news with the sound off. (Grandad doesn't want to miss any developments, but Granny doesn't want the TV on all the time.) We've just had lunch so within about five minutes both grandparents are asleep.

Me and Jed go and hang out in the garden. I'm drawing some more Bomb-busters strips. Jed is kicking his football against the kitchen wall, even though Granny always asks him not to, and humming the tune to *Match of the Day* over and over, getting a little louder each time.

I draw a picture of Stee-V tied to a giant aerial on the top of a skyscraper with a bomb belt strapped round her waist. '*Heeeelp!*' says the speech bubble coming out of her mouth.

Eventually, I say, 'Why didn't you want the police to know that you and your dad went back to the park after we saw your mum?'

Jed doesn't even turn his head in my direction. 'We didn't see anything, that's why.'

'You were gone for ages. You must have seen something.'

He just shrugs and keeps humming.

'Was Stevie still there when you left?' I ask.

'I can't remember,' says Jed.

The counter on Stee-V's explosive device reads, *10 . . . 9 . . . 8 . . . 7 . . .*

'You must remember something,' I say.

'Well I don't,' he says. 'Here, give us a look.'

He snatches the notebook out of my hands, flops down next to me on the step and stares at the picture of Stee-V for what seems like ages.

'What do you think?' I say.

'Yeah, it's good,' he says distractedly. 'Have you done any more of her?'

'Who?'

'The Stevie kid.'

'A few,' I say. 'She's in the new storyline.'

Jed flicks through the most recent pages of the pad. 'Look,' he says. 'If I tell you something, will you promise not to tell anyone?'

'I suppose so.'

'Cos I don't know if I can trust you not to go running straight to the cops. Do you swear on your mum's life not to tell anyone?'

I think about my mum, back at home, making a cup of tea in the kitchen, laughing with Gary, pale coral lipstick sparkling on her lips. 'I can't do that,' I say.

'Then I'm not talking,' says Jed.

I hesitate. 'OK then,' I say. I think of her turning to look at me, smiling, her eyes full of life again.

'On your mum's life?'

'On my mum's life.'

'OK, it was like this.' Jed talks really low, like

someone will hear us. 'That day in the park. Stevie was still there when I went back. And I was going to tell her to bugger off back to the party, but then Mik came along and he was dead angry.'

'What happened then?'

'Mik told the bikers to clear off, but they started throwing bottles at him.' Jed keeps bouncing the ball between his knees as he talks. 'I probably shouldn't be telling you this.'

'I said I wouldn't tell anyone, didn't I?' I say, trying to push the image of my mum's face to the back of my mind. 'Did they hurt him?'

Jed bounces the ball a little harder. 'No, but one of the bottles nearly hit Stevie, so she hid in one of the pipes.

I imagine Stevie hiding in the pipe, covering her ears so she can't hear the sound of smashing glass.

'What happened then?'

He keeps staring down and, apart from his hands on the ball, he is totally still. 'Then Zara comes running out of the woods and she's crying and her top is all ripped and Tyreese comes after her, shouting stuff.'

'What did Mik do?' I ask.

'He started to go for Tyreese. But then Tyreese pulls out this knife and says he'll carve Mik up if he tries anything. Just like he did to his cousin.'

'Is that what he said?'

'Zara was crying and telling him to stop and then Mik pulls out a gun.' Jed stops bouncing the ball.

I don't know what I was expecting him to say, but it wasn't this. 'A gun?'

Jed doesn't look up. He's holding the ball tightly in two hands. 'He starts waving it around, saying he'll shoot if Tyreese takes another step.'

'Was your dad there all the time?'

'No,' Jed releases the ball and starts bouncing it again. 'He arrived when Mik was waving the gun around. He told me to get the hell out of there, so I legged it down the alleyway.'

'Did Stevie run away too?'

'No, she was still in the pipe when I left.'

'And your dad?'

'I didn't see him again after that.'

I stare at Jed, but he doesn't look up. The ball keeps

marking out a nervous rhythm on the patio stone.

'Why didn't you tell the police any of this?'

'My dad told me not to.'

'When?' I ask.

'Later.'

'When later?'

'Just later,' he says.

And then we hear the patio door open. 'They've only gone and arrested that lad next door,' Grandad is saying. 'Come on or you'll miss it.'

'Remember, you promised,' Jed hisses. 'You can't tell anyone. Not even Priti.'

'I promise,' I say. And I can see my mum's face again, smiling, happy.

It turns out the police did find something when they combed the park – that's why they're taking Mik in for questioning. We watch them escort him out of the house. First we watch it live, then we see it again on the TV and for the first time we can see how badly beaten up he is. The whole left side of his face is swollen – red, black and blue – and one eye is completely closed.

He walks uncomfortably, like he's in real pain. The photographers crowd round the police car to take pictures.

'Why don't they question him at home if he's not a suspect?' asks Jed.

'Priti would know,' I say.

But we haven't spoken properly to Priti for a couple of days – and I kind of miss her.

'Dad says we need to keep an eye on her,' says Jed. Uncle Ian called last night to talk to Jed.

'On Priti?'

'On her whole family. He reckons they might be into child-trafficking. White kids. Better than a bomb, he reckons. Make a few little white kids disappear and you destroy the confidence of a community.' Jed doesn't look at me as he says this. He's flicking through my notebook, but he doesn't seem to be actually looking at the pictures.

'Mik looked pretty bad, didn't he?' I say.

'Did he?' Jed shrugs.

'Did you see him get beaten up then?' I whisper.

'I told you. I'd gone before it all kicked off.'

He doesn't say any more after that, but he looks uncomfortable. My big, cool, unflappable cousin looks almost – what? – scared? And now I'm sure that he's lying.

AUGUST 15TH

This morning, there's a little group of people at the bottom of the close holding banners with pictures of Stevie and slogans like, 'Give her back!' and, 'Pakis stole Stevie Sanders'. Grandad says we should take them tea and sandwiches, but Granny won't let him.

She won't let us go over to Priti's house either, although when Jed asks if this is because Mik has been arrested, Granny says, 'He's not been arrested. He's been taken in for questioning.'

But then we see Priti snaking her way through the reporters to get across to our house. For some reason she's wearing a sari and a headscarf, although she's still got her wheelies on, so some things don't change.

'They're like flaming piranhas out there!' she says, after Granny shows her up to our bedroom. 'Thanks, Mrs Evans,' she says, pulling off her headscarf and giving Granny her best smile.

Granny just nods and I don't know if I'm imagining

it, but I can't help thinking she isn't quite so friendly to Priti as usual.

'What's happening?' I ask.

'They took Mik in for questioning.'

'Yeah, we know that,' says Jed, who's staring out of the window with the binoculars and acting like he's not really listening.

'And a policewoman is talking to Zara. They know she was in the park. They want to know what she saw.'

'What did she say?' I ask.

'She still says she wasn't there, but they know she's lying.'

'What's going to happen to her, do you think?' I say.

'My dad will go mad if he finds out she was with Tyreese. And, even worse –' Priti looks almost excited when she says this – 'Tyreese got Mik taken in by the police.'

'How?'

'It turns out Stevie is Tyreese's cousin of some sorts.'

'No way!' I say and even Jed looks like he's vaguely interested in this new piece of information.

'Yeah, her mum and his dad are cousins or something.'

'But it's not like Mik knew that,' I say.

'I know, but Tyreese says he did and that Mik kidnapped Stevie as revenge cos he reckoned Tyreese had stabbed Said. Cousin for a cousin sort of thing.'

Jed puts down the binoculars, but he doesn't say anything.

'So what's going to happen now?' I ask, glancing at him.

'Well, for a start, Jed's going to tell the police what he saw when he went back with his dad so the police can get their story straight,' says Priti.

'What?' Jed spins around so quick he almost falls off the windowsill.

'You must have seen what went on,' Priti says. She's got a no-nonsense look on her face and her hands are on her hips. 'You can tell them he's innocent,' she says. 'And so can your dad, if he's not bent on trying to frame Muslims.'

'My dad is not bent.'

'No, but he is a racist bigot!'

'He is not!'

'Whatever. You have to clear Mik because they'll find out you're lying eventually.'

'Zara could tell them,' says Jed. 'She saw what went on too.'

'So you did see it then!' Priti says triumphantly.

'Maybe. But so did Zara. She can tell the police.'

'Two reasons why not – one, she's not going to tell my mum and dad she was making out with a biker or they will kill her, literally kill her. Two, she left the park long before you did.'

'Mik already knew about Zara and Tyreese,' says Jed angrily. 'He could have told your parents any time.'

For perhaps only the second time since I've known her, Priti is lost for words.

I imagine doodling a speech bubble above her head, filled with rows of question marks.

'He was going on about it that day,' Jed continues, 'like he'd known for ages.'

'I don't get it,' I say.

Priti still has her mouth open, like a fish. Now in my head I'm doodling flippers and a fin and air bubbles rising up out of her mouth.

'He was going on like, "I don't say nothing about your little meetings with my sister in the woods, but you lay another finger on her and I'll kill you!" that sort of thing,' says Jed.

'So Mik knew Zara was meeting Tyreese in the park all along?' Priti says quietly. She looks like her brain's working really hard to figure it all out.

'Mik must have seen that he'd hit her though,' she says.

'Who hit her?' I say. 'Why?'

'Tyreese,' says Priti. 'Zara told me that when she tried to end it, Tyreese got rough with her.'

'So that's why Mik got his gun out?' I say.

Jed glares at me.

'Mik had a gun?' For the second time in five minutes Priti looks gobsmacked.

'Jed saw it,' I say, ignoring the looks he's giving me.

Priti glances at Jed, who just shrugs.

There's a pause in which I can almost hear the cogs in Priti's brain turning. 'How did they manage to beat him up then?' she asks.

I've been wondering this too. Because even if the gun had no bullets or was a fake, how would the bikers have known? And they wouldn't have taken him on if he was waving a gun.

Jed just shrugs, but his face goes really red.

'You have to tell the police what you saw, Jed,' I say.

'And you have to learn to keep your promises!' he snaps back.

'Why won't you tell them?' demands Priti.

'I've got my reasons.'

'What are they?'

'Loyalty. That's something we have in my family!'

Priti pulls a face. 'OK, let me rephrase the question then: why doesn't *your dad* want you to tell the fuzz what you saw?'

'None of your business,' says Jed.

He refuses to talk about it any more after that. He just gets out his console, slumps on the bed and acts like we're not even in the room. Priti says she's not going to hang out with someone who is wilfully obstructing the course of justice and storms off home.

I watch her wheeling her way through the journalists then I pull out my notebook and start work on a new Bomb-busters storyline in which Jed-eye and Lil' Priti are arguing about whether to get the police involved or to mount a solo mission to rescue the kidnapped girl from the hostage-takers. But I only manage to do one frame because I keep thinking about what Jed said and I can't seem to concentrate on drawing properly.

AUGUST 16TH

When we wake up, we see that somebody has graffitied the front of the Muhammeds' door in the night: *Pakis, give her back!* it says in bold, red letters. Mr Muhammed tries to wash it off and the TV crews film him out there with his sponge and bucket of white spirit. But it won't budge.

Something else has happened too. Uncle Ian has told the police that Jed's mum was there on the day of the wedding party. He turns up at the house again, this time with the nice policewoman and the policeman, who say they need to ask more questions. And they bring a social worker, at Uncle Ian's request, supposedly to protect Jed's interests – although Jed doesn't look too pleased about it. In fact, he doesn't look too pleased about seeing his dad at all.

First the policeman asks Granny and Grandad about Auntie Karen coming over and 'harassing them' as Uncle Ian calls it. Uncle Ian sits on the arm of the sofa with his arm round Jed's shoulders and answers most of the questions for them, even though he wasn't actually there.

The social worker makes loads of notes and at one point she says, 'But Karen was granted contact rights by the family court, is that right?'

Granny looks up and Grandad is staring at Uncle Ian.

'Jed didn't want to see her and I wasn't about to force him,' says Uncle Ian. 'Isn't that right, son?'

Jed just nods. With his dad's arm round him, he looks smaller than usual.

Granny purses her lips tight and Grandad looks confused.

But then the police start asking me and Jed loads of questions, and Uncle Ian keeps his arm round Jed's shoulders the whole time as if he's afraid Jed might leg it out of the room. Jed keeps shifting around and scratching his head like he's got nits or something.

Were we aware of Auntie Karen's presence at the wedding prior to the encounter in the alleyway? the policeman asks us.

'No,' says Jed.

'Were you aware she'd been spying on you?'

'No – That is, yes.'

'Which is it?' The policeman asks all the questions this time, not the nice police lady who just stands in the background and takes notes.

'I suppose,' says Jed. He keeps scratching his head till I reckon it must really hurt, but he can't seem to stop.

'How did you know? Did she say she'd been spying on you?'

'She wanted to see me, yeah,' says Jed, still scratching.

Uncle Ian slaps his hand away from his head sharply. Jed twitches his head and holds his hand tight in his lap.

'Did she say whether she had ever spied on you before?'

'No.'

'And had she tried to make contact with you before this?'

I think of the letter under the bush, the letter Jed keeps under his mattress and which I've been tempted to read, but haven't.

'No.' The way he's sitting, it looks like Uncle Ian's arm round his shoulder weighs a ton or something.

'Has she or any member of her family ever tried to make contact with you outside the terms of the contact order?' asks the social worker, who is middle-aged and dressed in beige and talks with a fake, soft voice.

'I don't know what you mean.'

'Any secret meetings? Phone calls? That you weren't supposed to tell anyone about? Don't worry – you can tell us.' She smiles in that way that is supposed to make us feel we can trust her, but immediately makes me feel the opposite.

I glance quickly at Granny, who looks pale and washed out, her blue eyes suddenly grey like her hair.

'No!' says Jed.

'And on the day of the party,' the policeman says, obviously keen to stick to what's relevant to the Stevie Sanders enquiry, 'would you say your mother seemed desperate?'

'Yes,' says Jed.

'More so than usual?'

'I don't *usually* see her, so how would I know?' Jed

twitches his head again and stares down at his hands.

The policeman turns to me. 'Ben, do you think Jed's mum seemed agitated or distressed that day?'

'I guess so,' I say. I want to add that this isn't really surprising, but Uncle Ian is looking at me, so I don't.

'Did either of you see which way she went after she spoke to you?'

'No,' says Jed.

I say nothing.

'Of course, you ran off, didn't you?' says the policeman, looking back through his notepad, but I'm not sure if he believes Jed. 'You ran down to the other end of the cul-de-sac,' he says, reading from his notes. Then he looks up. 'So if she'd left that way, you'd have seen her, right?'

'I don't know,' says Jed, twisting his fingers in his lap.

'Answer the question!' says Uncle Ian.

'I suppose so,' says Jed.

'Did you see her leave that way, Mr Evans?' The policewoman turns to Uncle Ian. 'You were with Jed at that time.'

'No,' says Uncle Ian. 'No, I didn't.'

'So the only other way she could have left would have been through the park?'

Suddenly I see what they're getting at. They think she went back through the park and snatched Stevie on the way – just like Priti's mad theory.

'She didn't go through the park,' says Jed quietly.

'How do you know?' the policeman says.

'I just know,' says Jed. 'She must have left some other way.'

'What about you, Ben? Did you see which way she left?'

I glance at Jed.

'No,' I say, then, 'I don't know.'

But they don't seem that bothered about what I've got to say because then Uncle Ian starts talking about restraining orders and stuff and the police talk about getting Auntie Karen in for questioning. And suddenly it's like me and Jed aren't even there at all. I look at Jed, who's staring out of the window in the direction of the alleyway.

After the police have gone, Jed legs it upstairs.

'You did the right thing, Mum,' Uncle Ian says to Granny, who is looking shocked and upset.

'I can't help feeling sorry for Karen,' she says.

'That's what she wants, Mum. But she doesn't deserve your sympathy. She's an unfit mother.'

'No mother is perfect,' says Granny. 'I sometimes wish I'd done things differently with you and your brother.'

'Don't bring Andrew into this,' says Uncle Ian. 'She's dug her own grave. That's all there is to it.'

But Granny doesn't respond. Maybe there's nothing left for her to say.

MORE THINGS I'D LIKE TO KNOW ABOUT UNCLE IAN

1. Why did he and Auntie Karen split up?
2. Is he really brainwashing Jed, like Priti says he is?
3. Why did he lie to the police about Auntie Karen going off through the park?
4. Will the police find out that he's lying?

5. If he saw the bikers beat Mik up, why didn't he try to help him?

6. Did he tell the police about any of that?

7. Why does he look such a mess suddenly?

8. Why doesn't he like it when Granny talks about my dad?

9. Would my dad have been like him if he was still around?

10. And if he was, would I have still loved him, like Jed loves Uncle Ian?

'The crap's really hit the fan now!' Priti says when she pitches up, breathless and soaking wet, halfway through Granny's salad and corned-beef lunch. Uncle Ian left right after the police, and so it's just the four of us, eating in virtual silence until Priti bursts in. She's shivering and she looks kind of frightened.

'You poor thing, you're soaking,' says Granny. I don't think she wanted to let Priti in, but she didn't get much choice. Then Priti says, 'Shit,' just like that, right in the middle of Granny's dining room while me and Jed and Grandad are sitting at the table, forks halfway to our mouths, and I'm not sure who's the most shocked. I don't think anyone has used that word in this house for years (except maybe Uncle Ian).

'Tyreese has only gone and told the police about him and Zara,' says Priti, her words tumbling out of her mouth in a rush. 'And all about how Zara was scared my brothers would honour-kill her if they found out and so the police have told my mum and dad and now they're all kicking off!'

'Blimey!' says Jed.

'*And* Tyreese is claiming Mik kidnapped Stevie as revenge for the dishonour to the family. Only I reckon they did it and they're trying to frame Mik like they did to Said.' Priti barely pauses for breath. 'And Shakeel has gone storming out of the house and no one has seen him for ages and he's probably gone to hire the contract killer and now there's a big fight going on and who knows what will happen next.'

'Why didn't you stay to listen?' Jed asks.

'My mum sent me over here,' says Priti. 'She didn't want me to be exposed to it.'

'Oh, that's charming, that is!' says Grandad. 'I suppose she'll be wanting us to adopt the kid next!' But he doesn't look that fed up because this is a bit like one of those daytime TV shows with the lie-detector tests, and people crying and shouting at each other, happening right in his own dining room.

'You should have called my number then left your phone on over there, so we could have listened to what's going on. We could even have recorded it.'

'Jed!' says Granny. She's looking quite alarmed. The stuff with the police this morning has left her shaken, and she and Grandad had no idea about Zara and Tyreese or about the honour killing or the suicide bomb plot or any of it.

'Funny how I didn't exactly have time to think of that when my sister is about to be murdered by our own parents,' says Priti.

'They'll never get away with killing her now,' says Jed. 'The cul-de-sac is crawling with police and reporters.'

Jed's right. Grandad complained that he couldn't even get his car out of the drive yesterday. And there are loads more protesters now with their banners. Apparently, it's getting so bad that the police have had to draft in extra numbers for this service at the cathedral tonight in case there's trouble.

'What's all this talk of killing?' says Granny. 'I'm sure you're letting your imaginations run away with you.'

'We're not, Granny – honest!' I say. 'Zara was seeing this boy – Tyreese – and bringing shame on Priti's family.'

'And now they've found out they have to kill her,' says Jed.

'I'm sure this can't be true,' says Granny, but she's gone really pale and I notice that her hands are shaking.

'It is, Mrs Evans,' says Priti. 'And Dad says it's all Zara's fault that Mik's been arrested. And Mum is just crying all the time. I've never seen them so mad.'

'Well, the police don't want to go releasing your brother now,' says Grandad. 'Not now everyone thinks he's a kidnapper. They'll lynch him for sure.'

'That's why the bikers are trying to frame him,' says Priti, shifting anxiously from foot to foot, like she wants to go to the loo.

'He's perfectly safe in police custody,' says Granny.

'I wouldn't be so sure about that!' mutters Grandad.

Granny looks at him. 'Don't scare the girl, Barry,' she says.

'I'm already scared,' says Priti. 'My brother and sister can be really annoying, but I wouldn't want either of them bumped off.'

'Let's not be too dramatic,' says Granny. 'I'm quite sure nothing like that is going to happen.'

'And now Shakeel's gone missing too,' says Priti, hopping around some more. 'He said he was going to the mosque and then getting some stuff for his radios, but he's been gone for hours and no one knows where he is.'

'He's gone to get more radio equipment?' says Jed, raising his voice significantly.

Priti nods. 'He was going to go the service at the

cathedral later, to show that the Asian community care, but now no one knows where he is.'

'Radio equipment!' Jed repeats, staring at me and Priti.

There's a pause before Priti says, 'Oh, crap!' Granny opens her eyes wide with shock and Grandad chokes on a bit of lettuce. 'You don't think . . .?'

'Too right I do!' says Jed.

'This is all going too fast for me,' says Grandad.

'What are you all talking about now?' asks Granny. She looks like a fragile old lady.

'Nothing, Granny,' I say. 'Don't worry about it.'

'Shakeel wouldn't really though, would he?' says Priti, looking alarmed.

'Are you willing to bet a load of people's lives on it?' says Jed.

Priti glances at me and then back at Jed. For once she doesn't seem to be finding all the drama exciting. 'You're right,' she says. 'I'd better be going. Somebody has to stop him.'

'But what about your wet clothes?' asks Granny anxiously.

'I've really got to get back. Thanks anyway, Mrs Evans.'

'Are you sure you wouldn't rather stay here for a bit?'

'She's really got to go, Granny,' I say.

'Right,' says Granny as Jed bundles Priti out towards the door.

'The minute Shakeel gets back, you've got to put a tail on him,' Jed tells Priti as we all crowd into the porch. 'And text us about any suspicious movements'.

Jed's face lights up as something occurs to him. 'I bet he's targeting the service tonight,' he says. 'Think of all those Christians in one place and blowing up a massive cathedral – that'd be a good thing for an Islamic terrorist, don't you reckon? He'd get plenty of virgins for that!'

Priti nods, but she's got a faraway look in her eyes. She pauses for a second before she opens the door to the waiting media outside. 'Do you think he really is, you know, a suicide bomber?'

'I reckon so,' says Jed and it's almost like he wants it to be true.

'Do you, Ben?' Priti turns to me.

'Maybe,' I say and afterwards I wonder why I said it – something to do with being better safe than sorry, I suppose.

'All right then. I'll send Jed a text if anything happens.'

And then she's gone and it's too late to say I'm not sure.

Me and Jed spend all afternoon watching Priti's house with our binoculars. Shakeel comes back about 4 p.m., but after that no one else comes or goes for ages and we don't hear anything from Priti. I'm starting to get a bit bored, and I guess so are the cameramen outside the Muhammeds' house, but for some reason Jed doesn't get restless, which is completely unlike him. He just stares at the house through the binoculars, refusing to answer any of my questions.

Then, at 5.33 p.m., there's finally some action to wake up the sleeping paps. The front door opens and we see Shakeel come out, dressed in full robes.

'Suspect on the move,' says Jed.

Mr and Mrs Muhammed, and Zara (who's got

sunglasses on again), Ameenah and Priti all follow Shakeel out on to the driveway. It's like a family photo opportunity. They all look self-conscious, but there's nothing hurried about it. We watch as Shakeel says goodbye to them all in turn. The journalists' cameras click, click, click.

'Like he's going on a long journey,' I say.

'It's a long way to heaven!' says Jed ominously.

And there is something really formal about the way they all say goodbye to him – not like he's just popping out to the shops for some milk.

Priti looks up at the window and nods. We wave, but she doesn't wave back – she's got her hands thrust deep inside the folds of her sari, like she's cold or something. Then, when none of the others are looking, she quickly raises a hand to her ear and mimes holding the telephone. It's done in an instant then her hands are curled back round herself again.

'She's going to call us,' I say and a minute later, Jed's phone beeps.

'You've got a message,' I say.

'I know, dumbo,' he says, picking it up. 'It's from Priti.' He hands it to me.

Suichde bomber on the mov it says (I guess it's hard to text with only one hand when you're not looking).

'She must think Shakeel's really going to blow himself up,' I say.

'And he's taking Priti with him, by the looks of it,' says Jed.

He's right. Shakeel is getting into the car and Priti – who's dressed just like she was on the day of the wedding, in her very best sari, minus the wheelies – is getting in with him. The rest of the family stay on the driveway to wave as the car drives off.

Jed's phone beeps again. Jed reads the message then passes it to me. *Bom belt on* it reads.

'We should try and follow them,' says Jed.

'How?' I say. 'It's not like either of us can drive, even if we did have a car.'

'What do you suggest we do then?'

'Wait till she tells us where he's going,' I say.

'We know where they're going, don't we?' says Jed. 'She said Shakeel was going to the service for Stevie.'

'Well, what do you want to do then?' I ask.

Jed pauses for a moment. 'Let's just wait and see till we know for sure,' he says. I stare at him, wondering if he really believes all this is for real. 'Don't want to send the police on a wild goose chase.'

So that's what we do. We sit and wait. It's not dark outside yet, but we can already see our own reflections in the window and, for some reason, I can't look mine in the eye.

I suggest telling Granny and Grandad what's going on, but Jed says they won't believe us.

'They might,' I say, although I'm not sure I really believe it myself.

'Look, there are people's lives at stake here,' says Jed. 'We don't have time to waste trying to persuade two old fogeys there's a terrorist on the loose.'

'What if he isn't?' I say after a moment. 'A terrorist, I mean?'

'If some kid had known about the men who were about to fly their planes into the Twin Towers and he could have called the police and stopped them, you wouldn't have wanted him to waste time trying to persuade his gran and grandad it was the right thing to do, would you?' says Jed.

Yet again I see cartoon aeroplanes crashing into sketchbook towers, flames erupting, stick figures falling.

'No,' I say. 'Of course not.' And I think of Priti in her sari, looking scared.

We sit there for ages in silence and then I ask: 'Do *you* reckon Mik did something to Stevie?'

'No,' says Jed.

'But he had a gun. Maybe he shot her?'

'He didn't have a gun,' says Jed.

'But you said . . .'

'He had a gun at the beginning,' says Jed, not looking at me. 'But not after they beat him up.'

I want to ask him how he knows all this, but then suddenly the phone beeps again. Jed reads it out: *Citz cathedra ETA 5 mins.*

We both stare at the phone.

'We have to call the police,' says Jed.

'We'll get in loads of trouble if it's not true,' I say.

'And if it is?'

Jed is already ringing 999 on his mobile and he

426

doesn't look excited any more. In fact, he looks as scared as I feel and I find myself thinking how much braver he is than me. Perhaps that comes from having a dad. Or from losing a mum?

The police don't seem to believe him at first, but when he tells them that we live next door to the family of Stevie Sanders and that the potential suicide bomber is Shakeel Muhammed, brother of detained Mik Muhammed, it looks like they take him more seriously.

'They're sending an officer round right away,' Jed says, phone still to his ear. 'I have to stay on the phone till they come.'

So we stand there, looking at each other. We both know what a big thing we've started and I don't know what will be worse: if it turns out we're telling the truth, or if we're not.

'Jed,' I say, 'did you see the bikers beat Mik up?'

'Yes,' he says, not looking away now.

'How did they get his gun off him?'

Jed doesn't answer.

Just then the sound of voices makes us both turn

to the window. We see a policeman emerging from the Sanders' house; Mr and Mrs Sanders left for the service earlier so there's no one at home now. He's talking to someone on his radio, making his way in this direction.

'We'd better tell the wrinklies what's going on,' says Jed. 'Don't want them to have a heart attack.'

The sitting-room door is ajar and we can see Granny and Grandad, each in their favourite chair, watching the twenty-four-hour news channel, which is broadcasting live from the cathedral.

'Who's going to tell them?' I whisper.

'You'd better do it,' says Jed. 'They like you more than me.'

'No, they don't,' I say. It seems like such a funny thing to say, especially right now.

'Sure they do – your dad was the favourite and so are you.'

'That's not true.'

'Yes, it is,' says Jed matter-of-factly. 'Anyway, are we going to do this or not?'

'OK, I'll do it,' I say.

Jed nods and I push open the door. 'Granny, there's a police officer coming to talk to us,' I say quickly, before she's even had a chance to turn around.

'Why on earth would they come at this time?' she asks, looking startled.

The presenter on the TV is saying, 'We're broadcasting live from St Philip's Cathedral, Birmingham, where a service is being held for the Sanders family, who are still awaiting news of their missing daughter, Stevie. They are joined by a congregation of friends, family and well-wishers, all here to pray for Stevie's safe return.'

But before I get chance to explain, the doorbell rings and there, standing in the porch, is the police officer.

'Somebody rang to report a bomb threat?' he asks.

Granny looks bemused.

'That was me,' says Jed, stepping forward.

'Both of us,' I say, joining him. Because we're in this together.

We have to show the police officer Priti's texts and then he asks us loads of questions about our investigations into Shakeel. We tell him all about the radio equipment and the terror cell lists and the bomb belt and all the things we overheard. And the policeman says he's not sure this is enough to go on, to which Jed replies that Priti must have seen actual explosives or she wouldn't have texted.

'Can you text her back and ask her to verify that?' says the policeman sarcastically.

'You want us to text an eleven-year-old in the middle of a terror situation and alert the bomber that we're on to him?' says Jed. 'Oh, yeah, great idea, mate!'

'Nobody wants to create panic over a false alarm, *mate*!' says the policeman crossly.

'So you'd rather have a Midlands 9/11?' Grandad demands. Now he's worked out what's going on, he's wide awake and apparently enjoying every minute.

'Of course not!'

'Because our son died in the Twin Towers,' says Grandad, pulling himself up to his full height, and speaking with great dignity. 'And I wouldn't want any other families to have to know the grief we've suffered since.'

The policeman shakes his head and sighs. 'If I lose my job over this . . .' But he doesn't finish the sentence; he just gets on his walkie-talkie and starts telling whoever's on the other end all the stuff we just told him. He uses words like 'uncorroborated' and 'unsubstantiated reports', and all the while Granny just stares at me and Jed and doesn't say anything.

I'm wondering whether Priti has arrived at the cathedral, and how long it will take for the bomb squad to get there, and for all the people to be evacuated. And I imagine Shakeel with the bomb belt round his waist, imagine him pressing a button, imagine the cathedral going up in flames, people screaming.

'We'll try and apprehend him before he goes in,' says the officer over his radio.

But I can already see it's too late. On the TV the service hasn't started yet, but the cathedral is full to capacity. And then I see him. 'There he is!' I say.

The camera is panning round the cathedral, focusing on the faces of the congregation, and there, in the back row, with Priti sitting next to him staring up at the high-vaulted ceilings of the cathedral, is Shakeel.

'Positive ID of suspect,' the policeman radioes to his colleagues. 'Where is he, kid?' he says to me.

'There.' I point to Shakeel on the TV screen, leaving a fingerprint mark for Granny to clean off.

'Back row, right,' he says into his radio. 'Second from left. He's got a girl with him. Both in traditional dress.

'How old's your friend, kid?'

'Eleven and a quarter,' I say (knowing Priti would appreciate precision).

The camera pans back to them. Priti is fumbling with something in her lap, but she looks up startled when she realises she's being filmed and suddenly she's looking right at us down the lens of the camera. I wonder if she knows me and Jed are watching.

Then the camera moves away to focus on Mr and Mrs Sanders sitting in the front row – she's so big now she looks like she's about to burst, but he looks smaller somehow. A few seconds later, Jed's phone beeps again.

'Pass it to me,' says the officer. So we do and he reads it out, *Whr r th bleeding bomb squd whn u need thm?* The policeman relays this to whoever's on the other end of his radio and it is received without comment.

The camera is focusing on Shakeel again now and the commentator is saying how great it is to see people of all religions in the audience; how this tragedy has threatened to divide a community, but tonight those of different faiths are united in sympathy for the Sanders family as they await news of their daughter.

But despite what he's saying it's clear to me that the people sitting near to Shakeel are a bit uncomfortable with the presence of a man dressed in robes and a little girl in a sari (who keeps looking around nervously).

The service is starting now. The vicar (or is he a bishop – I'm not sure how you tell?) says a few words and then everyone is rising to sing 'I Vow to Thee My Country'. Grandad mutters something about Shakeel being more loyal to his warped faith than his country – he doesn't say it that loud though. And the policeman paces up and down, looking dead worried, clutching his radio like it's actually the bomb.

Then suddenly, out of nowhere, loads of black-

433

armour-clad police officers appear on the TV screen and our policeman groans and says, 'I'm definitely losing my job over this!' The camera has panned out to show an aerial shot of the whole cathedral, packed with people, and so we get a bird's-eye view of the little black figures swooping down on Shakeel. They've got massive machine guns and even over the singing, which keeps going because I guess the people in the front rows don't realise what's going on, we can hear them shouting to the people around them to keep calm and, to Shakeel, to get down.

The camera goes all wobbly and we lose them for a minute. 'Bet the cameraman is cacking himself,' says Jed.

'And I bet the producer of the show is laughing all the way to the bank,' says Grandad. 'TV gold, this is!'

Granny just looks at them both with eyes that are red and sad.

The poor commentator is trying to keep up. 'It's unclear what is going on,' he says. On screen there's just a picture of Stevie Sanders now, wearing a bikini and licking an ice cream. She has a massive smile on her face. 'But we are hearing reports of a bomb threat . . . The cathedral is apparently being evacuated.'

'Jed, are you quite sure he has a bomb?' asks Granny quietly.

'Priti said so,' he replies.

'You did the right thing, my boy,' says Grandad.

'He'd better hope so!' says our police officer, now clutching his walkie-talkie in two hands so he looks like he's praying.

'We are being told that a suspect has been apprehended,' says the commentator. Still all we can see on screen is Stevie Sanders' smiling face. But I imagine Shakeel, hands in the air, being surrounded by armed police yelling at him to get down on the floor.

'I'm hearing that trained explosive experts are on their way,' says the commentator. 'It's not yet clear whether reports that the suspect had an explosive device strapped to himself are correct, but the bomb squad has been called.'

'Dear Lord!' say Granny. 'What have you boys started?'

Next to me, the policeman stands very silent,

listening intently to the TV commentary.

'What's happening to Priti?' I ask.

'Perhaps they think she's a bomber too,' says Grandad.

Then the picture of Stevie suddenly cuts out, replaced with live images from outside the cathedral, where crowds of people are being ushered behind a cordoned-off section by police. I catch a glimpse of Stevie's mum climbing into an ambulance, clutching her tummy, her husband shouting something. The TV people clearly have no idea what's going on as they just keep repeating the same information over and over. And there's no mention of Priti.

We become aware of sirens approaching and, looking out of the window, we see three police cars come screaming up the cul-de-sac, scattering journalists in every direction. Out of the cars pour more armed officers who surround Priti's house.

Just moments later, the same scene is on the TV as some of the camera crews outside start recording.

'Reports are coming in that armed police have surrounded a home in the same street where missing five-year-old Stevie Sanders disappeared at the weekend,' says the TV commentator. 'Yes, we're getting pictures of it now. The police are, in fact, storming the house. There's a suggestion that this raid is – er – linked somehow to the incident in the cathedral, and – er – eyewitnesses are saying that the man in the cathedral may have been the eldest son of the Muhammed family, whose younger brother has been taken in for questioning in connection with the Sanders case.' The commentator stumbles as if the information is being fed live into his headpiece and he can hardly keep up with it himself.

'Bloody hell!' says Grandad as we see the police swarm into Priti's house. 'I really hope you kids aren't just making this up. This little stunt is costing taxpayers a lot of money!'

'Not to mention my pension!' mutters the police-man, whom I suddenly notice is crossing his fingers.

But it's not the taxpayers or the officer's pension I'm worried about right now – it's Priti.

'They'll be trampling all over the place, destroying all the forensics for the Stevie abduction too,' says the policeman. 'If this is a hoax, we're all in big trouble.'

'Still, if his own sister's trying to shop him,' says Grandad.

I glance at Jed and he looks at me, but neither of us says anything.

We watch policemen emerge from Priti's house with big boxes – full of evidence, I suppose. Maybe it's Shakeel's beloved radio equipment.

Then on the TV there's footage of a man wearing just a towel with a jumper over his head being taken out to an armoured vehicle behind the cathedral and driven away.

'Experts are suggesting that the suspect may have been stripped and searched at the scene,' says the TV man.

'Blimey!' says Grandad.

'We are being told that a child – believed to be involved in the incident – is being treated for shock before being questioned by police. Unconfirmed reports are suggesting that both may be related to Stevie Sanders suspect Mik Muhammed.'

'Poor Priti,' says Granny.

'What happens now?' I say, turning to the police officer.

'Depends what he had on him.'

'And when will we know?' Jed asks.

'Could be hours,' says the policeman. 'Even days.'

'And what about Priti?' I ask.

But the policeman just shrugs.

We get to stay up late. Me and Jed, Granny and Grandad and our police officer all sitting up in the front room as it gets darker and darker outside. Granny makes everyone a cup of tea and we all sit and drink in silence. Even Grandad doesn't have anything to say.

Granny makes us turn the sound off the TV because she says she can't stand listening to it any more, so we just watch the pictures and they keep showing the same footage over and over on a loop, with a running headline below.

I don't draw pictures and I don't even imagine any as I sit and watch the images on the TV.

The funny thing about waiting for the phone to ring is that when it finally does, you're still surprised.

We all jump up when we hear the telephone at about 8.30 p.m. Grandad gets there first.

'Hello?' he says.

Then he turns to me. 'It's for you, Ben.'

'Me?'

He nods and hands me the phone.

For a moment I think it must be my mum.

'It's Priti,' he says.

I take the phone off him and put it to my ear. I hear her voice on the other end of the phone. 'Hi, Ben, it's Priti!' She sounds all crackly and distant – like she's ringing from abroad or something.

'Priti, what are you calling here for?' I ask.

'I know my rights. I'm allowed one phone call. They said I hadn't been arrested, but I said I wanted my call anyway.'

'Are you OK?' I ask. They're all listening in – Grandad, Granny and the policeman – everyone except Jed, who legged it upstairs the minute he heard who was on the phone.

'I'm fine. Did you see it on TV?' Priti always said she wanted to be on TV.

'Yup,' I say.

'I wasn't sure if you'd really call the police,' she says.

'Neither were we,' I say.

'Do they know yet if he had a bomb?' she asks.

'Don't *you* know?'

'No, why would I?'

'I thought you said you saw one?'

'I saw him put that belt on, but that's not why I called.'

Then I hear Jed's voice on the line. He must have run up to Grandad's room and picked up the phone there. 'Are you OK?' he asks breathlessly.

'Like you care,' says Priti.

'Did they try to beat a confession out of you?' Jed goes on.

'No,' says Priti. 'I don't think they were very nice to Shakeel though. They stripped him down to his pants looking for explosives.'

'Did they find any?' Jed says.

'Not yet. It turns out the bomb belt is actually one of those bumbags – you know, for putting his keys and wallet and phone in and stuff!'

'Oh,' I say.

Jed doesn't say anything.

'I know, tragic, isn't it?' says Priti. 'I thought only tourists and American college students wore bumbags.' She pauses then says, 'Is it bad that I kind of hope they find something else on him? I get the feeling we're in big trouble if they don't.'

'We were only doing our civic duty,' says Jed.

'If you're so hot on civic duty, why don't you tell the police what really happened the day Stevie disappeared?' says Priti.

There's a pause on the line then Jed says, 'Is that really what you rang to talk about?'

'I figured it out while I've been waiting at the police station,' says Priti. 'I thought I might as well make my one phone call count.'

'So you didn't even ring your mum and dad?' I ask.

'I wanted to get Jed to confess.'

'I don't know what you're talking about,' says Jed.

'The police reckon Mik was the last person in the park. Except he wasn't, was he, Jed?'

442

Another long silence.

'Is this call being tapped?' asks Jed.

'Who cares?' says Priti. 'You're going to have to tell them anyway.'

'Tell them what exactly?'

'That your dad was still in the park after the bikers left.'

Jed doesn't say anything so Priti goes on, 'Zara and Mik said he was there the whole time. They also say he didn't do a thing to help Mik while the bikers beat him up.'

Another pause. Then Jed says, 'So?'

I wonder if his dad told him any of this.

'So it means Mik wasn't the last one to see Stevie alive. Your dad was.'

Jed doesn't say anything.

'And I've been thinking,' Priti goes on, 'if you let the police keep on thinking my brother did it then it'll be your fault if they never find Stevie.'

'They'll find her,' says Jed.

'Not if they're following the wrong leads,' says Priti. 'She might be alive still, but how are the police going to find her if they've got the timings all wrong?'

'She's probably dead by now anyway,' says Jed.

'Why doesn't your dad want the police to know what he saw? That's what I've been trying to figure out.'

I look around. Granny and Grandad are staring at me and so is the police officer.

'I don't know,' says Jed.

'I think he must have something to hide.'

'You reckon *he* took Stevie!' Jed tries to laugh when he says this, but it doesn't come out right: more like a cough or like he's choking or something. And I wish I could see his face because, even on the phone, I can hear that he's not certain as he says it. Not like he was when he was defending his mum.

'Maybe, I don't know. Maybe he and his phoney bomb squad – and they *are* phoney, I asked one of the real bomb-squad men and he'd never heard of them – maybe they had it planned all the time. Ben told me what that Tattoo thug said about kidnapping white kids.'

'That was just a joke!'

'Maybe. I just think you need to tell the police, that's all.'

'And if I don't.'

'Then I will.'

Pause.

'They're not going to believe you though, are they?' says Jed.

Just then the policeman standing next to me gets a call over his radio. I hear it crackling into life – a voice comes through on the other end, but I can't make out what it's saying.

'I have to go,' says Priti. 'Something's going on.'

'What's happening?' I ask – the first words I've managed to get into the conversation for several minutes.

'I don't know,' she says. 'Just make Jed tell the police, OK?'

'I'll try,' I say.

The policeman is listening intently to a call on his radio. Jed comes running down, taking the stairs four at a time.

'What's going on?' he asks, not looking at me.

'Negative for explosives,' we hear a crackly voice over the radio announce. Our policeman groans.

'That's negative,' he repeats. 'Can you confirm?'

A static pause then: 'Confirmed – negative.'

I hear Grandad moan. Granny lets out a little sob. I daren't even look at Jed.

I imagine a round, black bomb with a sparking fuse. A bucket of water dashing out the flame.

'What do you want me to do here?' the police officer asks his colleague at the other end of the radio. He's glaring at me and Jed – his hopes of a knighthood fading before his eyes.

'Await instructions,' the voice comes back.

'Roger that.'

The policeman puts down his radio, turns to look at me and Jed.

'The Muslim lad didn't have any explosives, did he?' says Grandad.

'No,' says the police officer. 'He didn't.'

'That's good news then,' says Grandad.

'It is,' he replies.

'But not for the boys?' says Granny.

446

'No, not for the boys,' says the police officer grimly. 'Or for me. I'll probably lose my job over this.'

'9/11 cost one of my sons his life,' says Grandad quietly. 'And it changed the other one so much it cost him his job and his marriage. He's so angry now, I hardly recognise him . . .' He pauses. I glance at Jed who is just staring at Grandad, his face pale, but his expression unreadable. 'Little wonder then if their boys see the world through warped glasses.' He puts an arm round each of us and the police officer gives a quiet huff and looks away.

'Why aren't they saying on the TV that he didn't have a bomb?' I ask. The running headline at the bottom of the screen still reads, 'Attempted terrorist attack at cathedral . . . Stevie suspect's brother named as bomber.'

'We can't convey that information to the public until the investigation is complete.'

'Why not?' I say.

'Police protocol,' is his reply.

'It's going to cause a riot,' says Grandad.

Jed doesn't say anything.

* * *

It's long after midnight by the time we finally get to bed. Granny says we'd better get some sleep because the police will want to ask us a lot of questions in the morning. Jed and I hardly say a word as we get ready for bed.

When Granny's gone downstairs, Jed reaches under his mattress and pulls out the note his mum left for him.

'You want to read it?' he says, passing it to me, but not looking me in the eye.

'Do you want me to?' I ask.

'Don't mind,' he says.

So I open it up, read what's inside, and when I get to the end, I say, 'It's nice.'

And Jed says, 'It is, isn't it?'

Then we both just sit there for a bit and eventually, Jed says, 'I've got to go and talk to Grandad.'

'Why?' I ask.

'He'll know what to do,' he says.

'Jed,' I say. 'How did the bikers get Mik to drop his gun?'

'They didn't,' says Jed quietly. (He so rarely talks at anything less than a shout that I find myself leaning forward to listen.) 'Dad did.'

I don't say anything. Just wait for him to go on.

'He told Mik not to be stupid. To hand over the gun before anyone got hurt. And Mik did.' He pauses. 'And then the bikers beat him up. And Dad just watched.'

I don't look at him as he says this and he doesn't look at me.

'Were you there?'

He nods.

'What happened then?' I ask.

'The bikers kicked Mik up real bad, then they dumped him over the fence into Priti's garden and then they all legged it.'

'What did you do?'

'I threw up. My dad didn't notice. He was just standing there. Then I legged it too.'

I pause for a moment, taking in what he's saying. 'So your dad was the last one left in the park,' I say.

Jed nods.

'With Stevie?'

Jed nods again. 'But I didn't think . . . I mean . . . he wouldn't really do . . . what Priti said he did – would he?'

I don't know how to answer this, so I say, 'What did he say when he took you out for breakfast?'

'He told me to keep quiet.' He stops for a second. 'I suppose I knew he wasn't really bomb squad.'

There's a long silence before I say, 'Are you going to tell Grandad?'

He nods again.

You'd think we'd both have had enough of telling tales for one night, but this time it's different. So we stay where we are and neither of us says anything for a long time. Jed sits there with the note in his hand and, after a bit, I sit down next to him and put my arm round him and he puts his arm round me and we sit like that for ages.

Then he gets up and goes downstairs.

For a while, I sit on Jed's bed, staring at the note his mum wrote for him. And then I take out my notebook and start to draw.

AUGUST 17TH

Grandad didn't go to bed at all last night. I know because I'm the first to wake up and when I go down, I find him still sitting in his favourite chair, still dressed in yesterday's clothes, still staring at the soundless TV screen.

No one else is up yet. Granny and Jed are both late sleepers and the policeman appears to have been released from duty.

'Do you want a cup of tea, Grandad?' I ask.

'Thank you, Ben, that would be nice.'

So I go and make him one and take it to him with a slice of toast. I want to take a blanket to put over his legs because, this morning, he looks like a really old man. Maybe that's what staying up all night does to you.

When I come back, he's taken his wallet out of his pocket and is pulling something out. He hands it to me: a small picture of two boys, one of those school photos when you have to sit side by side.

'Dad and Uncle Ian,' I say.

Grandad nods. 'Could be you and Jed to look at them though, couldn't it?' he says.

And he's right. Ian and Dad look a lot like Jed and me, although the haircuts are shorter and the shirt collars longer.

'My two boys,' Grandad says. 'They fought all the time when they were kids, but when your dad died, Ian cried like a baby and Granny had to comfort him.' Grandad looks at the picture again. 'I think it changed him, losing his brother like that.'

He pauses, staring at the picture, then he hands it to me. 'Here, put it in that memory box of yours.'

'No, you keep it, Grandad,' I say.

'I can't. Not now. Not with what I'm about to do,' he says, starting to rise stiffly out of his chair. 'I just hope your Granny will forgive me, because Ian never will.'

So I take the picture from him and then I help him to get his coat and shoes on because he is feeling stiff. He doesn't say where he's going, but I know and I also know he wants to go before Granny and Jed get up. 'Do you want me to go with you, Grandad?' I ask.

'Thank you, Ben, but no. This is something I need to do on my own.'

Then he shakes my hand – all formal, standing in the porch – and then he is gone.

The postman comes a few minutes later. Granny and Jed are still asleep. There's another card for me. This one has a picture of a pop band called the Boo Radleys on the front. I've never heard of them although I recognise the name as a character from an old black-and-white film my mum and I love to watch. On the back it says, *Remember Boo? Looking forward to you coming home so we can curl up with him again soon.* Just like the other cards, it isn't signed. But it doesn't need to be because the handwriting on this one is wobbly and uncertain – but definitely my mum's.

Stevie's mum gave birth to her baby during the night. They show her on the TV, climbing out of the ambulance at the hospital after all the stuff at the cathedral, puffing and panting like the baby is going to pop out any minute. The photographers all took pictures of her like that, panting like a whale with her hair plastered to her face, which Granny thinks is inhumane. Granny also reckons it's probably the shock that brought on labour.

And Grandad is right about the bomb scare causing a riot. On the news it says that gangs of skinheads marched into a part of the city where most of the Asian families live and started setting fire to cars and throwing bricks through windows chanting, 'Terrorists, give her back!' Some Asian youths tried to retaliate and the fighting didn't stop even when the police turned up. A fire bomb was thrown through a broken window and fire crews had to come and rescue three small children and an elderly lady from the upstairs of a burning building. Shops were looted, several arrests were made and a dozen people were taken to hospital, three with serious injuries.

'All because some kids want to play FBI,' says the policeman who comes to talk to us the next day. And I can't help thinking that Uncle Ian's buddy with all the tattoos was right about one thing – a little white kid goes missing and it kick-starts a war.

Shakeel has been released without charge and the news people are now talking about 'hoax callers' (that's us) and a full judicial enquiry into the police's handling of the case. They are also saying that the bomb hoax may have been a deliberate ploy on behalf of Mik's family to destroy evidence vital to the search for Stevie Sanders.

'That list you gave us – the terrorist cell. Want to know what it really was?' says one police officer who seems particularly fed up with us because, apparently, we ruined his darts night.

Me and Jed nod. It seems like the right thing to do.

'A list of wedding guests!' he says.

'Oh,' I say, which doesn't seem like a good enough response.

We get seriously told off by the police and then we get told off again by Granny. I feel stupid, ashamed, worried about all the trouble we've caused. But also worried about Grandad.

He still hasn't come back. I told Granny he went

out for milk, but I know she doesn't believe me – Grandad never goes out for milk.

'But even Priti thought he was a terrorist!' says Jed.

'More shame on her then,' says Granny. 'You know they only went easy on you because of what happened to Ben's dad?'

I nod.

'I told them you had been brooding about him a lot since you came here,' she says softly. 'They want you to see a counsellor.'

I nod.

'I've phoned your mum and told her what happened,' she says.

'My mum?' asks Jed, looking up suddenly. He's hardly said anything all morning. He just keeps watching the front door, waiting for Grandad to come back.

'No, Ben's mum.'

Jed doesn't say anything and neither does Granny for a moment. Then she goes on, 'When Shakeel returns home, I want you to go over and apologise to the Muhammeds for the distress you've caused. You

456

will no doubt want to apologise to Priti too.'

'But she was in on it,' says Jed.

'Don't argue with me,' says Granny in a firm voice I've never heard her use with Jed before.

Jed looks surprised, but says nothing.

'What did my mum say?' I ask.

'She'll call and tell you herself,' says Granny.

Grandad still isn't back when we go over to see Mr and Mrs Muhammed and Shakeel. They seem shaken and Mrs Muhammed in particular looks very angry when we first arrive, but they're both pretty nice about it when we apologise – nicer than we deserve, I reckon.

'We are just glad one son is now cleared and we hope the same may soon be true of the other,' says Mr Muhammed.

Jed and I say nothing. It won't take the reporters outside long to work out the identity of the hoax callers. Or the identity of Stevie's abductor.

'What happened to your father has made you see the world in a very bad light,' says Mrs Muhammed to me. She has red eyes as if she's been crying. 'We hope that you understand now that not all Muslims are terrorists.'

'I do,' I say.

She looks at me for a moment and then says, 'Do you want to go upstairs and see Priti? She has been sleeping. But I think she would like to see you.'

As we troop upstairs, we hear scurrying feet and the sound of bedsprings. We find Priti breathless, sitting up in bed in her pyjamas.

'Were you listening in?' asks Jed.

'Course I was,' says Priti. 'You got off far lighter than I did too. I've got to give Zara back all the stuff she gave me for protection payment, *and* clean Shakeel and Ameenah's bedroom every week forever, *and* write letters of apology to 'all concerned', and save up all my pocket money to buy new radio equipment for Shakeel and read *Northanger Abbey* –'

'Why?' I ask, confused about the last one.

'To teach me the consequences of an overactive imagination apparently. I've just started it and it's deadly dull, so I think it may actually be a cunning plan to bore me to death! "Honour killing by Jane Austen" they'll call it!'

'Anything else?' I ask.

'Yup, I have to paint over all the graffiti AND . . .' She places so much emphasis on the word that I'm expecting something truly horrendous. 'My mum says my wheelies have been confiscated for a MONTH!'

From the look on her face, I reckon her mum saved the worst for last.

'Ben's dad got us off,' says Jed, glancing out of the window in the direction of our house. The drive is still empty. Grandad isn't back yet.

'And you being at death's door didn't do any harm either,' says Priti.

'What?' says Jed, looking confused.

Which is when I realise I forgot to tell Priti that Jed isn't terminally ill after all.

'Oh, he's not dying,' I say quickly. 'He was just meeting up with his granny . . . his other granny that is . . . who he's not supposed to see . . . well, he is, but his dad won't let him.' I can see them both staring at me. 'It's complicated.'

'So basically, you're not going to die?' exclaims Priti, staring accusingly at Jed.

'What made you think I was anyway?' asks Jed.

'Just wishful thinking, I guess,' says Priti. 'So I needn't have gone to all this trouble trying to make your last days memorable.'

'Guess not,' Jed shrugs.

'Well, if I'd known that, I'd never have framed my brother as a suicide bomber!'

'Actually, I think that was my idea,' says Jed. Then he says a word I don't think I've ever heard him use before. 'Sorry.'

'No worries,' says Priti lightly. 'It was a stroke of genius – I just wish I'd come up with it myself.' I glance at her and see that she is being quite serious. 'I can't even take credit for the honour-killing storyline because that was Zara's idea. Still, I suppose we have to be careful not to let our imaginations run away with us in future,' she says, in what I suppose is meant to be a Jane Austen voice, and I guess this is her way of saying she's pleased he isn't dying after all.

'What *is* happening about Zara?' I ask.

'They've been pretty cool about it actually,' says Priti brightly. 'Turns out they don't mind her having boyfriends, so long as she tells them what's going on.'

'Oh,' I say.

'More importantly, what about the police, Jed?' says Priti, staring at him significantly. 'What about Stevie Sanders?'

'It's sorted,' says Jed.

My grandad still isn't back from the police station when my mum calls. Granny talks to her first. She's in the hall, sitting at the telephone table, and I'm in the kitchen, but I can still hear my mum's voice coming through, tiny and tinny, on the receiver.

Granny is very polite to her, but she's put on her smart visitors' voice, so I can tell she doesn't really know what to say. (I wonder if the two of them ever really got on or if they were just united in grief for my dad?)

'How are you, dear? . . . He's fine . . . All a bit upsetting, but we are OK here . . . How about you?'

Then I hear her say, 'Do you want to talk to

461

him? . . . Hang on, I'll go and get him.'

And then there she is at the doorway, saying, 'Ben, it's your mum. She'd like to talk to you,' like it's the most ordinary thing in the world.

She hands me the receiver. It's silent at the other end and, for a moment, I think Mum's hung up.

But she hasn't. 'Hi, big man, how are you?' she says.

'Hi,' I say. 'Are you better?'

'I'm on my way,' she replies.

'What did the doctors say?'

'I need to keep going to see them for a bit.'

'But you want to get better?'

'Yes,' she says. Then she asks if Stevie is a friend of mine.

'No, we weren't very nice to her.'

And Mum says, 'Who's we?'

And I say, 'Me and Jed and Priti.' And it's weird to think that Mum doesn't know who Priti is. (Although she probably knows what she looks like if she's had the TV on at all during the last twenty-four hours!)

'Sometimes we're not as nice to people as we should be,' says Mum. 'Even to ourselves.'

I glance in the direction of the sitting room where Jed is sitting with Granny, neither of them talking.

And then she says, 'Did you like the postcards?'

'Did you send them *all*?' I say.

'Of course. You didn't think I'd forgotten you, did you?'

I pause. 'Mum,' I say. 'Why didn't you ring?'

I think of birds sitting on telephone wires, mobiles held up to their beaks. I think of telephone numbers circling the air around them like clouds.

'I didn't want to put you through it,' she says.

'Through what?'

'I've leaned on you too much in the last couple of years. It hasn't been fair.'

'But I wouldn't have minded, Mum,' I say.

'I had to learn to do it on my own and to do that meant I had to let go of you for a bit.'

'Just for a bit?' I ask.

'I could never let go of you forever!' She laughs.

I imagine her hand, taking hold of mine, her fingers stroking the soft place between first finger and thumb. Just like she used to do.

'So do you think you'd like to come home?'

'Do you want me to?' I ask.

'Very much,' she says.

'Are you well enough?'

'I can't promise I won't ever get ill again, but I'll try not to,' she says.

'And you're not mad at me? You don't blame me?'

'What have I got to blame you for?'

'For letting you down.'

'Oh, Ben! Don't ever say that. You didn't let me down. You are the one who kept me going for all these years.'

'So why did you do it, Mum?' I say. 'Why did you stop eating?'

'I'm not quite sure, Ben.'

'Were you unhappy?'

'No,' she pauses. 'I was very happy – happier than I'd been since your dad died.'

'Then why?'

'Perhaps I didn't feel as if I should be,' she says.

'Because of Dad?' I ask.

'Yes. Because of Dad.'

'But Dad would have wanted you to be happy,' I say. And I don't see a stick man falling out of a tower: I see a smiling man playing football with a little boy on his shoulders.

'Would he?' She half laughs as she says this.

'Yes,' I say and I feel sure that I'm right because I know a bit about my dad now, thanks to Priti and my memory box. 'He would.'

'Then come home because I can't be happy without you.'

We're sitting at the kitchen table – me, Granny and Jed – when we hear Grandad's key turn in the lock. We're playing a game of cards and, for once, Jed isn't cheating. When we hear the sound of the front door opening, Jed is the first one on his feet.

Granny and I follow him into the hallway. Grandad is standing on the doormat. He closes the door quietly then turns and stands there hovering, looking as if he's about to topple.

'Where have you been?' asks Granny. She's holding her left wrist in her right hand and the bright little

465

spots of colour are in her cheeks again.

Jed is staring at Grandad, his eyes fierce. I know he wants Grandad to say he got it wrong, that it was all a mistake.

But Grandad looks at him and nods. Then he turns to Granny and says, 'It's Ian.'

Granny is still motionless. 'What about Ian?' she says. 'What's happened to him?'

Grandad turns to her. 'He . . . the police think he . . . they're searching his house.'

I glance at Jed, who is staring at the ground now. His face is closed, like he's not really there.

Granny lets out a little cry and seems to stumble.

Jed takes a step towards her, to stop her falling. I do the same.

Grandad stands on the mat and says, 'I'm so sorry.'

Granny has gone for another lie-down. Jed and I are in our room. Jed is on his bed staring up at the stars my dad stuck on the ceiling – or perhaps it was Uncle Ian who put them up there. I'm sitting on the windowsill, trying to finish my Bomb-busters cartoon.

We hear my grandad's heavy footfall on the stairs and the sound of china rattling as he pushes open the door to the bedroom opposite.

'I've brought you some tea,' I hear him say softly.

The teacup rattles again. My granny thinks mugs are too modern – along with mobile phones and the Internet and avocados.

Then we hear Granny say, 'Why did he do it?' Her voice sounds small and faraway.

Jed doesn't stop staring at the ceiling, but I can tell he's listening.

'He's been through a lot,' Grandad says. 'Losing his brother, losing Karen. It's been hard for him.'

'But to do something like this. To kidnap a child?' There is a question in Granny's voice. 'Didn't we teach him right from wrong?'

There's a pause. Outside, on the street, I hear the sound of a car pulling into a driveway.

'What happened to his brother, it changed him,' says Grandad.

'But he let the police arrest the Muhammed boy,' says Granny, her voice high and breaking on the final word. 'And it caused all that fighting. Riots. That's what they said on the news. Dozens of people hurt. In hospital.'

From outside, we hear a car door slamming, excited voices.

'Maybe that's what he wanted,' says Grandad quietly.

Granny says nothing for a moment. When she speaks, her voice sounds choked with tears. 'I just don't understand it, Barry,' she says.

From across the hallway, we hear the bedframe creak. I wonder if Grandad is lying down next to Granny.

'He was angry,' says Grandad quietly. His voice is muffled as if he is curled up close to her. 'It was like he blamed every Muslim in the world for what happened to his brother.' He pauses, coughs. 'For what happened to Andrew.'

There is another pause and I can hear Granny crying softly in low, rhythmic sobs.

'I think perhaps he wanted revenge,' says Grandad. 'That's the only reason I can think of for what he did.'

There is laughter from outside and loud cries of joy.

From my grandparents' room there is only the steady rise and fall of Granny's sobbing breaths. Then I hear her say, 'I'm not sure I can forgive him, Barry.'

'I know,' says Grandad. 'I know.'

There is a moment of quiet then I hear a low sound, something between a cough and a gasping exhalation of breath, and I wonder if my grandad is crying. And then the house is silent again.

I glance out of the window. The close is still full of journalists. There's a police car in Priti's driveway, and a couple of policemen are carrying boxes back into Priti's house, under Shakeel's direction. His radio stuff, I suppose.

'What happens at the end?' asks Jed.

I look down. He's not staring at the ceiling any more. He's looking at me.

'What?'

'In your cartoon,' he says. 'What happens at the end?'

'Oh,' I say, because I haven't totally figured out myself how it ends yet. 'Well, I thought maybe Jed-eye and Lil' Priti and Ben-D discover that they'd got it all wrong: that Stee-V was never in danger of being blown up, but had just gone to the funfair with her grandma.'

'That could work,' says Jed.

'And then Da Hona Killaz and Da Bikaz turn out to be undercover police units, so they make up and become best of friends,' I add, glancing at him quickly before going on. 'And the Pub Men turn out to be the real baddies, so they get arrested for perverting the course of justice.'

'Cool,' says Jed. He once teased me for using the word 'cool'. He told me it was dead old-fashioned and that I should say 'Rad!' or 'Insane!' instead. But I don't remind him of that now. 'What happens then?'

'Um, well, Jed-eye, Ben-D and Lil' Priti eat garibaldi biscuits and then set up their own pirate radio station.'

'And become millionaires?' says Jed, glancing up at the stars again.

I think of Shakeel, unpacking all his radio equipment. I wonder if any of it's been damaged, and if he'll be able to make his radios work again. Maybe he'll let me and Jed and Priti help him if we ask.

I can feel Jed looking at me again, waiting for an answer.

'Yeah,' I say. 'They become millionaires.'

Stevie Sanders' baby sister is born about the same time that they find Stevie. A little girl, Billie Maud Sanders, weighing just 5 lbs 10 oz. ('What on earth else did she have in that bump?' says Grandad.) She was born at 3.45 p.m. and shortly after her birth, Mr and Mrs Sanders received the news that Stevie had been found safe and well. Both sisters arrive back in the cul-de-sac within half an hour of each other the very same day.

We watch it all happen in duplicate – live outside the window and, just a second later, on TV. Mr and Mrs Sanders give an interview at the door of their house. They are holding their new baby daughter and saying how happy they are to know their elder daughter is safe. They thank the police and everyone who helped with the enquiry. They do not offer an apology to the Asian community.

Half an hour later, a police car draws up and a little girl with her face covered by a towel is carried inside by two female police officers. The door shuts behind them and the curtains are closed, so we don't see the reunion.

TV commentators discuss the ordeal Stevie has been through and the help she will need to recover from it. They talk of the loving family around her and they stress that police have no reason to believe that she was harmed in any way, although they will continue to question her and to search the premises where she was found. The motivation for her abduction is still unclear.

Then they start to talk about the man they have in custody, who is helping the police with their enquiries, and Granny turns off the TV. She doesn't look at Grandad.

She makes us ham sandwiches as we watch another family reunion going on across the road. Mik – who has been released without charge – is dropped off by a police car.

'I expect all the reporters will be gone in a few

days,' says Granny quietly, coming in with the plate of sandwiches.

Grandad doesn't say anything. The police haven't yet released the name of the man they now have in custody. But as soon as they do, the press will be knocking on our door – even I know that. And then Granny will have lost two sons.

My mum's coming later. She won't take me home with her right away – I said I want to stay here with Jed for a few days, until they know what's happening with him. Jed asked Granny to call his mum – Granny Brenda gave her the number – but I don't know what's going to happen there. Granny says that Jed can stay here as long as he likes, so who knows?

For now, Granny, Grandad, Jed and I sit in the front room and eat our ham sandwiches. Grandad looks at us both and says, 'My two boys.'

THINGS THAT HAPPEN AFTERWARDS

1. I end up staying on at Granny's for the rest of the summer. Mum and Gary come to visit lots – Mum is wearing see-through lipgloss, her hair is shiny and she looks happy. She asks if I want to come home right away, but I decide to stay on a bit longer because of Jed.

2. Jed is a mess after his dad is arrested. He cries all the time and no one can cheer him up except Grandad – and sometimes me. For the first time ever, it's kind of useful that I've lost my dad too.

3 Granny calls Auntie Karen, but then Jed changes his mind and says he doesn't want to see her. He doesn't even want to see Granny Brenda. Grandad says we need to give him time.

4. Jed is going to stay with Granny and Grandad 'for the time being' and go to the school Zara goes to, and where Priti is starting in September, which I say will be really cool although Jed doesn't look so sure suddenly.

5. Priti's latest scheme is to set up a Muslim matchmaking business to 'put the spark back into arranged marriages'. Zara obviously isn't on her books because she starts dating a boy from school who Priti says 'is hardly the person she – or her parents – would have chosen for her'.

6. Mik stops wearing jeans and Converse trainers and starts wearing Muslim robes and the little Muslim hat thing all the time. I don't know if he's still mad at us, but we don't see him much any more and Priti says he spends all his time at the mosque.

7. Tyreese gets arrested for stabbing Said, although Shakeel reckons he'll wriggle his way out of being charged.

8. The Sanders won't let Stevie play with me or Jed or Priti. They won't even let her play out on her own in the road any more, so the rest of the summer she's stuck in the hot house with her new baby sister who screams all the time. Sometimes we see her looking out of the window, her face pale now that her tan has faded. We wave, but she doesn't wave back.

9. The Sanders decide to sell their house, which contains 'too many unhappy memories', they say. They throw a farewell party and invite all the neighbours except Granny and Grandad. To everyone's surprise, the Muhammeds are invited, but they don't go either.

10. At the end of the summer, when I finally do go home, Priti writes me letters on *Twilight* notepaper, with swirly handwriting in pink ink. I send her postcards (which Mum helps me choose) with short messages and cartoons on the back. Priti and Jed are going to come and visit us at half-term.

11. I start a new comic strip about three kids who think they're hotshot teen-spies, but always get things wrong. Gary shows me how to make my own website to post the strips on and pretty soon I'm getting hundreds of hits.

12. And Priti gets her wheelies back at the end of the summer, but loses them again a week later after 'reckless wheelying on school grounds'. Some things never change!

This is how my Bomb-busters story turned out in the end. I kept changing it and I couldn't work out how it finished for a while but Jed said we all needed to be heroes, and Priti wanted Zara placed in mortal danger – and then grovelling in gratitude – and my mum said she liked the bit about biscuits, so I tried to put all that in. I don't think I got it totally right and some of the pictures don't exactly look like they should, but anyway, this is it.

I figured I might put it in my dad's memory box. Mum says she thinks he'd have liked it, because he was a bit of doodler – like me. She told me some other things about him too. Things I didn't know. I wrote them down and put them in the box as well.

Anyway, you need to read it backwards (turn to the bit about 2012 – that's where it starts) because that's how manga works. Back to front, topsy-turvy. A bit like that summer.

IN 2012, THE UK GOVERNMENT LAUNCHED A NEW OPERATION IN THE WAR ON TERROR, RECRUITING AND TRAINING AN ELITE TEAM OF TEENAGE CRIME FIGHTERS. THE OPERATION IS A CLOSELY GUARDED SECRET. THESE TEENAGE SUPERHEROES WORK ALONE, OUTSIDE THE RESTRICTIONS OF THE SECURITY SERVICES AND SOME SAY THEY MAY - JUST MAY - HAVE TOP SECRET SUPER POWERS.

THEIR MISSION:
BUSTING TERRORISTS
& SAVING LIVES
THEIR NAME:
BOMB-BUSTERS

ACKNOWLEDGEMENTS

With grateful thanks to everyone at Tuesday's Children, especially Brielle Saricini, Erik Abrahamson and Bridget Fisher; to Peaceful Tomorrows, Families of September 11th, Voices of September 11th, the Child Bereavement Trust; Mothers Apart from Their Children (MATCH). Thanks to Dr Cynthia Pfeffer of the New York-Presbyterian Hospital/Weill Cornell Medical Center, Dr Claude Chemtob of the Trauma Recovery Program at the Mount Sinai School of Medicine in New York, the late Dr Richard A Gardiner and the BBC Newsround website for their invaluable research. Also to Martin Hart, Patricia Bingley, Marian Fontana, Alissa Torres; and to Elizabeth Turner and William who I hope will like the book.

Many thanks also to all the amazing children I have the pleasure to know and to teach: to my uber-cool nephew, Nye; to Joshua Butler, Skye Lawrence and the wonderful Sawyerr kids; to the Year 6s at Otjikondo; my U4As from Habs (1996/7); to

Paulinas each and every one; to the KES Manga boys of Years 7 and 9 (2009/10), to Max Lury, Hannah Gibs and Adam Dudley Fryer; and my 'insane' KES Year 11s (2011), particularly Ollie Chadwick who, 'used to draw cartoons of aeroplanes flying into towers'.

Thanks to the following people for support and inspiration: Naomi Rich, Joanna Nadin, Kit Watson, Claire Baguley, Paula Trybuchowska, my lovely book group, the Freshford playground gang and the English department at King Edward's School, Bath.

Massive thanks to both Caroline Montgomery and Ali Dougal for loving my little book and making it better than I ever could; to Stella Paskins and to everyone at Egmont for general loveliness, Mr Gum and chocolate cake.

Especial thanks to my family – in and outlaws included – for their love and support. To Granny's table; Graham Avenue and Wellington Grove; to my much-missed dad, lovely mum and bonkers brother and sister; and to Jonny, Joe-Joe and Elsie Maudie whom I love up to the moon and back again.

EGMONT PRESS: ETHICAL PUBLISHING

Egmont Press is about turning writers into successful authors and children into passionate readers – producing books that enrich and entertain. As a responsible children's publisher, we go even further, considering the world in which our consumers are growing up.

Safety First
Naturally, all of our books meet legal safety requirements. But we go further than this; every book with play value is tested to the highest standards – if it fails, it's back to the drawing-board.

Made Fairly
We are working to ensure that the workers involved in our supply chain – the people that make our books – are treated with fairness and respect.

Responsible Forestry
We are committed to ensuring all our papers come from environmentally and socially responsible forest sources.

**For more information, please visit our website at
www.egmont.co.uk/ethical**

Egmont is passionate about helping to preserve the world's remaining ancient forests. We only use paper from legal and sustainable forest sources, so we know where every single tree comes from that goes into every paper that makes up every book.

This book is made from paper certified by the Forestry Stewardship Council (FSC), an organisation dedicated to promoting responsible management of forest resources. For more information on the FSC, please visit **www.fsc.org**. To learn more about Egmont's sustainable paper policy, please visit **www.egmont.co.uk/ethical**.